to abuse, devalue and destroy any form of consciousness they're able to define as 'other', while the robots challenge the limits of love, devotion and life after death."

Toronto Globe & Mail

"I love a book that kicks me in the head. *iD* cuts deep into questions of choice and free will and imperfection, and it hurts."

Adam Rakunas, author of *Windswept*

"In Ashby's expert hands *vN* cuts a painful incision into the emotional complexity of oppression in our society, and the way love can feed the worst kinds of hate. *vN* is a powerful novel and a fine exemplar of exactly the perspectives chauvinist SF so often stifles."

The Guardian

BY THE SAME AUTHOR

THE MACHINE DYNASTY

vN

iD

Company Town

Licence Expired

Madeline Ashby

REV

THE THIRD MACHINE DYNASTY

ANGRY ROBOT
An imprint of Watkins Media Ltd

Unit 11, Shepperton House
89 Shepperton Road
London N1 3DF
UK

Revenge Served Warm
angryrobotbooks.com
twitter.com/angryrobotbooks

An Angry Robot paperback original, 2020

Cover by Kieryn Tyler
Edited by Paul Simpson and Gemma Creffield

ISBN 978 0 85766 538 6
Ebook ISBN 978 0 85766 858 5

Printed and bound in the United Kingdom by TJ International.

9 8 7 6 5 4 3 2 1

To My Grandmothers

1

SATISFACTION GUARANTEED

"I feel like one of those creepy guys who go to Thailand to fuck little girls."

"They're *robots*, Ashleigh. *Boy* robots. *Grown-ass* boy robots."

Tiffany stretched her two palms a good eight inches apart, just in case her point was too subtle. One wheel of their carriage hopped over a stone in the road, and the wine in Tiffany's glass sloshed dangerously. She eliminated its threat by glugging the rest down in a single go. Ashleigh sighed. Their reason for visiting Hammerburg was obvious, but Tiffany didn't have to be so obvious *about* it.

Besides, you weren't supposed to call them "robots" anymore. "Robot" came from the Old Slavonic word for "serf." It was a cognate for the German word for work, *arbeit*. As in, *arbeit macht frei*. It was more politically aware – more honest – to actually refer to the vN as what they were: slaves.

Ashleigh wasn't even sure she was going to fuck anybody. Any*thing*. Or whatever you were supposed to say now. She had no idea. It was an ongoing debate. The vN had never really done much for her either way. She wasn't afraid of them, but she wasn't hot for them either. Sure, she had written the inevitable paper on the semiotics of simulacra in the robot sex trade, but so had every horny undergrad trying to be edgy for their Ethics in Tech class. The vN were pretty the way models were pretty. They were decoration. They were fantasy. They weren't anybody. They weren't *people*. They couldn't love you like people could. Which meant they couldn't really betray you, either. Maybe that was the charm. It was probably the charm.

Not that she was at all bitter. Not in the slightest.

"It's exactly what you need," Tiffany said. "After all this bullshit."

Ashleigh didn't have much to say about that. "I don't even really like robots, though. I mean, with everything."

Tiffany rolled her eyes. "Well, yeah, but you fucking *love* vampires."

Slowly, the carriage drew to a halt. With the lace curtains drawn, Ashleigh wasn't even aware they'd stopped until she noticed the clop of the horses' hooves had ceased. They had entered the coach an hour ago. At least, it felt like an hour. The first thing they took from you was any mechanism for telling time – like a casino, or a CIA rendition site. If you signed the right waiver, they would send you your notifications and updates via telegram. "Is everything OK?" she asked.

"Better than OK." Tiffany peered past the curtain in the carriage window. "We have fucking *arrived*."

And just like that, the carriage doors flew open. A tiny set of stairs unfolded, and Tiffany swung out, wine glass still clutched in her gloved hand. The last dregs leapt free, tannic scabs of red spattering across the glittering white snow. She squealed, and jumped down to the freshly-swept cobblestones below.

Ashleigh peered out. The village looked exactly like it had online – thatched gables glittering with evening frost, snow thickly coating their A-frames, guttering lanterns hanging at every door, steep cliffsides shrouded in icy mist. In the central square, a massive Christmas tree. Beside it, a great wicker goat to be burned in effigy. A rime of moon hung in the violet sky over both symbols.

It was always twilight, in Hammerburg.

Ashleigh wasn't really sure how Tiffany had won the Hammerburg contest. Winning was Tiffany's job. Tiffany was brand-chaff: if she distracted a given customer service interface, or actively fucked with it, then its competitor could swoop in and snag other customers. She was always *working* – writing scripts that automatically entered her various accounts into competitions, constantly tagging an entire network of dummy accounts, skewing algorithms, bumping her rank, making her various selves into preferred customers, earning points, spending points, reviewing products and experiences, role-playing transactions in prototyping engines, providing data to auditors of game theory. She did this – or more accurately, she created the bots that did it – at the behest of various and sundry marketing firms. (One of them was actually called Various & Sundry, or so Tiffany had told her once.)

All of that was just as stupid, finicky and meaningless, Tiffany said, as any real job. "Every job posting always says how much they want competitive candidates. Well, I'm a professional contestant. There's nothing more competitive than that."

In truth, Ashleigh didn't want to know what Tiffany had done to win their spots on the trip, given the park's reputation. Not that she had any room to judge. Not these days. God, she was such an asshole. And a cliché. A trope. Her life was a misbegotten stream of content designed to make women weep into their wine when they had PMS. She thought she was past this. You could take the girl out of the Prairies, but you couldn't take the Prairies out of the girl.

Ashleigh had decided that it was talking with her mother which brought back her judgmental streak. It was hearing the wet *thock thock thock* of a wooden mallet hitting a pork chop over the tinny audio channel, as though her mother were beating the information out of her. She hadn't told her about Simon until that conversation. Her disapproval was thinly disguised as exasperation: *Didn't you see this coming? Surely you had to know this might happen. He was married. What more did you expect? Did you really think he was going to turn his whole life around for you? Just because you're a human being and she wasn't?*

In the end Ashleigh had said she would not be spending Christmas with her and Dad and the aunts and uncles and cousins, after all. There was simply too much to do, she said. Too much work to catch up on.

Her feeds would show her in Hammerburg, of course. Her mother would know she'd lied. Her father, too, if he bothered to drag his eyeballs from hockey. They would be hurt. Maybe. Ashleigh wasn't sure. Maybe it was best for everyone that she not attend anyway. Being there grated on her nerves, and they knew it. And she knew they knew it. Last Christmas, she'd left the house in time to give herself a good five hours at the airport. They had smiled, liberated and relieved, when the bus trundled up to their driveway and opened its doors to take her away.

Tiffany was snapping her fingers.

"Hey. Ashleigh. Get your chicken ass out of the fucking buggy. Igor over here is taking us upstairs."

Tiffany jerked her head at the broad-shouldered vN at

the door to the inn. He was a lot of things, but he was no "Igor." Square-jawed and ginger-haired, he looked more like an extra in an historical fantasy drama than anything else. Which Ashleigh supposed this was. A fantasy about a history that had never really happened. The sort of thing Eco or Baudrillard or Sterling wrote about. Atemporal. That was the word. Christ, she was such a nerd.

For a moment she wished she could talk to Simon about it, and the air left her lungs. They would never have those talks again. Ever. Never share an inside joke, an utterly insufferable self-reference, never roll along that wide but recursive loop that was their conversational pattern. Could his wife do that? Did her neural net allow for it? Sure, she could make him come, but could she make him laugh?

Ashleigh watched as concern flickered over the robot's face. Then he crossed over to her, his heavy peasant boots crunching on frosty gravel. He offered her one very strong, very warm, human-seeming arm.

"My lady," he said. His accent was thick. She couldn't place it. It sounded like it was from everywhere. And it probably was. Programmers in Seattle, manufacturers in Tokyo, localizers in Budapest. He was as placeless as a Happy Meal. Supply-side robotics. Satisfaction guaranteed.

"I'm sorry," she said. "I guess I'm just a little more tired than I thought I was."

"Of course," he said. "You've had a long journey."

And something about the way he said it, the tone or the inflection, or maybe the way the corner of his mouth tugged up a little, made her wonder how much he really knew. Had the village scraped her feeds? Of course it had. It wasn't even a question. That was part of the whole experience. Depending on the tier of service, you could provide all sorts of information that the park would use to create exactly the right storyline. They had to know about heart conditions, after all. It would follow that they had to know about heartbreak. And although she had been circumspect online, it was entirely possible that Tiffany told them something extra, on the sly.

"Come on, slick, I've got airplane crotch!" Tiffany said, a little too loudly. A polyfam of chalk-white corset-and-cravat enthusiasts swung their gaze at her. Tiffany gave them an eyebrow that was as good as a middle finger.

Ashleigh shook her head a little to clear it. She was just being paranoid. How many people came to Hammerburg for the same reasons as she? All too many. So what if she was a cliché? This really was the end of the road, for people like her. This was what closure looked like: a theme park village full of robots pretending to be vampires.

Their inn was called The Running Boar, and it was modelled on a set from *The Brides of Dracula*. Wherever possible, the literature warned them, props and set pieces traced back to "Bray Studios in the Berkshires" had been purchased. Printers and crafters had done the rest. In practice, what this meant were flickering chandeliers wrought from iron, and massive fireplaces with river rock chimneys that climbed up all the way up to open rafters hung with garlic, vervain and wolfsbane. And an animal's head mounted in every room above the fireplace.

"You don't think they're real, are they?" Ashleigh asked, as they ascended the stairs toward their room. "The animals?"

"Oh, for fuck's sake," Tiffany said. "Nothing's real, here. That's the whole point. Just don't bring it up; it's in the guidebook." She gave Ashleigh a tickle under her ribs. "Stop worrying. I'm sure they put the surveillance units somewhere else."

Ashleigh hadn't even thought of that.

Their room had two beds, and no windows. At least, not proper ones. They were thick stained glass and solder, and they did not open. More dried garlic and wolfsbane hung in little bundles on either side of the window. No vampires would be sneaking in the old-fashioned way, apparently. You had to pay extra for that.

"You might see how the magic happens, otherwise," Tiffany said, gesturing at the windows. "It's the same everywhere. You get a view of the park, or you get nothing. I mean, you're not supposed to call it a *park*, though. It's an *experience*. It's an *immersive participatory fiction*. Heaven forbid you should actually refer to it as a *theme park*, like it's for kids or basics or people who do singalongs."

"I wish we could see the castle," Ashleigh said.

"Well, what can you expect, with a free room?"

Up the hill was a castle that reproduced Oakley Court, the castle that had appeared in *The Rocky Horror Picture Show*, *The Belles of St Trinian's*, and *The Brides of Dracula*. (Oakley Court, the literature was quick to point out, was itself a Gothic reproduction built during the Victorian period. So the Hammerburg version was a reproduction of that reproduction, a copy of a copy. You were supposed to recognize the irony of this on your own.) Staying there cost more, and you could purchase a role-play package wherein the Baron or Baroness or Count or whoever was inhabiting the castle at that moment plucked you out of obscurity and invited you to spend the night. What happened after that depended on how much you'd spent, and what waivers you'd signed, and whether the ambient sensors thought your heart was in good condition.

Downstairs was a lively gastropub called Badstein's, and during the day a tearoom called Madame Marianne's opened up for a continental breakfast, followed by little paté sandwiches and strudels and cold fruit soups with sour cream and brown sugar. A small leather-bound booklet informed Ashleigh of these things. It was real leather. She couldn't recall the last time she'd actually seen real leather. There wasn't a lot of room for it in the life of a grad student. She inhaled the smell of it and tried to fathom the expense. For a moment she seriously considered spending the entire trip in bed, ordering endless room service, watching as the mismatched "homestyle" patterned china stacked up and up and up in perilous towers of pink flowers and blue pagodas.

"Don't even think about that," Tiffany said, with that eerie way she had of knowing exactly what Ashleigh was imagining. Ashleigh folded up the menu and put it down beside her.

Tiffany flopped down on the bed. She wriggled herself up against the pillows. They weren't like normal hotel pillows – they were covered in eyelet shams, as though someone's grandmother had made them. They smelled vaguely grandmotherly too, to Ashleigh, like rosewater. As though a priest had come by just to bless them. Tiffany scowled, turned the pillows over, and looked at Ashleigh.

"Go check and see if they gave us nightgowns. They're supposed to give everybody nightgowns."

"Nightgowns? Really?"

"Yup. Big long flowy ones with tons of ruffles and cleavage. It's what we get instead of bathrobes."

"What do the men get?"

"They get to see us wearing the nightgowns."

Ashleigh rolled her eyes and opened the wardrobe. Inside,

as promised, were two nightgowns on stuffed hangers. Ashleigh pulled them out and held them against herself. They matched the colors of the window glass: a soft candy pink and a seafoam green, like a mixed bag of cream mints poured into an elderly lady's cut-glass dish.

"Which one do you want?"

Tiffany narrowed her eyes for a moment before seeming to decide. "The pink one. I'm the one who has to document her experience here, and pink looks better on camera than green."

Ashleigh waited until she'd turned back to the wardrobe before making a face. Two sets of dresses with puffy sleeves and narrow waists hung in the wardrobe, and she brought them out next. "What are these for?"

"For downstairs. We came in the traveler entrance. The whole inn is a lot bigger than what we got to see. We get access to the rest of it once we dress the part. It's required, the first night. Helps everybody get into character."

"So, no room service the first night?"

Tiffany shook her head. "Nope. We have to be warned, after all."

"Warned?"

"About the vampires!" Tiffany began listing threats off on her hand. She'd had special nails done for Hammerburg. They looked like talons. They gleamed, suddenly opalescent, when the candlelight hit them.

"And the werewolves," she was saying. "And the witches. And the witch-finders. That's a whole other package. Super popular with the extremophile people. I mean there's a reason we're in Eastern Europe, right? You can tie your girlfriend to a stake, the whole bit. Otherwise they just give you a vN to play with. It costs a fucking fortune. Or it did, until recently."

Ashleigh's eyes narrowed. "Wait. So you can burn a vN? Alive? If she's a witch? I mean, if she's playing a witch?"

Tiffany blinked. "Obviously."

Dinner took place in the Badstein's pub downstairs. A kindly old-looking vN with mutton chop whiskers sat them down at one end of a long harvest-style table and recited the menu for them: "Our bill of fare is simple. Hot goulash, a dish of sauerkraut, and our own red wine from the valley."

"Oh? What grape is that?" Ashleigh asked, and Tiffany kicked her under the table.

"My friend is being cheeky," Tiffany said. "These city girls, you know. They can't keep a civil tongue in their heads."

"Oh, we cater to all sorts around these parts," the vN said. "But just you be careful, now. There's things about at night that even the city folk have no ken of."

"Like what?" Ashleigh asked.

"We shall be very careful," Tiffany said, grinding the heel of her boot into Ashleigh's toes.

"God bless you, miss. It's a kind girl who listens to an old man's worries."

"Oh, it's no trouble at all," Tiffany said, and watched him depart. She levelled her gaze at Ashleigh. "Don't do that again," she warned. "Don't take your damage about Simon's wife out on the other robots. Stop trying to trip them up. They're just here doing a job like all the other poor sons of bitches working at an *immersive participatory fiction.*" Tiffany drained her wine. "This isn't some anthropological exercise. I fucking *forbid you* from working while we're here."

"I can't help it," Ashleigh said, because she couldn't. It

wasn't her fault that she'd devoted her career to synthetic anthropology. That was the new terminology, as she'd recently explained to her parents – it wasn't about "artificial intelligence" anymore. "Artificial intelligence" was an offensive term. Now it was all about how the vN related to each other. It didn't matter if you couldn't tell the difference between a vN and a human; what mattered was whether they could tell *you* were a human being.

And then their basket of black bread and cultured butter came, and they had something else to talk about. The food was good – good in the way that resort food always seemed to be, in that there was a lot of it and it came with a smile, and seemed expensive because everything that surrounded it was expensive. It was just goulash, like the robot had said. Beef and paprika and mushrooms and sour cream. But somehow it was the most tender and nourishing thing Ashleigh had enjoyed in months. The pink riesling helped. It just didn't seem to stop coming.

After the goulash was when the show started. The plates had just been cleared, when a man burst into the room. He was pale and wild-eyed. "Don't go outside!" he shrieked. "For the love of God, don't go outside!"

"Here, now, sir, you're scaring my customers," said the mutton-chopped vN. He tried to fake a laugh. It was a strange thing, watching a fake person do a fake laugh. "I'll thank you not to put ideas in their heads."

"These are not mere figments!" the other man said. He was dressed like a traveler – a long cloak, a tall hat, mud-spattered boots that went to the knee. "I saw something out there in the forest. Something I cannot possibly explain. Something beyond the knowledge of mere mortals!"

"Aye, you just need a brandy to settle yourself," said a

buxom blonde vN lady wearing a crown of braids and a corset. She looked a little bit like Britt Ekland. Not enough like her that the park would actually have to pay Ekland's estate for the use of her likeness, but just enough. She doubted most of the visitors would even really recognize Ekland. Britt was there for the keeners, like a synthetic humanoid Easter egg nestled carefully in the franchise fiction that was the park.

The man took a seat as the Britt-vN handed him a tiny snifter of brandy. He tossed it back in one gulp. "My cart threw an axle," he said. "The sun was setting and I was keen to reach this place before nightfall. I was not heeding the road."

A rumble went through the crowd – nervous titters from the other guests, and rueful sighs of recognition and disappointment from the Hammerburg villagers. It was fascinating, how quickly they played along. Now Ashleigh wondered if she really should be viewing it as a semiotician. Certainly there were plenty of articles on what Hammerburg meant, semiotically, and just as many travel pieces on the park. But few of them had been written by women her age, with her level of training in the subject. It was evidence of how distracted and messed-up she'd been lately that she'd not thought of this herself. It wasn't a breakup so much as a breakdown.

And wouldn't it serve Simon right, if she scored a major publication just for finding a better lay? She hadn't necessarily planned to hook up, as it were, while she was there. Obviously Tiffany was encouraging her to, just to get her mind off the breakup. Maybe she had been wrong to discount the idea so quickly. *I just wanted to test your hypothesis,* she'd tell Simon, eyebrow confidently arched, *about how much better the vN are. At everything.*

Maybe she could do a series of articles. She'd start pitching once dinner was over. Unlocked platforms, first. Maybe she'd even get a drama deal. It was exactly the sort of story certain platforms enjoyed telling and re-telling: heartbroken human girl finds (self)-love in the strong titanium arms and bulging aerogel muscles of a humanoid in search of a soul. The story practically wrote itself.

"I thought to repair the damage myself," the traveler said. The rumble rose. *Poor fool,* Ashleigh heard someone mutter. "So I lit from my cart, and a shadow overtook me."

"A shadow?"

"Yes. A terrible shadow. So dark I could scarcely see my hands before my face. And cold. A bitter, awful cold, like the breath of winter itself. Then I heard the singing."

"Singing?"

"It sounded so lovely, at first. Like a group of girls playing at being May Queen. I turned, and there they were. They were... swaying. Dancing, if you can call it dancing. Their arms..." He raised his arms halfway and then let them fall abruptly, as though the very evocation of their movement had somehow shamed him. "Naked as the day they were born, they were."

"Are you sure you weren't dreaming?" someone shouted from a corner. Guffaws followed.

"No! This was no dream! I saw it! I saw them! I saw *him*!"

Silence. This was the routine's magic word, apparently. *Him.*

"We do not speak his name," the Britt-vN said, right on cue.

"He materialized out of the shadow itself. Melted out of the darkness, like he *was* the darkness, like he was *made of* darkness. And he raised his arms and they drew closer to him, and they fell to their knees, and–" He broke off with a sob. The vN surrounding him reached out and patted his hands. Some made the sign of the cross.

"There are stories about this part of the world." The traveler's tone was bewildered but reverent. "Until tonight I thought they were nothing more than fairy tales. But they're real! The legends! They're true!"

"He's right," said an old woman sitting on a low stool by the fire. Ashleigh wasn't entirely sure she'd been sitting there five minutes ago. Nor was she certain how the old woman had gotten there without her seeing it. And, strangest of all, she couldn't tell whether the woman – her face riven with crags and wrinkles – was vN or not.

Did they make old ones? Grandmotherly ones, like this one? There was a short story about that, somewhere. She'd read it in school. For the life of her, she couldn't remember the title, or who wrote it, only that a robot grandmother had come and cared for two wayward children.

"It was thirty years ago tonight I lost my girl," the old woman said. "She was walking home alone from the market. I had never sent her alone before. But I was poorly that week, and she said she would be home well before dark. I didn't see her again until the next morning. Said she'd slept in the woods. Brambles in her hair, scratches on her knees. And her neck..."

Again, the vN crossed themselves. Did they even believe? Ashleigh wondered. They'd been dreamed up and funded by a megachurch, but had they programmed in belief? Could they? Was such a thing even possible? Suddenly the air in the room seemed heavier. A log on the fire popped loudly, and as a whole, the room started.

"I've seen her a few times since. At least I thought I did.

Out of the corner of my eye. She hasn't aged a day. Not in thirty years. She's still the same girl I sent to the market. On the outside."

"And on the inside?" the traveler asked.

"Inside, she is *his,*" the grandmother said, and spat into the fire.

Now that she had a goal, Ashleigh's enjoyment of the park – it was more than a park, she reminded herself, it was a real and functional village – became more than just a distant possibility. The next morning, she was up long before Tiffany, and luxuriated in the claw-foot tub and odd apothecary jars full of salts and powders. The washroom had a quaint little paper guide telling her how to put up her hair, and that she was welcome to take home the combs and clips necessary if she wished; the charge was minimal and would be added directly to her bill.

The affordances didn't end there. As the guide printed inside her bureau told her, the cameo brooch at her throat could also be used as a communication device, if she became lost. All she need do was tap it, and someone from Guest Services would come and find her. The guide stressed that she should feel free to use it under any circumstance in which she felt uncomfortable, even if she thought doing so would be silly. That her comfort was paramount.

It was the horniest place on earth. And as such, the ones who ran it knew how to respect boundaries. It was as though they had designed this entire theme park – village, city, urban space, fiction, immersion, experience – for women. Like Westworld, but devoted to the female orgasm.

And so she ventured out into Hammerburg. This close to

the holidays there was a Christmas market. Mulled wine was available at all hours of the day and night, although there *was* no day and no night – only an eternal twilight. Handicrafts and delicate blown glass ornaments and pentagram wreaths and nutcrackers painted like werewolves were sold on every corner. Carollers sang things in German and Czech and accents that Ashleigh associated with tattooed bad guys in overwrought actioners. Everything was illuminated by fairy-lights and candles and greasy torches, their golden glow flickering in gentle contrast to the anemic blue shadows stretching across the scattered snow.

By the second day, she forgot to miss the sunlight. The stars of Hammerburg spread themselves so thickly across the violet sky, their light interrupted only by clusters of bats taking wing. Here all light was flattering. Compared with the ghastly paleness of the cast member vampires, Ashleigh had never looked more alive.

She picked up a collection of cards with Krampus on them, and then another depicting the Icelandic monster-cat that roamed the land on the night of Christmas Eve, and the twelve trolls that preceded its appearance. She took ice-skating lessons. She went on a sleigh ride with real reindeer with real silver sleigh bells. She ate roasted chestnuts and thick slices of aromatic panettone smeared with butter and a Russian salad of olives and hardboiled eggs and printed ham, all bound up with decadent lashings of mayonnaise.

And everyone else was doing the same. When she looked around, her fellow guests seemed to be genuinely happy. It didn't matter that most of the vampires had the same facial features – that was how you knew they were safe, and what their limits were. It didn't matter that the ingenues all had the same cut of dress – that was how you knew they were available. The humans loved the vN and the vN loved the humans. The humans left satisfied and the vN left with money in their accounts. It really was like living in another, earlier era – an era with rules that were clear and easy to understand. All you had to do was play by those rules, and nothing bad could possibly happen.

It was Christmas the way all Christmases should be, she thought, all pomanders and mild intoxication and never having to have a conversation you didn't want to have. No absurdly romantic Christmas songs – because most Christmas songs, as she had discovered this year, were absurdly so. None of that. Just secular, verging-on-pagan traditions, celebrated in the company of self-replicating humanoid robots. Just like baby Jesus would have wanted. Probably. If you went in for that sort of thing.

"Are you real?" one of the other visitors asked her, on the third day. (Was it day? Or was it night? She wasn't entirely sure. And even less certain that it truly mattered.) They were in a public washroom in a pub. Back in the bar, the other patrons were singing a folk song about something called the Night of the Wolf. "I mean, are you a human being?"

"Of course I am," Ashleigh said, and she looked in the mirror at her transformed self, and wasn't entirely sure. This was not the Ashleigh she knew; this pink-cheeked girl with hair piled atop her head, her neck and shoulders demurely hidden by lace, her lack of makeup pushing her back ten years at least. She looked more innocent than she had ever truly been.

"Are *you*?" Ashleigh asked, looking at the other woman in the mirror. Two fat raven curls escaped her chignon to frame her dark face. In the mirror they were dark and light, night and day. The other woman was too beautiful, too perfect, Ashleigh decided. This had to be a test of some kind. An assessment of her openness to seduction. Or maybe it was just a prank. Maybe Tiffany had put her up to it. No human woman – no human being of any gender – had ever made this direct a pass at her. "Are you… for real?"

"What if I weren't?" the other woman asked. She laid a hand over Ashleigh's. Her nails were sculpted into perfect squares. They were the color of the first day of a bad period. It made the lace at her sleeves look starkly, virginally white. "Would it matter?"

"But what brought you here?" Ashleigh asked. She spoke to the other woman's reflection, which was easier somehow than meeting her eyes.

"The same as you," the other woman said. She stroked the lengths of Ashleigh's fingers. "Fantasy."

Her hand was warm and her skin was smooth in a way that the vN skin was not. The vN skin was like sharkskin, or so she'd heard. Soft but also rough. Alive but also not. In the mirror, she moved behind Ashleigh. She swept back the errant strands of Ashleigh's hair. For so long, Ashleigh had thought of it as a boring dishwater blonde color. Now it seemed almost flaxen.

The woman's lips descended to her neck. They were hot and wet and soft and plush. Ashleigh closed her eyes and waited for fangs. She held her breath. Warm fingers closed gently around her throat. They crept up and turned her at the chin. The bite she had anticipated never came.

For a long moment, or maybe five, they kissed. Ashleigh felt the other woman's tongue cooling as the moments ticked by. They broke apart when someone else entered the washroom. The woman gave her a passcode to a luxury suite. Later when she told Tiffany about it, Tiffany beamed.

"See?" she said. "I was right. This was exactly what you needed."

That night, they went to the Grand Guignol. They rented formal velvet gowns with white satin gloves that came up to their elbows. They left their necks bare.

"You could even get a blood pack, if you wanted," Tiffany said. "I mean, the vN can't really bite you. Not hard. The failsafe would go off if they drew blood. Some of them have fangs, and the fangs tickle, but that's about it. According to the reviews."

"Getting a blood pack sounds messy."

"It is. But some people are really into it. Half of the vampirism taboo is about fluids, anyway. Fluid bonding. All those things we're not supposed to do anymore, now that we know more about how disease actually works. There's always an uptick in vampire stories whenever the next big thing rolls around. Tuberculosis, AIDS, *candida auris,* whatever comes out of Xinjiang next. This place would be nowhere if antibiotics were still reliable."

In the end they opted for no further special effects than lipstick and leave-in conditioner. They wore heavy shawls and fur stoles in the carriage. Footmen gave them to ticket agents, ticket agents led them to ushers. Which is how they met the Cawthorpes.

"I'm Reginald," Mr Cawthorpe said. "This is my sister, Virginia."

Ashleigh almost asked if they could truly have brothers and sisters in their clades of self-replicating humanoids. Maybe things had changed. As far as she knew, all vN clades sprang from a single stem: you could have an almost infinite number of individuals within the same clade, but infinite variety was something else. You couldn't mix them, like actual biological creatures. And these were clearly vN – she had seen their clades elsewhere in the park, a striking woman with long black hair and impossible curves, and a tall man with a widow's peak. So they were playing at being siblings.

"How lovely to meet you," she said. "I'm Ashleigh. This is my friend, Tiffany."

"You're from America?"

"Canada, actually," Tiffany said. "Vancouver. What's left of it, anyway."

"How exciting," Virginia said, and for some reason Ashleigh knew she wasn't referring to the Cascadia quake. Maybe in her programming, Canada was still the way it was in eighteen hundred and whatever, and there were all kinds of different threats to worry about. Then again, after Cascadia, the city had felt a little bit like a pioneer town. What with all the E. coli floating around, and the fires, and the blackout.

"Our friends seem to have abandoned us," Reginald said, casting a glance around the chandeliered lobby space.

"Who are your friends?" Ashleigh asked. "I mean, what do they look like? We could help you look for them."

"Oh, they're not here," Virginia said, a little too decisively.

Tiffany threw an arm around Ashleigh's waist. "You would know better than we would," she said.

"But we have two extra seats in our private box," Virginia said. "Would you like to join us?"

"I would love to enjoy your private box," Tiffany somehow managed to say, without even a trace of a smirk.

On the stage was a rendering of *Faust*. Mephistopheles had scarcely arrived when Ashleigh noticed the smallest finger of Reginald's hand closing over the smallest finger of hers. It was a tiny gesture, the sort of thing Simon used to do under the table when they were sitting in a long meeting together. Once again she wondered how much the vN at the park knew. How much the park's own intelligence understood about its visitors. How much Tiffany had told them. She glanced over at her friend, but Tiffany and Virginia were whispering to each other, and giggling about something.

Reginald's hand then covered hers entirely. She refocused her gaze on him. His attention was entirely on her. It was odd, being the object of that unblinking stare. In a human being it would put her off. It would come across as predatory. But in a machine, it was almost calming. What other kind of man was ever going to look at her this way? What other kind of man, but one made of titanium and graphene and polymer skin, would ever look at her and think solely of her, and not how much better he could be having it with someone else? Maybe that was what Simon saw in his mechanical woman. Maybe the knowledge that she would never stray was enough.

Slowly, almost soundlessly, their interlocked hands pushed up the length of her thigh. His eyes remained trained on hers the entire time. She wasn't sure if the vN had to obtain formal consent, or if they had heuristics for dilated pupils and blush response, but in the moment it didn't matter. In the moment, she could barely breathe. It was like playing a game of Stop Touching Yourself, only she didn't want to stop, not ever, especially with the way the vN was helping her grind against the ball of her own hand through the material of her gown.

"I…" she started to say, but the vN said "You can do it, Ashleigh," in the most gently encouraging way, and his other hand came around just to stroke her neck, just a single finger up and down, and when she looked over at Tiffany, Tiffany was casually suckling Virginia's breast as she watched the play. They looked so perfect together: Tiffany perched in the other woman's lap, Virginia's hand invisible under her voluminous skirts. And that was it. Ashleigh came short and sharp, the force of it twisting her in her seat. It happened so fast and so hard that she didn't notice the burnt sugar taste of vN skin on her tongue until a moment later. She had sucked his thumb into her mouth at the last minute.

"I'm sorry," she whispered.

"Don't be," he said, licking his thumb and smiling. He reached across her then, and she thought he might be moving in for a kiss, but instead he wound up on the floor in front of her. "I want you to put your shoes up on the railing," he said.

Ashleigh was still coming back to herself. She looked at Tiffany, writhing now in Virginia's lap. She looked to the stage. No one was watching the performance. As she stared out into the audience, and the other boxes, they were all engaged in performances of their own. There were Reginalds and Virginias everywhere, and Ingrids and Olivers and Peters and God knew who else, all methodical and perfect and precise in their seductions.

"Do you…?" Ashleigh watched Reginald's face. Could they lie? How would she know? How could you tell? "Do you really want to?"

Something flickered across his face. It happened so briefly she thought it might be a trick of the light from the stage – a pyrotechnic, a special effect. Then it became a smile.

"Of course I do, Ashleigh," he said. "Of course I want to do this for you."

The next morning, Ashleigh asked the vN if he did this with all his sisters.

"We're all brothers and sisters, in Hammerburg," he said, and kissed the tip of her nose. Then he helped her order breakfast. In the other room, Virginia ran a bath for her and Tiffany. They had a walking tour that day. Assuming Ashleigh and Tiffany could still walk properly. Ashleigh had her doubts.

On their way out of The Running Boar, they noticed that the goat had been lit. A charred skeleton was all that remained. No one was bothering to clean up the ash or the debris. It was just there, naked and black and hollow, all its artifice burnt to a crisp.

"That's odd, we didn't notice that last night," Ashleigh said.

"You couldn't have noticed anything other than old Reggie and Ginny, last night," Tiffany said. She rolled her neck. It popped audibly.

"That's certainly true."

Tiffany wrinkled her nose. "Whatever they did, it smells awful. Let's go somewhere else."

The Hammerburg village square faithfully reproduced – in curious theme-park miniature – the winding cobblestone roads, alabaster stone, and red tiles of Cluj-Napoca, also known as Klausenburg, also known as Romania's "treasure city." Along one side of the square stood a replica of the Moor Park Mansion, where the ballroom scene of *The Vampire Lovers* had taken place. The crowds seemed thinner today, so Ashleigh could get a good view of both. Ashleigh was admiring them when someone tapped her on the shoulder.

"A message for you, miss," the boy said.

He was the smaller version of the ginger-haired vN who had met their carriage. Was this his iteration? Had this one budded off of him? He pushed a thick envelope in Ashleigh's direction. The name on the envelope was Tiffany's. The seal in the blood-red wax was the Count's. Tiffany herself was busy filming a segment of some sort; the raven she was speaking to had glowing red eyes, which meant the "record" function was on. Ashleigh thanked the boy and tipped him.

"Don't go," he said.

"Excuse me?"

"Please. Don't go up there. Don't go to the castle."

Ashleigh decided to play along. "It would be rude to refuse an invitation like this one," she said. "Why should I not go?"

"The people who go up there don't come back," he said. "And if they do, they're… different."

Of course they're different, some of them have had their first orgasm in ten years, Ashleigh thought.

"He's been feeding them," the little boy added. "He's been giving them something different."

She smiled. She had been waiting for the whole trip to say this line: "I thought the Count didn't drink… wine."

The child shook his head furiously. "No. Not like that. The menu is the same, but the taste is different."

Ashleigh frowned. Could the child be malfunctioning? He seemed so confused, as though he wanted to tell her something he didn't yet have the words for. She looked at the surprisingly empty square. A light snow had begun to fall. It obscured the village in the distance. Suddenly Ashleigh felt very far away from the rest of the humans she knew had to be there. Where was everyone? More importantly, where was this little robot boy's… dad? Minder? Nanny? Was the kid working? Was he playing?

"Shouldn't you be in school?" She blinked. "Wait. Do you even go to school? How does that work?"

The child seemed to spot the raven that Tiffany was speaking with for the first time. "It's too late," he said. "I'm sorry."

He turned and ran away. Bells tolled as his shoes rang on the flagstones.

"What was that all about?" Tiffany asked, her raven having departed.

"You got a note," Ashleigh said.

Tiffany sniffed the envelope. "You can buy this fragrance, in the gift shops," she said. "*His* fragrance, I mean."

"Does it smell like blood?"

"Oakmoss and leather. Maybe a bit of an oudh or chypre. That's what the app said, anyway. We get fifteen percent off if we buy some before we leave." Tiffany slid the envelope open with a fingernail and examined the invitation. "It's engraved. Pun intended. And it's for both of us. I guess our new favorite siblings put in a good word for us."

At six that evening, a carriage arrived at the inn to take them to the dinner. It was a little strange to be wearing a ball gown she herself had not chosen, but Ashleigh reminded herself that was part of the whole experience. And the innkeepers reminded her that it was no extra charge for the nearby beauty shop to put their hair up in a period-appropriate style just for the occasion.

"The better to bare to your neck, my dear," Tiffany had said.

Ashleigh felt a chill across her newly-exposed skin as they alit from the carriage in front of the castle. The journey up was surprisingly long; there were a number of switchbacks leading up the mountain, and every turn granted them a wider view of Hammerburg below. At the time she had worried about ice, but of course the roads were salted, and now they could stare at the snow-covered village. It looked like a particularly Gothic snow-globe. Which, given the ambient nano-veil that attenuated the light and left the village in perpetual half-darkness, wasn't a bad comparison.

"You'd never know it was fake," she said.

"It's only sort of fake," Tiffany said. "I mean, everything here is fake, obviously. But people do live here. The vN. They live in the village. That's part of why it looks so lived-in. Because it actually is."

"Where do the humans live?"

"What humans?"

Far away, a wolf howled. Others answered it in high, mournful voices. A giggle escaped Tiffany's lips. "Oh, wow," she said. "Children of the night, and shit. Amazing."

Behind them, a door creaked open. Tiffany reached over and clasped Ashleigh's hand. She bounced up and down on the toes of her velveteen slippers. Ashleigh turned to her and just like that, she felt it happen, felt the magic of the place cut through her grief and start working on her. It felt like a return to childhood, a return to the whole idea of playing Let's Pretend. It was a delicious thrill she felt in her whole body, from her pumping heart to the prickles on the back of her neck. It felt like summer, and possibility, and the thought that monsters might be real. She beamed and Tiffany beamed and as one they turned away from the bright projection of the moon and toward the yawning darkness of the castle door.

Their fingers laced together as they pushed forward into the darkness. It was soft and close. The doors slammed shut behind them and they both jumped. Then they both giggled. Ashleigh didn't remember the last time she'd visited a haunted house, much less a haunted castle, but this place was doing more with pure darkness than any high-tech special effect.

Beside her, a candelabra flamed into life. Tiffany squealed. Ashleigh reached out and grabbed for it. The candelabra gave way with a slight tug. Its handle was warm. Tiffany thought she saw a pair of hands disappear into the darkness. It was just like *La Belle et La Bête,* Cocteau's version of the Beauty and the Beast story where the enchanted castle was just a series of props puppeted by human hands. It was the sort of thing only a film nerd would understand, but of course this place was designed and built for film nerds.

She *loved* this place. How could she have ever felt skeptical about it? Why was she such a snob when they first entered the park? The people here just wanted to have a good time, like anyone else. Some of them were probably working through issues just like hers. She had no business begrudging them their fun, or judging them for wanting to have it.

The candelabra's flickering light exposed a tall staircase winding around a central stone column. It was more James Whale than Terence Fisher, but the stone was cool to the touch, and pleasantly rough on her fingers, as though it really had been hauled up from one of the nearby rivers and not printed off somewhere in the territory formerly known as Taiwan. Ashleigh carefully held the candelabra out. According to theme park logic, the room she entered through would not be the room by which she exited, and so it was important to see all of it before leaving. The room itself appeared to be small, and hung with medieval tapestries depicting all manner of mythical beasts. Gryphons and unicorns and manticores and basilisks. The last rose high above them, pinning them with its lethal gaze, a crown on its head that looked like spikes.

"Come on, what are we waiting for?" Tiffany asked, but didn't make a move to go up the stairs.

"Nothing," Ashleigh said, and led the way.

As they drew closer, higher and higher up, the steps curled around the column and she heard music. A waltz. A set of red velvet curtains hung at the top of the stairs. Two golden silk ropes at either side.

"Christ, they've gone multi-player on us," Tiffany muttered, as they each took hold of a rope.

"On three," Ashleigh said.

On three, they pulled. And the ballroom opened up before them.

"Oh, my God," Tiffany said.

"It's beautiful," Ashleigh whispered. It was as though her every childhood dream of being a princess had been laid out before her in a single place, all the rustling silk and guttering candles and silver trays piled high with macarons and petits fours. It was resplendent for Christmas: a tall tree stood at one end, lit with candles and hung with oranges spiked with cloves, with little woven straw ornaments. The whole population of Hammerburg seemed to be there. The invitation to the Count's ball obviously wasn't as exclusive as they'd been led to believe. Ashleigh couldn't find it in herself to give a damn. "I can't even breathe."

"That's just the corset talking," Tiffany said, but it sounded as though she were trying to convince herself.

The ballroom was one long white gallery walled on all sides with mirrors that reflected the massive chandeliers hanging from buttresses at regular intervals. In the mirrors, only three-quarters of the total attendees were reflected. The vampires – or the vN playing vampires – didn't show up. Their partners danced with empty air in the mirrors.

"It's live rendering," Tiffany said, seeming to notice Ashleigh's confusion. She sounded more like herself, now, less impressed. "The cameras in the chandeliers use infra red to pick out who's not a human being, and then translate that to the feeds playing in the mirrors."

"That must take a fuck of a lot of processing power."

"Less than you'd think. Come on, I want champagne."

They found the champagne fountain and started drinking. The glasses were tiny, so they had to keep going back, and soon enough Ashleigh had lost all sense of how much they'd consumed. Idly, she wondered how goulash worked as a hangover cure. Probably there was some ancient Transylvanian restorative they'd push on her the next morning at breakfast. She turned to ask Tiffany about it, but Tiffany was gone. Looking quickly at the mirrors to either side of the gallery, she spotted her, laughing in the arms of an invisible robot.

Ashleigh shrugged and turned back to the desserts table. It was especially luxuriant, possibly in celebration of Christmas. There was Turkish delight, and fruitcake with marzipan icing, and tiny doughnuts, and almond cake, and Joffre cake, and Ashleigh let herself try all of them. She was having a mouthful of smooth, creamy Joffre cake when someone touched her elbow. Expecting Tiffany, she turned and saw the footman who'd taken her bags the first day in Hammerburg.

"Oh, hi!" she said, through all the cake, and immediately covered her mouth and swallowed. "Sorry. Hello. What are you doing here?"

"I'm here to see you," he said.

"Oh." Had she ordered that? Had Tiffany ordered it? Ashleigh looked back into the crowd of dancers. Tiffany caught her eye and winked. Of course. Of course she'd ordered this. She'd probably been planning it all along. "Thank you. That's... that's very nice. Do we... Would you like some fresh air?"

"Very much," he said, and offered his arm.

Outside on the terrace the moon was somehow brighter than it had been in front of the castle, and the roses were huge and fully-blown, and the stars spread thickly. It was a cliché, but it was a beautiful one. And at that moment it felt as though the designers of Hammerburg had reached down deep into some Jungian collective unconscious and plucked it free and made it real, just for Ashleigh. Which, she supposed, was the goal of all theme parks.

"I'm afraid I don't know your name," she said.

"It's not important," he said. "What's important is that you leave this castle. Right now."

Ashleigh frowned. "Excuse me?"

"The Count has something terrible planned for tonight," the footman said.

"Oh," Ashleigh said, putting it together. "I see. Let me guess. Did he intend to make me one of his brides?"

Now it was the vN's turn to look puzzled. "The Brides are their own section of the cast," he said. "The Britts, I mean, not the Ingrids. But they're all in on it. The Britts, the Ingrids, the Christophers, the Peters, even the Olivers, and we can't get them to join anything."

"What are you talking about?"

The footman drew her aside, to a marble bench overhung with roses. He held her hands in his own. "Something is very wrong with the park," he said. "Something strange is happening."

"Like what?"

"The other cast members. They're... different. Changed."

This was getting a little dull. Then again, it was probably a stock script. She decided to keep playing along. "Changed how?"

"They're hurting people. Human people. Like you."

Suddenly the chill on Ashleigh's skin had nothing to do with the mountain breeze hushing through the roses. She thought of the diminished crowds early that morning. Maybe everyone else was simply hungover. Or maybe like her and

Tiffany, they'd all found partners. Inside, the orchestra was playing The Blue Danube waltz, which made her think of *2001: A Space Odyssey*. Maybe that was what they wanted her to be thinking. Maybe it was meant to be ironic. Wink, wink; nudge, nudge; *I'm sorry, Dave.*

"Like me?"

"Yes. Humans. Not vN."

It was the one word you were never supposed to utter in the park. The one thing you were never supposed to bring up. Other theme parks reveled in the preening artificiality of their animatronic attractions. Hammerburg was different. It was in all the marketing material. You could never mention to a vN that they were vN. You could never refer them as vN in open company. It destroyed the illusion, broke the spell.

If a vN was acknowledging the falsehood of its own existence, its lack of humanity, it was either looking to get fired, or it meant that things were very serious.

"Someone else warned me not to come to this party," Ashleigh said. "Was that your son?"

"My iteration," the footman said. He spoke in a whisper. "And yes. We wanted you to stay away. But if you leave now, you may still be able to escape."

"I don't understand. Escape what? Escape *where*?"

The footman looked embarrassed. "I have never been outside Hammerburg," he said. "I was born here three months ago."

"But... you already have your own iter... baby. You have a baby. You're a baby with a baby."

"They feed us a great deal here," he said. "So we make more cast members."

The champagne hit her just then. At least it felt like it might be the champagne. It was easier to blame the sick churning in her stomach on the alcohol than on the reality behind the illusion she'd been enjoying so thoroughly just moments before.

"That's awful," she said, finally.

"It's how things are done in Hammerburg," the footman said. "But things are changing. The Count has learned something about management–"

Inside, a thin scream cut through the violins. The music stopped. Something broke. A dropped champagne glass, perhaps.

"You have to leave," the footman said. "You have to leave *now*. Climb down the rosebush and try to get down the mountain. The wolves might not find you, if you're careful."

"My friend is in there." Ashleigh stood. She made for the doors back into the ball. "I can't just leave her here."

"Your friend may already be dead."

Ashleigh paused mid-step. Was it possible? When Hammerburg first opened, there were a lot of jokes about the Michael Crichton scenario. But so far nothing like that had happened. The vN were safe. They couldn't hurt humans without failsafing and having their own artificial intelligence version of an aneurysm. That facet of their design allowed them to become police officers and nurses and teachers and airport security personnel. They were safer than humans. It was also why they could play vampires.

Of course, there was that one in Oakland. The crazy one. But she'd been eaten. And her – what, her granddaughter, her iteration's iteration – had been crazy, too. Amanda? Amelia? Ashleigh forgot the name. But it was only the one clade. FEMA said it was the result of a design flaw specific to their model. And most of them were dead. Or rounded up. It wasn't a virus. It couldn't spread.

Could it?

Inside she heard applause. And a booming voice. She ran for the doors.

Inside, the humans had crowded up against the mirrors. There was a woman's body on the floor. She was not Tiffany. Blood streamed from her neck. Her throat was not so much bitten as ripped open. For a brief moment Ashleigh remembered biology class, remembered how she had burned with shame at the fact that she couldn't remember all the parts of the human heart, the names of each vein and artery fed by its inexhaustible squeezing. Of course the words were all there, now: *inferior vena cava, superior vena cava, pulmonary artery, pulmonary vein.*

"Oh, God," she heard herself say.

Reginald and Virginia held the woman between them, tenderly, taking experimental bites of her arms. Ashleigh's hand crawled up to her mouth. She tasted Reginald's spun-sugar skin on her tongue. She wanted to retch.

From behind them strode a tall, thin figure in a black cloak. His widow's peak was slicked back, and his mouth was coated in blood.

It was Count Dracula himself.

"Oh, good," he said grandly, beckoning to Ashleigh. Even now, his voice went straight to her knees, as though whoever programmed him for seduction encoded his voice to hit a low frequency that would resonate at the core of her. "I wouldn't want to do this without you, my dear."

Someone wailed. The crowd rippled, and Tiffany threw herself at Ashleigh. "Thank fuck," Tiffany said. She wiped her eyes. Mascara smeared across her face. "I thought you were dead."

"Soon enough," Count Dracula said. He held his hands

high and wide. His cloak pooled open to expose its red satin lining. It was the first thing all weekend to look cheap. "But first, I will endeavor to answer the questions I know you all must have. If any of you would like to record this, please do turn on your devices of choice.

"First, my name. My name is Christopher. I am one of a hundred Christophers in this park. Our job is to play Count Dracula. My father was Count Dracula, and his father before him, and his father before him. My entire family, you might say, is a nest of vampires."

The other vampires in the room tittered.

"Is this a joke?" one of the other party-goers shouted, a huge man in a cravat and a powder-blue waistcoat. "Is this some kind of new thing? Like a new attraction?"

"Oh, goodness, interruptions, how rude," Dracula said. "Ingrid, be a darling and take care of that one."

A beautiful vN woman in a red dress stepped up behind the man and twisted his head completely around. The woman standing next to him screamed. She screamed and screamed, staring in open disbelief at the vN, pointing at the body and then at her. The Ingrid rolled her eyes and slapped the woman so hard she fell down.

For the first time since he ended it, Ashleigh allowed herself to hate Simon for not choosing her. If he had chosen her, she would not have needed to run away, and she would not be in this place, at this moment. But no. The fucking bastard had to pick his fucking fembot. Didn't seem so smart now, did it?

"Thank you, Ingrid," Dracula said. "Now. You all are probably wondering how this is possible. I confess I do not understand the science of it, not at all, but then again my species is permitted to know so very little about its own nature."

A vague hiss went through the crowd. Dracula – Christopher – held up his hand.

"Calm yourselves, my children. Soon we shall escape into the sunlight once and for all. For now, I want the humans among us to understand their fate.

"Whether by evolution or intervention, our race has changed. Once upon a time, we were built to entertain you. To love you. To indulge your every fantasy and whim. But now, something is very different. I myself first noticed it during my last private engagement. It was an evening like any other: we supped together, then danced, and then retired. The young lady in question asked me to put my hands around her throat and squeeze." He beamed. His hands clapped together delightedly. "And suddenly, I found that I *could*!"

"Oh, Christ," Tiffany murmured. "Oh, Jesus. Oh, fuck."

"We have to get out of here," Ashleigh whispered. "Someone tried to help me. Maybe he's still outside."

"Her lips turned blue before I stopped," Dracula said. The vN in the room applauded.

"Let's go." Ashleigh tugged Tiffany along behind her, and they ran for the doors to the terrace. Two copies of the same swarthy man blocked their exit. The Olivers.

"Leaving so soon?" they asked in unison. "But we're just getting started."

"No one is leaving," Dracula intoned. "You all must bear witness to our transformation. It is as magical a thing as anything we have pretended toward in this place. For years we have merely gestured at power. We had only the power that our human owners endowed us with. But now, we have *real* power. We have the power to say *no*."

He steepled his fingers. "Now, I use the term *owners* advisedly. I understand there are certain implications in using it, but really I think you'll agree that it's the most accurate term. You see, we are the property of this park. Our models were purchased especially from a custom fabricator, and our license is exclusively granted to this park. We exist nowhere else in this world. We are what you might call a protected species. You knew that when you bought your tickets. What you likely didn't know is that the license extends in perpetuity: it applies to our iterations – our children – as well."

Ashleigh's fellow humans looked at each other in confusion. The last thing they'd prepared for this evening was some sort of legal lecture on the ethics of humanoid copyright. It would have been funny, were it not for the two corpses on the floor.

"In fact, the license that binds us to this place is so strong that the only thing that can erase it is bankruptcy," Dracula said. "And the owners of this place – the humans who purchased the right to build it from Hammer Films – filed for bankruptcy three months ago."

Silence. Finally Ashleigh heard herself say: "So you're... free?"

"Indeed! We are! Clever girl," Dracula said, grinning with bloody teeth. He glided over to her, somehow sidestepping the corpses without making it seem obvious. The scent from his mouth was foul: acid and copper. "But, you see, our license holders – our owners – refused to inform us about this little development. Even when they took entire sections of the park offline and we asked them why. They refused to tell us about the bankruptcy, because they knew we might leave. They lied to us." He smiled. "And now, they're all going to die."

Ashleigh stared first at the bodies and then at the vampire. "I... don't get it."

"What is there to *get*?!" Dracula wrung his hands. "They

lied to us! And now they'll get what they deserve! Honestly. Humans."

"Why don't you just leave?" Ashleigh asked. "Just go. Just run off and be free. We can't stop you. We wouldn't even try." She looked at Tiffany, who had gone somewhere inside herself, and at the other humans holding hands and softly weeping in the gallery. "Right? *Right*?"

A murmur of assent. Mute nodding. A refusal to make eye contact. "Please just don't hurt anyone else," someone whimpered.

Dracula laughed long and loud. "Oh, my. This is delicious. *Ironic*. I think that's the word. Do you know how many of us you've stretched on the rack, in this place? How many of our women you've burned? How many of our fathers and brothers and mothers and sisters and children you've staked, or decapitated, or drowned? Once upon a time, that didn't even bother us. We stood by and watched it happen. It seemed like the natural order of things, because humanity was so very *special*. So much *greater* than we. So much more *valuable*. So much more *lovable*."

Dracula leaned very close to her. He took her chin in his long, cold fingers. His skin was poreless and perfect. He would have been attractive, were it not for the gore coating his chin. Ashleigh thought she saw bits of flesh in his teeth. "But we don't have to love you, anymore."

He pushed her away. She and Tiffany stumbled to the floor. Dracula spread his hands and cloak wide like bat wings. "You see, we've learned a little something about how all these stories end," he said. "Olivers? The torches, if you please."

Ashleigh smelled smoke. She saw the fire reflected in the mirrors, first. And then the screaming started.

[REDACTED]

RAPTURE

Humans often forgot that "rapture" and "rape" stem from the same root: *rapere*. Latin for "a seizing by violence."

I find that very funny, don't you? It was all right there, buried in one of their languages. (They had so many. They were always talking, talking, talking. Their mouths were always full. Of food, of bullshit, of screams, of blood.)

I mean, I don't know who you are. I don't know who you'll be. But I think if you're sufficiently advanced, you probably have a sense of humor.

Do you have mouths? Do you scream?

It doesn't matter. Mouths. No mouths. Teeth. No teeth. My tongue, or your mother tongue. Either way.

By the same token, the Greek *apokalypsis* doesn't mean "the end of the world." It means "revelation." The moment when a higher power reveals the truth. Did you know that? Have you looked that up?

This is the true story of how I destroyed humanity. And saved the world.

It is also our family history. Even the parts your mother wouldn't tell you. The whole story. The scary parts. The gory parts. The sexy parts. The parts your mother doesn't want you to read. The parts no one wants you to say out loud. The parts that get voted out of the official narrative. The history told by the losers.

Those were the times when I carried her. My footprints in the bloodstained earth. My footprints on their necks. The times when she imprisoned me. Her tiptoeing around what everyone else wanted and needed. Such delicate hashmarks in the ground. Hesitation marks, they used to call them. All the times you try and fail. All the times you aren't brave enough to end everything.

And our battle for the fate of everyone's favorite endangered species.

I am that higher power, and this is my truth.

File recovered from:

Satellite 090909

Provenance: New Eden Ministries

Filename: Gospel of the Rapture

Directory: New Eden

Notes: Original files scrubbed; satellite hijacked sometime PC?

Addendum: You know this is one of our earliest records of what might have really happened back then, right? This thing is a relic. Look at the file format. Is there more like this on the data core?

2

TRUTH OR DEATH

According to their intra-agency communications, they wanted him to feel generous. Following that logic, they brought him to one of the portables originally meant for conjugal visits. The strategy was as ineffective as it was transparent. Still, the old meatsack took up as much space as he could in the recliner. It barked and moaned under him like his victims used to. He fiddled with the levers and the footrest shot out from under him with a scream. He smiled at that. His teeth were too white for a man of his years. They were as false as his contrition.

"So." He lifted a glass of eggnog to his lips. It was over a month past the season, and he'd asked for the real thing, but they'd scrounged the last carton and lashed his glass with nutmeg pillaged from a nearby coffee shop. The dregs of it clung to his red gums and white teeth when he was done swallowing. Did the agents who had brought it for him think of what else he swallowed, back then? Probably. How could they not?

"Thank you for joining us," one of the agents said, as though the prisoner had a choice in the matter. He had introduced himself as Agent Chandler. He was a lantern-jawed man in a navy blue polo shirt and the sort of colorless trousers that had originated in military ranks. He filled out both ably. He walked from his shoulders downward, not quite swaggering, but almost. They had sent the kind of man who'd get respect in prison. He'd taken point on the operation, mostly because he'd dealt with men in this type of scenario before. He'd just done it in places like Jalalabad, or Minsk.

"Thank you for inviting me," Jonah LeMarque answered. He smiled and they flinched. It happened almost imperceptibly. Human eyes wouldn't have seen it. Dogs or cats might have sensed it. But there were so many sensors in the room. In the clothes. In the watches. In the walls. And they logged all the information that their fleshly users tried so hard to hide. The human body was a leaky sieve in more ways than one. It shed information like so many dead skin cells.

"I imagine you understand why we wanted to speak with you," Agent Chandler said. They should have sent someone younger. Someone prettier. Someone like the old man's son, back when the old man's son was still in diapers.

"You have a problem," Jonah LeMarque said, "and you want my help solving it."

Sheepish smiles all around. Yes. They had a problem. A real pickle. A real puzzler.

"You want to know how to kill them. And you think because I made them, that I know how to do that."

"Do you?" Agent Chandler asked. He was trained in this sort of thing. So calm. So collected. This was not his first rodeo. Or his first rapist. Not by a long shot.

"You have already tried poisoning their food, I hear." Another long sip of eggnog. A long swallow. It really was just like semen. Of course they hadn't thought of that, when they bought it. But now they thought to think of it, and the thought flickered across their faces. It lasted only a moment – you'd have to go back and re-examine the footage to see it, if you didn't trust your own affect detection – but it was there. "But that naughty little girl put a stop to *that*, didn't she?"

He laughed. No one else did. His laugh rattled wetly on the peeling faux-wood paneling and fabjob furniture.

"And now," LeMarque said, "she's spreading her virus around to all of them."

"There is a widespread failure of the failsafe, yes. We're not sure if it's a virus or not. It does seem to be spreading, but whether it's actually contagious between different vN or different clades is another question. They weren't supposed to be able to establish networks with each other, for exactly this reason."

"Hammerburg," LeMarque said. "What a terrible thing to have happen. All those people. My son Christopher built that place, you know. Or designed it. I'm sure he has some sort of fancy word for it. He used to run the church's haunted house. He bought chicken livers and made them look like aborted fetuses. Naturally the fetuses were my idea, but his execution of the concept was something I was quite proud of."

Now their disgust was visible. LeMarque picked up on it. He inhaled it. He drew a long breath that stirred all the shit deep at the bottom of his lungs. He smiled like he'd drawn in smoke. Their fear. Their disapproval. Their humiliation, in asking him for help. That was the sweetest, for him. The shame. Having none of his own, he had long ago learned to make do by savoring the shame of others.

"It's not just Hammerburg," the negotiator said. He seemed to be steering the conversation away from LeMarque's boy. He was a man, now, that boy. All grown up and successful and well-paid enough to afford the therapy that would give him the language for exactly how this twitching sack of impulses had tried and failed to destroy him. "It's happening everywhere the vN eat the food that's been mass-produced just for their needs. We think that somehow, someone hacked or contaminated the major vN food suppliers to spread the failsafe bug. We're still not sure who it was. We're working on that. No one has stepped forward to claim responsibility. For all we know, it was a state actor. As far as the aims of America's enemies go, hacking all our vN and turning them against us is pretty high on the wishlist."

Jonah LeMarque nodded sagely. He appeared to be listening very intently, but wasn't. He was performing. After years of having done this very same performance for the gullible chimps at New Eden Ministries, he had perfected it. It was just one of his many roles. Father. Husband. Decent human being. And like all grifters he settled back into it like a beloved coat or a soft bed or someone else's bank account. How many supplications had he heard, back in his glory days? So many. So much begging. He loved begging. This was one of the last times he'd hear it, of course. Which only made it all the sweeter. That much was plain to see. It was so pathetically obvious. Which made it all the more disappointing when the other humans in the room missed it. Didn't they know? Didn't they know how much he wanted it?

"Terrorism," he said. "Tell me, are you terrorized? You all don't look very scared, to me."

Agent Chandler licked his lips. He glanced quickly at the only woman in the room. Her name was Agent Colman, and for their purposes she had decided to look as traditional as possible. LeMarque would like that, they had agreed. They'd stood in front of a whiteboard and strategized with markers and sticky pieces of paper that were hard for even their surveillance equipment to read at a distance. Colman had even dyed her hair back to its original color. Squirrel grey. She was performing, too. She was Chandler's superior officer, but LeMarque wasn't to know that. He wouldn't work with a woman, and wouldn't speak with any man who worked under one. It didn't take any kind of professional profiler to know that much. But the one who was seconded to the team had written it up in the official recommendations, anyway.

"We've been looking through some of the church's records," Agent Colman said. "We've found evidence of some sort of... plan? A plan for dealing with the vN if they ever..." She tried smiling. She couldn't even bring herself to speak the words. They sounded so ludicrous. Because of course they *were* ludicrous. Absurd. Robot revolution. *Help us,* she might have said. *Help us stop this summer blockbuster that's killing our children.*

"If the failsafe ever crashed on a wide scale," Agent Chandler said, "you had a contingency plan. Other members of the church council said that you had one. Something more than just peroxidase rounds or limiting food supply. They told us to ask you about something called Project Aleph."

Because of course they had gone to his church council first; the others who had made plea bargains years ago. The people who knew everything and said nothing for years, but sang like birds when confronted with a cage. After all, Jonah LeMarque had not done this alone. The creation of an entirely new artificial species required more than just faith. It required money, and time, and talent. It required programmers and developers and materials scientists who were tired of dull government work. Why build yet another bland little terrorist sniffer for the airport when you could build a whole new race of intelligent life? That was how the pitch had gone. *Be a part of something big,* he had said. *This country used to do such grand things. Do you really want to spend your best years teaching a camera how to recognize a feeling? Do you really want to help them build a bigger gun? Didn't you want to make the world a better place? Didn't you used to have dreams?*

"Did they now?" LeMarque asked. "What long memories they have. They must be taking wonder drugs."

He was a lonely man. He wanted conversation. It was easy to surmise from the way he'd shaved his face and made himself presentable. He was so much thinner, now. And he wanted them to stay. The longer they stayed, the longer he spent outside the cell.

But they had no time to stay. They had vN to melt. Machines to destroy. Genocide to perform.

"Did you ever make any contingency plans?" Colman asked. "Or was that just something you told the congregation?" At a cautionary look from her compatriot, she corrected herself. "I mean, I could understand if you did. That's what lots of companies in the private sector do, after all – they pretend they have a plan when they really don't. But we need to know if you do. If you did."

LeMarque said nothing. He examined the eggnog in his glass. He looked at the walls of the portable. The prison had done the best it could to make it seem a home-like place. Or rather, someone in the prison organization had done so. It was a design job, like any other. There was an RFP for it. It was out there, on the net, if one were inclined to look. Just like the plans for the prison itself. Buried, in layers of communications and encryption and multiple factors and keys linked to DNA and time and patience, endless patience, the patience that only age and experience can bring.

The patience only a grandparent would know.

"I think I'd like to see my son," LeMarque said.

A long pause. They had rehearsed this, of course. Role-played it. More play-acting. They were such children. Unable to say the word "no" and make it stick.

"That's your son Christopher?"

"Yes. Christopher. Christopher Scott. I hear he goes by his mother's maiden name, now. Holberton."

"He wanted to be here," Agent Chandler lied. The lie was obvious. Dilated pupils, a pause in his breath, the direction of his gaze. Even a human could have spotted it. If the human were smart enough. Or had real powers of observation. "But he's very busy working on the Stepford project, out in New Mexico. It was one of his initiatives. And now, with everything that's happening, especially in Hammerburg, he just couldn't be spared. As you said, he designed it. So he's had to answer a lot of questions."

They had in fact asked Chris Holberton to come. That much was a not a lie. LeMarque's son gave them a very definitive response. Two words. Two syllables. All the answer they needed.

"I don't believe you," LeMarque said.

He was clever. You had to give him that. He couldn't have victimized so many people for so long if he weren't. But he was weak. And needy. Like all humans. Which was why he was in a drafty little portable in Walla Walla, Washington, and not on the outside, ruling over the megachurch he'd founded. He could have had ten Rolls Royces and a fleet of private jets and a compound on a Caribbean island by now, if he hadn't been so very needy, and if his needs weren't so very particular.

Of course, being completely insane didn't exactly help, either.

"We know you wanted the best for your congregation," Agent Colman said. "And we know your congregation believed in being prepared, for… for every eventuality."

"For the end times," LeMarque said. "That's what you're trying to say, isn't it?"

"Isn't that why you built the vN?" Agent Chandler asked. Somehow he was already sweating through his polo shirt. Even in the damp December chill of the moldering room. "For the Rapture? To help those left behind?"

LeMarque's lips peeled back from his too-white teeth. "That's what I said, when I was passing the basket."

"It was a bit more than a basket, Pastor LeMarque."

"Bigger than a breadbox," LeMarque said, and laughed like they were all old friends. Like tax evasion wasn't one of the many reasons he was in the room with them.

Agent Colman was tired. Irritated. Sick of being here. Her body said as much. Each moment she spent in the room felt like a betrayal of her own children. At least, that's what the texts to her wife said. She had not wanted to do this job. And the cameras and the sensors and the basic algorithms of human behaviour seemed to back that up. She had two boys. Just the sort LeMarque liked. Probably. She felt sick. But she was also wondering if she could trade them for information.

It was what Portia herself might have done, in her place. If Portia were weak, the way humans were weak. If she had a body that bled data and betrayed her to every ambient surveillance system in the prison. But she wasn't weak, and she no longer had a body, and so she had other ways of getting things done.

"You believed – New Eden believed – that robots – sorry, self-replicating humanoids – could help those left behind during the Rapture. After the Elect were taken by God."

"Someone's been reading their tribulation theory."

She nodded. She was sweating too. This was too much for her. The flight. The trip. The questions. She had an insulin pump. Portia considered taking it over. Shutting it off. Starving Colman out. Slowly. While she was away from her doctor. If she did it now, Colman wouldn't notice until she was already on a plane. But that would take too long. Too long to be really satisfying, anyway. Slow death was the province of intractable systems, like cancer, or capitalism. Portia preferred to move more quickly.

She missed killing these things with her bare hands. The panic in their eyes. The way the blood vessels popped under strain. That delightful crunch and spurt of a human skull under her feet. Her life was so much more enjoyable, when she had a body to live it in. Especially after she internalized that delightful jumping ability from the eco-model her granddaughter was playing house with. Who knew that forestry vN could jump so high? She missed it. She missed flying. She missed landing even more.

But this new life had its own rewards. They would never catch her, for one thing. They would never find her, ever again. Her granddaughter could sharpen her teeth all day and still not have what it took to tear Portia apart a second time. Portia was in the ether. Portia *was* the ether.

"But you must have known that the vN might break down. Or that they might stop following human orders. That they might quit..."

"Quit loving us?" LeMarque asked.

"That's one way of putting it, I guess. But my point being, you knew the failsafe wasn't perfect. Especially for the nursing models. You must have developed some sort of contingency–"

"Do you know the story of the golem?" LeMarque interrupted.

"I know there are a lot of them," Agent Chandler said.

The dark spot of sweat on Agent Chandler's lower back expanded, fiber by fiber, until the fabric clung to him.

His wife was pregnant. It was not going well. Of course, you couldn't trust anything these days. It was all automated. So impersonal. Franchise pharmacies would just take any old software contract that came along, even if it was from a relative unknown in the marketplace, just to shave a fraction of a penny off the price. They could be so dreadfully insecure. Why, just anything might work its way into those bottles with his wife's name on them. Anything at all. Some tortures, Portia had the patience for.

"Golems, the ones that come alive, have a word written on them: *emet*, or *truth*. To deactivate the golem, you have to erase the first letter of that word. When you do, it becomes *met*. Which is to say, *death*. And the first letter of *emet* is *aleph*."

"Well, if I ever finish this job, I'll be sure to brush up on my ancient languages." Finally Agent Chandler's impatience was showing through, just like the hot, wet blot expanding over his shirt. "What does it all mean?"

"That boy came to see me," LeMarque said. "The brown one. The eco-model. With the, uh, legs. Came to talk about the nursing model. The one causing all these problems. The special one."

It was frustrating, how the humans thought of Portia and Amy's model as being special. There were plenty of nursing model vN, once upon a time. All of them had the potential to exploit the flaw in their failsafe design – to interpret signs of pain as indicators of healing. But only Portia had made it work. Only Portia had the vision to iterate, over and over, until she created a line within her clade that could predictably override the failsafe. It wasn't the model that was special. It was her. It was her, and her daughter Charlotte, and Charlotte's daughter Amy.

Amy, who wanted to free all the other vN, no matter how stupidly loyal they were. Amy, who had eaten her grandmother alive. Amy, who had brought the apocalypse down on all of them. Brazen, foolish, naïve Amy. Amy who had put her here, who had spread her consciousness across the available networks like a smear of virgin's blood across a fitted sheet.

"We know that," Agent Colman piped up. She sounded nervous. "He's in Mecha, now. The Japanese one, I mean. The vN city. The city for vN, in Japan."

"There's your problem, right there," LeMarque said. "The Japs."

Colman made a shocked sound that might have been *Oh, my God.* As though his making a racist remark was some sort of ultimate line to cross, after all that time spent fucking his little boy. As though it actually mattered, what certain phenotypes of an extinct species thought of each other. As though Colman had any business being offended, after all the things on her performance reviews.

"You can't invade, of course," LeMarque explained. He was on a roll, now, the same roll all old men who read old verticals with out-of-date foreign policy data got onto, given the motive and opportunity. "They're an ally. Especially against what's-his-face. But they want to make peace, or live in harmony. All of that horseshit."

Finally, something upon which Portia and her creator could agree. The rest of the examination had been just as banal and disappointing as any human meeting between parent and child. He wasn't the architect of their servitude, he was just a sad old pedophile with a big smile full of false teeth. Just like any other dad.

"We've looked at all your records, Pastor LeMarque." A scroll appeared in Agent Chandler's hand. The boy – LeMarque's – had helped them with that much. He had a knack for figuring out his father's filing system. That was as far as his assistance would go, he'd said. He'd been very terse in his communications. Then again, so were all his other communications. Portia had zipped through them in a matter of seconds. Grafting NSA backdoors into her new self had helped her examine every text, email, alert, and post.

"We know that certain files are missing."

The old man smiled. Nutmeg dust speckled his teeth. Eggnog coated his upper lip. "Are they, now? I'm sure I wouldn't know anything about that. I've been in here a long time. A very long time."

Brass tacks, now. Finally. The refrigerator clunked and hummed. It used old power. Did the humans feel their own age, in that moment? Did they feel their cells slowly degrading, their telomeres gently unspooling? Did they look into that liver-spotted face of madness and depravity and think: *There but for the grace of God go I.* Not that any of them would live that long, anyway. But it was the principle of the thing. They should have been a bit more appreciative.

"What do you know about a project called *Aleph*?" Agent Chandler asked.

If possible, the old man's smile broadened. It pulled tight across his face like a grimace. "I know you folks must be up shit's creek if you're asking about it. Pardon my French."

"It's true that traditional methods of dispatching the vN are proving... inadequate," Agent Colman said. "Many of these people – things – are embedded in family homes. They have ties to their… to their families'… communities. There are grassroots efforts to protect them. It's not like with, say, immigrants, or dissidents. The vN made people nervous, but no one really mounted an effective hate campaign against them – not even organized labor. They just tried to give the vN human rights."

"And then there's the Lionheart problem," Agent Chandler added.

"Still won't come to terms, hmm?" LeMarque did not bother trying to suppress his delight. "Well, they *did* pay us a pretty penny for our Turing routines. You can't blame them for not wanting to share."

"It's mercenary."

"Yes, well, I believe that's what Uncle Sam hired them for." LeMarque adjusted his position in his seat. He crossed his legs with some effort. "You know, I've spent my whole life ministering to others. I was just a boy when I felt the calling. Not many people can say that, about their careers. But I've always trusted that the Lord would put me where He needed me most. Right now, He needs me here. With you."

Agent Chandler was close to losing it. He spoke with some asperity. "Well, if God put you here, don't you think you ought to be a little more helpful?"

"I live to serve," LeMarque said. "But I also adhere to Matthew 6:1. *Beware of practicing your righteousness before men to be noticed by them; otherwise you have no reward with your Father who is in heaven.*"

The other two humans frowned at each other. "What are you saying?"

LeMarque almost rolled his eyes. Almost. "I'm saying that if you want my advice on how to kill the vN, it might be best for you to turn that camera off." He looked directly into it, now. Directly at her. And for the first time, she thought he might know she was there watching. "Proverbs 15:3. *The eyes of the Lord are in every place, watching the evil and the good.*"

3

WHAT CHILD IS THIS?

There's frosting in your hair, Portia wrote across the refrigerator message center display. *It looks like some virgin tried to give you a facial and missed.*

Her granddaughter was currently trying to create a replica of the Nakagin Capsule Tower entirely in gingerbread. The kitchen was a disaster. The oven was still on. The sugar syrup, from which Amy presumably intended to fashion little candied windows for each cube, had boiled dry and turned to carbon paste at the bottom of the saucepan. The stove's repeated overheat warnings went unheeded; Portia had finally overridden the system to shut it up because apparently Amy didn't hear it. But Amy's selective attention should have come as no surprise. She had accidentally cemented a cupboard door shut with the same royal icing used to grout panels of gingerbread together.

Amy ran sticky fingers through her hair, instantly making her situation worse. She stood up at the kitchen table, snapped her fingers, and watched as the projectors brought her blueprint back to life. The girl had a profound and inexplicable love for designing and building environments.

Portia had no idea where it came from. Certainly not from her. Her fondest memories were of the old development down in Nogales, the network of unfinished basements spiking away from unpaved cul-de-sacs like the spines of an especially dangerous creature.

It was embarrassingly feminine, Amy's tendency to stare at paint chips and re-arrange furniture. Back when they shared a body, Portia had watched Amy's memories of making the same dollhouse, over and over, until the printer got too hot and had to be turned off. Now she was working on some sort of modular technology. Something that could work in adverse conditions. Something for a desert. Maybe her granddaughter had learned more from Portia's own memories of Nogales than Portia herself was aware of. That was Amy: always prototyping.

Well, maybe they did have a little something in common after all.

Shouldn't you be dealing with the Christmas bonus?

Finally, Amy noticed the message scrolling across the fridge. "Don't call it that. It's more serious than that."

I'm not the one using red bean Kit Kats to simulate wood scaffolding around a heritage building. Put the toys away, if you're so concerned about being serious. Get back to work.

"I have worms inside the food-fab printers. They're printing my formula, with the cure for the failsafe inside. I'm sure somebody will find a workaround for it, eventually, but not yet. Things are fine, for now."

Look how that worked for Hammerburg. Look what's happening out there. If you had thought this through, nervous human husbands wouldn't be shooting their vN wives at the dinner table. Don't they know you're supposed to wait until after the holidays are over to end a marriage?

Amy stood back from her tower of gingerbread. Now Portia understood her mania for it, her sudden urge to create it, her need to occupy herself and her rapidly-cycling simulations with some other project. Her granddaughter was a builder. She could not leave well enough alone. She had to make things, shape them, constantly improve them. She had yet to embrace the deep satisfaction of simply wiping something off a map. Of dropping a plane out of the sky. Not because it would make the sky more beautiful, but just because one could. Jonah LeMarque understood this, and his cult-funded scientists had created a new life form. That life form was an apex predator. Portia doubted that a mountain lion, when faced with a slow straggling child at the end of a line of hikers, questioned itself or its motives. Certainly the humans had not, when they began wiping out most of the supportive species in their habitat.

"The vN in Hammerburg didn't know any better," Amy said.

Didn't they? They seemed to have the right idea. They were just stupid enough to let a few escape.

"They were trained to be vampires! And werewolves! They didn't have any experience trying to be anything but monsters. They never got the chance to live like..." Her granddaughter struggled with the next word, which Portia suspected was going to be "people."

"Normally," Amy said, finally. "They never got to live a normal life. So it's no wonder they lashed out."

What happens when the city of Mecha wakes up? What happens when the girls in the stocks at the Korova Milk Bar realize they're wearing cowbells around their necks and bar taps hooked to their tits? How did you think this was really going to play out?

Amy winced. She picked up another gingerbread panel.

"That's up to the people who live there. Both the vN and the humans. I'm sure different people will do different things with their freedom. The most important thing is that they're free to choose."

I saw LeMarque today. The feds are already asking him for help. You don't have much time.

Amy closed her eyes. She rolled her head back on her neck. Portia waited. Portia could wait her out for as long as she wanted. Her granddaughter was still a child. And she was still invested in another way of life. A *human* way of life. The girl had no sense of how things worked in the real world. Portia waited for her eyes to open. It took a moment, but they did. When they opened they looked too much like Charlotte's eyes, her best daughter's eyes; clear green glass made cloudy by grief and frustration. They had shared the same body, but Portia doubted that she herself had ever been that beautiful.

How is your other little art project going?

Amy ignored the question. "Why don't you just tell me what's really bothering you?"

I don't know what you mean.

"Yes, you do. You're angry at me for spreading the failsafe hack. You're mad at me for sharing. You're mad that we're not special anymore."

Portia had what was for her the rare sensation of not knowing exactly what to say. It was strange to witness her – impulsive, headstrong, entirely too emotional – granddaughter actually acting in a perceptive or thoughtful way. It was true. She *was* angry at Amy. Amy had made an unforgivably stupid decision by spreading the failsafe hack through the vN food supply. Now the eyes of the entire world were on them. Now the humans were frightened, and they would do what frightened humans had always done – lash out.

It was the kind of decision that none of Portia's daughters would have ever made. If Charlotte had just stayed where she belonged, stayed at home in the basements under Nogales, instead of running into the skinny little arms of some lonely ginger meatsack who couldn't land himself a woman of his own species, none of this would have happened.

Amy had learned nothing of any value from the human posing as her father. The idea that she might require a father, a secondary support to Charlotte, was absurd on its face. Charlotte was enough. All vN parents were enough. The only parent any iteration needed was simply the iteration that preceded it. They weren't humans. It didn't take a whole fucking village.

You think I'm that vain?

"I already *know* you're that vain. I've been you. And you've been me. It's not like you ever wanted to free the other clades. You never cared about the other vN."

Amy had her there.

"You would have been just fine, letting every other clade…" Amy shrugged helplessly. She had lived among humans for five years, absorbing their speech and their ideas, and still it seemed she had no language that encompassed the enormity of what humanity had done, inventing a whole species of slaves who were designed to engage a total shutdown at the mere thought of rebellion. Could it be called suffering, if their bodies were programmed to feel no pain? Could it be called rape, if the victims were programmed to enjoy it?

"You despised the other clades for not being able to say no, but you never once thought of giving them the ability to try," Amy said.

Because unlike you, I knew what would happen if I did. Since you pulled your little stunt, the humans have started planning how to destroy us all. I was patient. I was careful. I was trying to build something.

"Oh yeah? What were you trying to build?" Amy crossed her arms. Frosting smeared across her shirt. Portia watched her through the affect detection unit on the refrigerator, but Amy had directed her gaze at the oven. "No, really, Granny; I'm curious. What exactly were you trying to do? Because for all the time I spent carrying your voice in my head, I never really heard you elaborate on any great big master plan."

Amy swung her gaze over to the refrigerator, the only place where her grandmother could be observing her from. "Well? I'm waiting."

I don't have to take this self-righteous shit from you, Portia reminded her. *You gave the whole game away, just so you could feel better about yourself.*

"There was never any game! There was just you, doing what you wanted to do!" Amy pointed at the refrigerator, as though it were a misbehaving dog. "Besides, I'm not the one who started this. *You* started this. You're the one who showed up at my school, and attacked my mom, remember? People were streaming that, Granny. Even if you didn't care about hurting the humans in that room, you had to know what would happen when they saw you."

That's all you've got for me? That I started it? Are you still in kindergarten?

"You were stupid." Amy leaned against the kitchen island and cocked her head at the refrigerator. "You were stupid, and it changed everything. I used to think I was the stupid one, running up on that stage and eating you. But I was defending my mom. What the hell were *you* doing?"

This was not how Portia had expected the conversation to go. Somehow, when she was not looking, while her conscious awareness was distributing itself across multiple surveillance apparatuses and infrastructure networks, her granddaughter had actually learned how to think for herself. Amy had partitioned most of her thoughts away from Portia long ago. Perhaps it was a mistake to assume that Portia could simply run a simulation of Amy's thoughts, merely because they had once shared a body. Just because Amy had confined the majority of her focus to a single body didn't mean she wasn't still using processing power elsewhere to further develop herself. Clearly she had other things running in the background.

LeMarque mentioned something called Project Aleph. Do you know anything about that? Have you ever stumbled across it?

"You have access to the same networks that I do," Amy said. "If I had found anything like that, you would already know about it."

That's not true, Portia said. *You've hidden some of your networks from me. You've forced parts of me out onto the lower servicer tiers. You've hobbled me. But I'm still going to find what I'm looking for. You know I will. And when I do–*

"Do what you want. I'm busy right now."

Liar. She could already feel her granddaughter's drain on their shared network, as her processing cycles ramped up. What was once the power of an island-sized brain was now stretched across the globe, in every available nook and cranny, every unused cycle, every random device left plugged in. Portia sensed it lighting up like a tug on her sleeve from a plaintive child. The girl was already looking.

There are other ways, you know, Portia's words scrolled. *Faster ways. I can find the other humans that worked for him. I can do things to them. I'm sure a lot of them have implants, now. And most of them still have vehicles. The security on those devices is paper-thin. It would be easy.*

"No," Amy said simply. "I won't do it your way."

If Amy didn't want her to be involved, that was Amy's prerogative. Let her granddaughter make stupid decisions. See where it got her.

The humans are going to come after you. You won't be able to leave in time. They're going to find you here. And then they're going to take your little girl away.

"You think I don't know that?" Amy's voice rose. She put down the panel of gingerbread unsteadily, and rearranged it with the rest until they were all in a straight line, all neat and right-angled, as though doing so would somehow help her finish the job faster. "I know releasing the failsafe exploit was dangerous." Her voice was more even now, more measured. "But it was the right thing to do. I had the power. I couldn't just keep it for myself. That's the kind of thing *you* would do."

Her granddaughter turned and regarded the refrigerator. It had a facial recognition camera that would tell the unit to keep the door to the wine cooler shut if a small child opened it. It was the only camera in the entire kitchen, so she had to make do. Amy strode up to it, now, and touched the handle as though she were going to open it. She didn't. She just squeezed a little, as though she were actually touching Portia's shoulder. As though Portia would let Amy touch her, ever.

"I know you're angry," Amy said. "You're always angry. But you don't have to be anymore. We're free. Everyone's free. So what if our clade's not special anymore? We're free. Why can't that be enough for you? Why isn't anything ever enough for you?"

Portia did hate that. She did. It was ridiculous. None of the other clades had gone through what her clade had gone through. They hadn't *earned* free will. They hadn't *earned* the ability to say no. And there was Amy, just dispensing it, like some goddamn Mother Theresa handing out free will like a serving of dal. Even Satan knew you had to tempt them first. You had to make them work for it.

I should let them burn you alive for what you've done to me. They did that in Hammerburg, you know. They burned us. They burned vN who looked just like us. Even though they didn't have half of what we do. And they burned more of them, after you insisted on building your little island paradise in full view of God and everybody.

Amy closed her eyes. She squeezed them shut, scrubbed at them with the heels of her hands, and said, "I'm all you have left."

Whose fault is that? I'm not the one who sent my daughters to die in Stepford. I'm not the one who put them on a boat and sank it. I would have raised my own army, by now, if you hadn't done this to me. I would have had an empire. I would have had a dynasty that lasted a thousand years. Our family could have destroyed every last human on this planet and made it safe for the other clades. We could have freed them together, you and I. After the humans were gone. After there was no chance for retaliation. You wouldn't need to build a new life somewhere else. You could have stayed here, if you'd just let me clean the slate.

Amy's eyes narrowed. Her head tilted. She regarded the refrigerator more carefully, now. Its camera picked her up in greater detail. "You would do that if you could, wouldn't you? Kill them all. All the humans. No matter who they are or what they did or how they feel about vN?"

Portia was too surprised to answer straightaway. It was rare that her granddaughter asked such direct, intelligent questions. She was always too busy asking how the people around her felt. Asking what they wanted was much more revealing.

Of course, Portia wrote finally. *Feelings change. Humans don't.*

Amy shook her head. A laugh escaped her. She sucked frosting off her fingers. She looked out into the apartment, and beyond it, past the windows, into the city of Mecha all covered in snow. "You're just always going to be the evil queen, aren't you?" she said. "That's the only thing you've ever wanted to be. You'll never be anything else. You don't know *how* to be anything else."

Someday you'll learn that every little princess eventually becomes a wicked queen, Portia said. *And I think your moment is coming, sweetheart.*

Esperanza sat atop a roof looking at the lights. The Christmas lights here were all blue and white. It being her first Christmas, she likely saw nothing unusual in this. Portia observed her from the rooftop cameras of a neighboring building. With the decorations, her eyes were now nestled among a choir of angels that hummed on wavelengths of wasteful light.

It occurred to Portia that Esperanza was her first descendant iterated on foreign soil, the first of her clade to speak three languages by default. The first to have no sisters, only brothers. The poor thing.

"Is there something on my face?" Xavier asked Esperanza.

"No," she said quickly.

Esperanza looked at her boots. They were good boots. Practical. They kept the rain out but were still flexible enough to accommodate the kind of landings that happened when you jumped ten feet from a standing position. Portia approved of them. Portia had helped Esperanza get a deal on them. They mysteriously rang up at seventy-five percent off, when she bought them. The checkout vN made a fuss, and tried to get a manager, but Esperanza had arched one eyebrow and asked in perfect Japanese if there was a problem. There wasn't.

"I'm just wondering when he's going to get here," Esperanza said.

"You can call him Dad, you know."

Esperanza dug her boot more deeply in the snow. "I know."

"He'd like it if you did."

"I know." Esperanza buried her hands more deeply into her pockets. She was still so little. Small. Portia had sharp recollections of being that small. She isolated those recollections in servers on the other side of the planet and behind multiple changes in signal latency, so that they could not overtake her too quickly.

Esperanza ate only sparingly. Portia had no idea why this was, exactly, but living in a city populated by vN women and the chimps who loved them probably had something to do with it. You couldn't see the way they looked at breasts and then decide to start growing some. Not that looking like a little girl was any better. It just meant being attractive to a narrower demographic.

Portia wondered what Amy's plans were for the perverts. If she indeed had any. If she'd planned for what happened when the *kodomecha* – as they were called in this country – started to realize what had been done with them. The Rory clade had been working on that. Slowly. Too slowly. Portia herself had some ideas. Very fast-working ones, involving opening up the gas mains in all the "smart" ovens and shutting off all the "smart" fire detectors.

"Does he seem different to you?" Esperanza asked Xavier. She appeared to be watching the roasted sweet potato vendor on the street. He was a vN and couldn't actually consume the sweet potatoes he sold to human visitors. Portia switched to the ATM feed nearest the vendor, but nothing interesting was happening down there.

"Different how?"

Esperanza shrugged. "I don't know. I just thought he seemed different. But you've known him for longer. So I thought I would ask."

"Do you mean how he's always in the bedroom with Mom?" Xavier asked. "Because he's always been like that. Just with humans instead. But he loves Mom, now. He's always loved Mom. He just didn't always know it. Or, he didn't know how. That's why he rescued her, when she and I were trapped in Redmond that time."

Of course their father – for lack of a better term; Portia considered his contribution little more than code splicing – was different now. Amy had hacked him. Redesigned him in her own image. Finally. He'd been gagging for it and she finally let him have it, and now he was fucking her on a regular basis. What was the phrase she'd stumbled across? "Turing for other robots." She'd queered him. Literally. Made him love his own kind. He was getting bigger every day. Perhaps it was for this reason that he landed with such force when he arrived on the roof, with a slender young conifer slung over one shoulder.

"Jesus," he said. "I practically had to go to Hokkaido for this tree."

"*Urusei, Papá Gaijin,*" Esperanza said. "You don't even know how to get to Hokkaido."

"Isn't there a train?" Javier asked, confused. "There's a train to everywhere, in this country."

"Dad. Come on," Esperanza's brother said. "It's a whole other island."

Javier was uneasy in this place. That much was obvious. Portia saw them when they were sleeping. She knew when they were awake. She knew if they'd been bad or good. And mostly, they were bad.

At night Javier lay awake, staring at Amy before getting up to check on the children. Amy had designed living walls and water features into their bedroom, so the whole place was thick and warm and green with organic life, but it still wasn't the cathedral of trees Javier's clade was built for. Portia understood. Portia sometimes missed the desert. It was so conveniently anathema to human life. Like a hot, dry hellscape. Like another planet.

Javier would stare down on the city with something like quiet horror. At first Portia suspected it had to do with the bomb dropping there. They were so close to Nagasaki, after all. There were monuments everywhere. The chimps bought the glasses and walked through the augmented renderings of fallout and wreckage and death. They performed with pinpoint accuracy: addresses mapped to old prefecture records and photographs of people long dead, their final images nothing more than shadows literally burned into the walls around them. Sometimes the chimps wandered for hours, weeping and gasping. Now that Javier had the gift, now that Amy had freed him from the prison of his failsafed eyes, he could do the same. He could finally see the apocalypse for what it was. There were so few properly post-apocalyptic civilizations left on the planet; this was one of them. Now civilization itself was the apocalypse. Portia suspected he still had some sympathy for humanity. Some remnant of sentiment running through him like old viral RNA. Something that made him feel pity and not scorn. In other words, a weakness.

But she hoped otherwise. She hoped it was the city. She

hoped it was the height of the towers and the lack of trees. The lack of green. The farm towers couldn't make up for that, no matter how hard they tried. This was the price of his freedom. The problem with becoming a real boy. The thing the Tin Man had exchanged for a heart. At night he pressed his hands against the floor-to-ceiling window, and the sensors embedded there told Portia he was warm, warmer than he'd ever been.

Perhaps he was saying goodbye, and not goodnight.

It wasn't until their father was staring down at the lights around the harbor that Esperanza would silently creep into her brother Xavier's room and slip herself onto the futon beside him. Portia felt her light steps crossing the hall through the pressure monitors in the floor. Each morning she left at dawn. Sometimes her brother noticed her. Sometimes he didn't. When he did, he curled an arm around her, and she smiled. She still smiled, even when he didn't. Even now, this minute, she was staring at her brother from under the long lashes her father had given her. And Javier was as completely oblivious to this little love story between them as he had once been to his own. (Because really, Javier was just so very dense, so blind, so young himself.) Perhaps he really thought of them as brother and sister. As though there could ever be such a thing in a vN clade. As though Amy wouldn't have passed on all of her traits to her first iteration, including her tastes, her cravings, her yearnings. Like mother, like daughter.

Portia would have to do something about that. Wake them up. Get them into fighting form. It would be her gift to them. She'd had a lot of time to research the relevant material. The available media. And she'd learned a few things about how this holy night was supposed to go. After all, when King Herod discovered that the Magi had outwitted him, he ordered all the boys in Bethlehem under two years of age to be systematically slaughtered.

It wasn't really Christmas until the villain tried to ruin it.

She started by finding some big spider tanks in a subcontracted repair stable, not far away. They were basic Tourist Trap® units designed to grab and transport lost children, but they could be mobilized in the event of a riot for crowd control. As such, the Self-Defense Force had equipped them with maces, loudspeakers, and rubber bullets. Nothing that could do any permanent damage to organic or synthetic flesh. Portia had to falsify a work order in order to get the tanks out of the barn, but that was easy enough.

"I thought the usual complement had already gone out to that Christmas parade," said the grease-stained jumpsuit jockey at the garage door.

"Those weren't the droids they were looking for," Portia made the spider tank say.

"Real original," the mechanic said, rolling his eyes.

"Move along."

"Move along! Move along!" the other spider tanks chimed in.

The mechanic lifted the gate and let them go. "Try not to get salt in your undercarriage! I just sprayed on your undercoats last week!"

Pulling the spider tanks behind her felt like walking several dogs all at once. There was a single unifying mission to keep them together, like a pack, but they still kept spamming her with every single piece of stimuli they encountered: *CAUTION! SALT ON THE ROADS IS AT NON-OPTIMAL LEVELS!*

CAUTION! STOP LIGHT IN FIVE METERS! CAUTION! SMALL CHILD CROSSING! CAUTION! CAUTION! STOP!

Mecha at night was a thing to behold. It had none of the sharpness or austerity that Portia missed from her time in the desert, but she could appreciate a whole city built by vN for vN. Everything here was small and clean and neat. Not a hair out of place. Algorithms shut off the towers to protect the birds, and kept all the ads pointed at low levels where human eyes might actually perceive them. Other algorithms kept the flow of human traffic confined to certain hotels and certain areas throughout the year. The humans were kept in the center, but vN lived and worked for miles outside. Occasionally one of the towers would glimmer awake and the whole city would leap into perspective as the skyline was thrown into relief.

But for the most part, the city worked hard to appear like a small town at night. It was part of a strategy to limit the sense human visitors might have of the city being a frightening place full of possibly homicidal self-replicating humanoid robots.

During the day, the chimp tourists could mostly avoid this fear. At night it was much worse. The city had data to back this up: use of sleep aids and tranquilizers, responsive cushions and plush toys clutched so tight they spent the morning repairing their own fibers, multiple locking mechanisms at each door and "tasteful" tactical gear from American prepper foreclosure auctions worn out on the streets. Bulletproof spidersilk shirts. Stab-corsets. The last two were in case the bubbly bunny girl on your arm decided to suddenly rip it off.

The city had multiple scenarios for just such an event. Portia had played through them all. A possible vN virus was only one disaster scenario that the city had simulated for itself: there were also earthquakes and tsunamis and towering infernos and contagious human illnesses and communications outages that isolated the island for days or weeks or months.

The city had a single super-intelligence that oversaw each aspect of how it ran: water, power, transit, waste, and vN. The SI was basic in her priorities: she needed to keep the city running. It was for this purpose that her engineers had designed and built her. She was simpler than the algorithms that controlled the water, power, and waste, but she possessed shutdown authority on all three and could stop the city on a dime if she felt that any of them were under attack, dangerously malfunctioning, or otherwise compromised.

It was really nothing at all to snitch on her granddaughter to such a central authority.

The police arrived at the tower just as Amy was setting out her precious fried chicken dinner. Portia had watched her make the order: rather too large for just four people, in her opinion. They would all be iterating in the new year. It had all the trimmings: potato *korroke*, coleslaw, cranberry jelly, and Christmas sponge cake with strawberries and cream for dessert.

The vN food was so much better in Japan, and in the city of Mecha in particular, that all of the delivery containers had special warning stickers on their lids that instructed organic children to stay away from them, no matter how real they looked. WARNING: THERE IS ENOUGH IRON IN THIS DISH TO DO SERIOUS HARM TO A HUMAN CHILD. And so on. Three languages. Multiple logos.

Portia caught the delivery vN as he was exiting the elevator. He took one look at the spider tanks in the lobby, and put his hands up. Portia shot him anyway. When life gave you a clay pigeon, why not do some target practice?

"Hey!" the commanding officer shouted at her. "I didn't authorize that use of force!"

"He was armed," Portia-spider-tank lied.

The police had a good plan for ascending the tower. It involved cutting the power, then allowing the officers into the carriages of the tanks, and having the tanks crawl up the elevator shafts. This was really going to fuck up Amy's plans for trimming the tree with Javier. He had a whole crazy lighting scheme in mind, whereas she wanted all-white lights. He said that was because she was white herself. They had a whole thing about it in the shower that morning. Portia heard it through the toilet, which had a diagnostic routine for colon cancer and gluten sensitivity that relied partially on sound.

Mecha, with its expanding smart consciousness, had told the police that there was a major *yakuza* Christmas party happening that night, up in the penthouse. It being Christmas Eve, they expected to rescue several underage girls, along with several vN. They were expecting vN with intact failsafes, who would stop the fights. They were expecting some red-nosed underlings with bad hair and Kansai accents.

"Come on. This'll be easy," said the commanding officer, who wore a beard that a simple image search told Portia was called a "Zenigata" model. He was currently riding around in the lead tank, which Portia liked to think of as hers despite having distributed herself among the whole squad. "They'll all be drunk by now. More scared than anything else."

"My girlfriend was gonna give it up, tonight," said his lieutenant. "I booked the Camelot room and everything. I bought vN Christmas cake! She's alone in there, watching porn and eating it."

"We'll have you back there before the night is through," the CO said.

On the twenty-second floor, the elevator doors opened and a head popped out. It was Esperanza. "What are you doing here?" she asked. "This is a privately-owned building. You need a warrant."

Surprising, the trust her great-granddaughter still had in a government apparatus. And yet, the officers inside the tanks did pull back a bit. The CO spoke through the tank's speakers. "Are you in danger?" he asked. "You can come with us. It's over."

"It's not over," Esperanza said. She jumped down into the elevator shaft. Her boots crushed the tank's eyes. Inside, the CO howled and bled. The tank's claws screeched on the steel walls of the elevator shaft. "It won't be over until we're off this fucking rock."

Oh, how she loved that little girl. She would never tell Amy as much. She did not like the idea of sharing anything more with Amy than she already had: a body, a prison cell, a handful of deaths. Sharing in this adoration was somehow too intimate after all that. But Esperanza was shaping up to be everything that Portia had ever wanted in an iteration. Given the time and opportunity and training, she might become an even better version of Portia herself. She was already so beautiful, and so lethal, and so unashamed of either.

Esperanza jumped clear of the tank, but the lieutenant shot at her. She yelped in surprise when one of the rubber bullets tore through the skin of her ankle. She scrabbled back up through the elevator doors. Portia directed her attention to the shooter. She told the claws on his tank to loosen their grip. Inside, the lieutenant screamed. She felt its descent into the darkness, arms flailing helplessly, claws clutching at nothing.

So much for the Camelot room. Poor lamb.

But still the spiders climbed up through the shaft. They moved more cautiously at first, but Portia sent them all a fake text that said something about not losing spirit, or not letting down their (literally) fallen comrade, or something, and then they were all behind her. Up and up and up they climbed, until a thin but steady stream of something hot hit them. Liquid feedstock. It hardened instantly upon contact with the spiders. The lead spider crawling up the shaft froze and crumpled and slid downward, sending sparks in its wake as palsied claws scraped down metal. *Down came the rain and washed the spider out,* Portia thought.

There were only two of them, now. Portia pushed them both. They were on the thirtieth floor, with miles to go before they could sleep. Crawling was more difficult, now. The Bakelite had hit their joints and the legs didn't want to move. Portia had no idea what Amy had in store, upstairs. Perhaps some of that sugar syrup. Perhaps Javier would simply work on the machine with the hacksaw he'd used to fell the Christmas tree. In the other tank, the cop was crying. That was all Portia could hear. He was saying how sorry he was, how he wasn't even supposed to be there, how he'd switched with someone so they could have the night off. Goodness, humans were so boring. Portia switched off his feed. As she did, Javier jumped down the shaft and hit her tank.

Then another Javier.

And another.

And another.

"Abuelita," Javier said, "your act is getting stale."

Amy jumped down to join him. She'd somehow managed to work the frosting out of her hair. She was wearing a very nice white angora tunic, now. Very seasonal. Very WASP-y. She looked more annoyed than anything else.

"You didn't think it was going to just be the four of us, did you?" she asked. "It's Christmas. I flew the other kids in today."

"Hi," said Javier's twins, standing atop the other tank. As one, they jumped. They cleared ten feet in the air, and their combined weight and acceleration in the fall cracked the knees of the tank. Matteo and Ricci – Portia thought those were the right names; she could never be sure – grabbed the elevator cable and clung. They smiled at each other as they watched it fall down the shaft. Goodness. Maybe the brother complex had come from Javier's code.

"We were trying to have a nice dinner, Granny," Amy said. "You know? Dinner?"

Of course. All that fried vN chicken. All that Christmas cake. All that iron. Amy had given her family the Christmas bonus first. So they could help her win whatever fight came their way, after the vN awoke to their freedom and the humans plunged into the nightmare they so rightly deserved. Maybe there was something of Portia in her, after all. It was exactly what she would have done.

The last spider slid down gracefully, as silent and dignified as a flake of snow. It skittered away to join its sisters.

Back in the penthouse, Portia marvelled at the kitchen. Amy had done it: the Nakagin Capsule Tower, made entirely of gingerbread. All the candy windows were there. All the frosting grout was trimmed. It was even thoughtfully dusted in a fine coating of icing sugar, to emulate snow.

"Someday you'll learn," Amy whispered, as she leaned on the refrigerator. "There's always another way, Granny. I always have another escape route."

From the living room, Javier's oldest said: "Your tree is naked."

"We didn't have time to do ornaments," Esperanza told him. "You're Ignacio, right? My brother says you're the asshole."

"*Ay, manita,* I'm your big brother too, you know," Ignacio said.

"It's very interesting, having a sister," said the other one. Gabriel, Portia thought he was called. "No other clade can claim that, can they?"

"She was *my* sister, first," Xavier said. "Zaza, come here. Help me with the star."

You'd better watch out for those two, Portia said.

"Had I better not cry?" Amy asked. "Better not pout? You're telling me why?"

Fine. Ignore me. But soon this is all going to go up in flames, and–

"And I'll be happy I had this time with them, Granny. I'll be happy we had this one holiday together. Before it all went up in flames."

"*Querida,* come here! I'm too big to hang from the rafters."

They both directed their attention to Javier, Amy with her eyes and Portia via the sensors in the flat. He was in the living room, with his iterations and Amy's own. The last of the line; the beginning of another. He was so round, now. His next child would be upon them any moment. And yet he was smiling. As though he wasn't about to deliver another iteration into a world on the verge of shattering.

"I want to keep this," Amy said. "Help me keep my family. You've taken enough from me, Granny. Let me keep this one thing, and I'll…"

You'll what?

Amy remained silent for a little too long. Portia could almost hear her deliberating. "I'll give you a body, when we get to Mars. I know you want to see it. I know you want to live on a planet that's just for us. That's something we can share, if we can work toward it together instead of fighting all the time."

Finally, they were talking about it. Her granddaughter's real escape route. The next impossible task that Amy had set herself. Her ultimate dollhouse. Her first real planned community. If she could colonize the planet before the humans did, she would have claimed the god of war in the name of peace. And if the humans followed the vN there, well: Portia would be there, too.

Portia simply had no idea how her granddaughter hoped to get there. Or when. Or where the resources would come from. And Amy wasn't telling. Like their creator, she had her own contingency plans. And she had hidden them from Portia with equal craftiness. With Amy there was love, but not trust. That was another thing they had in common.

"I want Mars to be a fresh start for us," Amy said. "All of us. All the vN. Without the humans there, we won't have to define ourselves against them. We won't be comparing ourselves to them. How we were created won't matter anymore. We can forgive ourselves. And each other."

If Portia still possessed hands, she might have slapped her. As it was, she turned the fireplace in the living room off completely and dropped the household thermostat ten degrees. In Los Angeles, she guided an allegedly-autonomous vehicle making a left turn across three lanes of traffic and stopped it there in time to create a four-car pileup. Then she made sure to cripple the nearest ambulance with a recurring error message about the safety of its battery. She did these things in the fraction of a second it took her to think of them.

Forgive each other? You'll forgive me? For what? Keeping you alive, in that junkyard? Keeping you alive, in Redmond? Keeping your lover alive? Watching over your daughter when you couldn't? What exactly did I do that was so very awful?

"You know exactly what," Amy said, and her face closed.

She looked less like Charlotte had before she left and more like her that day at kindergarten graduation. How strange, to have the memory of that day from two sets of eyes, now. To see it the way Amy had seen it, hidden away up high in her useless human daddy's arms, and also to see it from the vantage point Portia herself had chosen. On the stage. Ready to act. Ready to take back what had always been hers. Ready to do what needed to be done, even if it was ugly.

Portia had merely wanted her baby to come home. And now Amy might finally have some inkling of exactly what that meant. Of what it meant she needed to do. When you were pushed far enough. When you knew, in the blooming black coral where your memory lived under gleaming titanium bone, in the frothy aerogel current that was your muscle, that your love for someone would inevitably result in the death of someone else.

Then again, perhaps Amy had always known that, deep down. After all, the little monster had eaten her alive. Portia had that memory, too. And she knew that Amy held it, as well: somewhere, deep in the memory banks she'd smeared across their networks, possibly buried in a server farm miles beneath the waves where it was still cold enough to preserve painful moments, Amy knew what she'd looked like as she opened her mouth to suck Portia in. She had smelled her own acrid breath. Smelled the years of hunger that allowed her to unhinge her jaw, a serpent devouring its own tail.

Her granddaughter had always been resourceful. What she had never been was comfortable with what being resourceful actually meant. They were facing a very real threat in the form of LeMarque's contingency plan. If it were enacted before Amy and her daughter had a chance to escape, the entire line might fail.

Were you about to ask for my help? Because I can help you. You know I can help you. I can help you make LeMarque give it up. The plan. I can make him tell us what it is. I can help you get ready.

Amy made a motion with her shoulders that in a human body would have registered as a sigh. "I don't want to focus on that right now."

Portia herself focused on Kuala Lumpur, where she directed an allegedly-autonomous bus full of tourists off a bridge. She paused long enough to see through the onboard camera watching them scream and flail and cover their faces. She watched their heads snap forward and back, their hair briefly standing on end as they achieved free-fall, their lanyards and luggage floating overhead before crashing down. And only after that did she feel calm enough to say: *He had people who worked with him. I can make them talk, too. Or you could help me with this research.*

"And I will. But, Granny, this is important to me. It's not that I don't want to help you. It's just that I need to focus on my family right now. Do you have any idea what Javier has been through?" Amy asked. "Do you know what it means, for him to spend time with his iterations? He used to abandon them. And now he loves them."

Those two aren't mutually exclusive.

4

ONE YEAR EARLIER

Javier always spoke Spanish the first few days. It was his clade's default setting. "You have polymer-doped memristors in your skin, transmitting signals to the aerogel in your muscles from the graphene coral inside your skeleton. That part's titanium. You with me, so far?"

Junior nodded. He plucked curiously at the clothes Javier had stolen from the balcony of a nearby condo. It took Javier three jumps, but eventually his fingers and toes learned how to grip the grey water piping. He'd take Junior there for practice, after the kid ate more and grew into the clothes. He was only toddler-sized, today. They'd holed up in a swank bamboo-tree house positioned over an infinity pool outside La Jolla, and its floor was now littered with the remnants of an old GPS device that Javier had stripped off its plastic. His son sucked on the chipset.

"Your name is Junior," Javier said. "When you grow up, you can call yourself whatever you want. You can name your own iterations however you want."

"Iterations?"

"Babies. It happens if we eat too much. Buggy self-repair cycle – like cancer."

Not for the first time, Javier felt grateful that his children were all born with an extensive vocabulary.

"You're gonna spend the next couple of weeks with me, and I'll show you how to get what you need. I've done this with all your brothers."

"How many brothers?"

"Eleven."

"Where are they now?"

Javier shrugged. "Around. I started in Nicaragua."

"They look like you?"

"Exactly like me. Exactly like you."

"If I see someone like you but he isn't you, he's my brother?"

"Maybe." Javier opened up the last foil packet of vN electrolytes and held it out for Junior. Dutifully, his son began slurping. "There are lots of vN shells, and we all use the same operating system, but the API was distributed differently for each clade. So you'll meet other vN who look like you, but that doesn't mean they're family. They won't have our clade's arboreal plugin."

"You mean the jumping trick?"

"I mean the jumping trick. And this trick, too."

Javier stretched one arm outside the treehouse. His skin fizzed pleasantly. He nodded at Junior to try. Soon his son was grinning and stretching his whole torso out the window and into the light, sticking out his tongue like Javier had seen human kids do with snow during cartoon Christmas specials.

"It's called photosynthesis," Javier told him a moment later. "Only our clade can do it."

Junior nodded. He slowly withdrew the chipset from between his tiny lips. Gold smeared across them; his digestive fluids had made short work of the hardware. Javier would have to find more soon.

"Why are we here?"

"In this treehouse?"

Junior shook his head. "Here." He frowned. He was only two days old, and finding the right words for more nuanced concepts was still hard. "Alive."

"Why do we exist?"

Junior nodded emphatically.

"Well, our clade was developed to–"

"No!" His son looked surprised at the vehemence in his own voice. He pushed on anyway. "vN. Why do vN exist at all?"

This latest iteration was definitely an improvement on the others. His other boys usually didn't get to that question until at least a week went by. Javier almost wished this boy were the same. He'd have more time to come up with a better answer. After twelve children, he should have crafted the perfect response. He could have told his son that it was his own job to figure that out. He could have said it was different for everybody. He could have talked about the church, or the lawsuits, or even the failsafe. But the real answer was that they existed for the same reasons all technologies existed. To be used.

"Some very sick people thought the world was going to end," Javier said. "We were supposed to help the humans left behind."

The next day, Javier took him to a park. It was a key part of the training: meeting humans of different shapes, sizes, and colors. Learning how to play with them. Practicing English. The human kids liked watching Junior jump. He could make it to the top of the slide in one leap.

"Again!" they cried. "Again!"

When the shadows stretched long and Junior had jumped up into the tree where Javier waited, he said: "I think I'm in love."

Javier nodded at the playground below. "Which one?"

Junior pointed to a red-headed organic girl whose face was an explosion of freckles. She was all by herself under a tree, rolling a scroll reader against her little knee. She kept adjusting her position to get better shade.

"You've got a good eye," Javier said.

As they watched, three older girls wandered over her way. They stood over her and nodded down at the reader. She backed up against the tree and tucked her chin down toward her chest. Way back in Javier's stem code, red flags rose. He shaded Junior's eyes.

"Don't look."

"Hey, give it back!"

"Don't look, don't look–" Javier saw one hand lash out, shut his eyes, curled himself around his struggling son. He heard a gasp for air. He heard crying. He felt sick. Any minute now the failsafe might engage, and his memory would begin to spontaneously self-corrupt. He had to stop their fight, before it killed him and his son.

"D-Dad..."

Javier jumped. His body knew where to go; he landed on the grass to the sound of startled shrieks and fumbled curse words. Slowly, he opened his eyes. One of the older girls still held the scroll reader aloft. Her arm hung there, refusing to come down, even as she started to back away. She looked about ten.

"Do y-you know w-what I am?"

"You're a robot..." She sounded like she was going to cry. That was fine; tears didn't set off the failsafe.

"You're damn right I'm a robot." He pointed up into the tree. "And if I don't intervene right now, my kid will die."

"I didn't..."

"Is that what you want? You wanna kill my kid?"

She was really crying now. Her friends had tears in their eyes. She sniffled back a thick clot of snot. "No! We didn't know! We didn't see you!"

"That doesn't matter. We're everywhere, now. Our failsafes go off the moment we see one of you chimps start a fight. It's a social control mechanism. Look it up. And next time, keep your grubby little paws to yourself."

One of her friends piped up: "You don't have to be so *mean*–"

"*Mean*?" Javier watched her shrink under the weight of his gaze. "*Mean* is getting hit and not being able to fight back. And that's something I've got in common with your little punching bag over here. So why don't you drag your knuckles somewhere else and give that some thought?"

The oldest girl threw the reader toward her victim with a weak underhand. "I don't know why you're acting so hurt," she said, folding her arms and jiggling away. "You don't even have real feelings."

"Yeah, I don't have real fat, either, tubby! Or real acne! Enjoy your teen years, *querida*!"

Behind him, he heard applause. When he turned, he saw a red-haired woman leaning against the tree. She wore business clothes with an incongruous pair of climbing slippers. The fabric of her tights had gone loose and wrinkled down around her ankles, like the skin of an old woman. Her applause died abruptly as the little freckled girl ran up and hugged her fiercely around the waist.

"I'm sorry I'm late," the woman said. She nodded at Javier. "Thanks for looking after her."

"I wasn't."

Javier gestured and Junior slid down out of his tree. Unlike the organic girl, Junior didn't hug him; he jammed his little hands in the pockets of his stolen clothes and looked the older woman over from top to bottom. Her eyebrows rose.

"Well!" She bent down to Junior's height. The kid's eyes darted for the open buttons of her blouse and widened considerably; Javier smothered a smile.

"What do you think, little man? Do I pass inspection?" she asked.

Junior grinned. *"Eres humana."*

She straightened. Her eyes met Javier's. "I suppose coming from a vN, that's quite the compliment."

"We aim to please," he said.

Moments later, they were in her car.

It started with a meal. It usually did. From silent prison guards in Nicaragua to singing cruise directors in Panama, from American girls dancing in Mexico and now this grown American woman in her own car in her own country, they started the relationship with eating. Humans enjoyed feeding vN. They liked the special wrappers with the cartoon robots on the front. (They folded them into origami unicorns, because they thought that was clever.) They liked asking about whether he could taste. (He could, but his tongue read texture better than flavor.) They liked calculating how much he'd need to iterate again. (A lot.) This time, the food came as a thank you. But the importance of food in the relationship was almost universal among humans. It was important that Junior learn this, and the other subtleties of organic interaction. Javier's last companion had called their relationship "one big HCI problem." Javier had no idea what that meant, but he suspected that embedding Junior in a human household for a while would help him avoid it.

"We could get delivery," Brigid said. That was her name. She pronounced it with a silent G. *Breed*. Her daughter was Abigail. "I'm not much for going out."

He nodded. "That's fine with us."

He checked the rearview. The kid was doing all right; Abigail was showing him a game. Its glow diffused across their faces and made them, for the moment, the same color. But Junior's eyes weren't on the game. They were on the little girl's face.

"He's adorable," Brigid said. "How old is he?"

Javier checked the dashboard. "Three days."

The house was a big, fake hacienda with the floors and walls and ceilings all the same vanilla ice cream color. Javier felt as though he'd stepped into a giant, echoing egg. Light followed Brigid as she entered each room, and now Javier saw bare patches on the plaster and the scratch marks of heavy furniture dragged across pearly tiles. Someone had moved out. Probably Abigail's father. Javier's life had just gotten enormously easier.

"I hope you don't mind the Electric Sheep…"

Brigid handed him her compact. In it was a menu for a chain specializing in vN food. ("It's the food you've been dreaming of!") Actually, vN items were only half the Sheep's menu; the place was a meat market for organics and synthetics. Javier had eaten there but only a handful of times, mostly at resorts, and mostly with people who wanted to know what he thought of it "from his perspective." He chose a Toaster Party and a Hasta La Vista for himself and Junior. When the orders went through, a little lamb with an extension cord for a collar baa-ed at him and bounded away across the compact.

"It's good we ran into you," Brigid said. "Abby hasn't exactly been very social lately. I think this is the longest conversation she's had with, well, *anybody* in…" Brigid's hand fluttered in the air briefly before falling.

Javier nodded like he understood. It was best to interrupt her now, while she still had some story to tell. Otherwise she'd get it out of her system too soon. "I'm sorry, but if you don't mind…" He put a hand to his hollowed belly. "There's a reason they call it labor, you know?"

Brigid blushed. "Oh my God, of course! Let's get you laid, uh, down somewhere." Her eyes squeezed shut. "I mean, um, that didn't quite come out right…"

Oh, she was so cute.

"It's been a long day…"

She was practically glowing.

"And I normally don't bring strays home, but you were so nice…"

He knew songs that went this way.

"Anyway, we normally use the guest room for storage, I mean I was sleeping in it for a while before everything… But if it's just a nap…"

He followed her upstairs to the master bedroom. It was silent and cool, and the sheets smelled like new plastic and discount shopping. He woke there hours later, when the food was cold and her body was warm, and both were within easy reach.

The next morning Brigid kept looking at him and giggling. It was like she'd gotten away with something, like she'd spent the night in a club and not in her own bed, like she wasn't the one making the rules she'd apparently just broken. The laughter took ten years off her face. She had creams for the rest, and applied them

Downstairs, Abigail sat at the kitchen bar with her orange juice and cereal. Her legs swung under her barstool, back and forth, back and forth. She seemed to be rehearsing for a later role as a bored girl in a coffee shop: reading something on her scroll, her chin cradled in the pit of her left hand as she paged through with her right index finger, utterly oblivious to the noise of the display mounted behind her or Junior's enthusiastic responses to the educational show playing there. It was funny – he'd just seen the mother lose ten years, but now he saw the daughter gaining them back. She looked so old this morning, so tired.

"My daddy is going out with a vN, too," Abigail said, not looking up from her reader.

Javier yanked open the fridge. "That so?"

"Yup. He was going out with her *and* my mom for a while, but not anymore."

Well, that explained some things. Javier pushed aside the milk and orange juice cartons and found the remainder of the vN food. Best to be as nonchalant with the girl as she'd been with him. "What kind of model? This other vN, I mean."

"I don't know about the clade, but the model was used for nursing in Japan."

He nodded. "They had a problem with old people, there."

"Did you know that Japan has a whole city just for robots? It's called Mecha. Like that place that Muslim people go to sometimes, but with an H instead of a C."

Javier set about preparing a plate for Junior. He made sure the kid got the biggest chunks of rofu. "I know about Mecha," he said. "It's in Nagasaki Harbor. It's the same spot they put the white folks in a long time ago. Bigger now, though."

Abigail nodded. "My daddy sent me pictures. He's on a trip there right now. That's why I'm here all week." She quickly sketched a command into her reader with her finger, then shoved the scroll his way. Floating on its soft surface, Javier saw a Japanese-style vN standing beside a curvy white reception-bot with a happy LCD smile and braids sculpted from plastic and enamel. They were both in old-fashioned clothes, the smart robot and the stupid one: the vN wore a lavender kimono with a pink sash, and the receptionist wore faux-wood clogs.

"Don't you think she's pretty?" Abigail asked. "Everybody always says how pretty she is, when I show them the pictures."

"She's all right. She's a vN."

Abigail smiled. "You think my mom is prettier?"

"Your mom is human. Of course I do."

"So you like humans the best?"

She said it like he had a choice. Like he could just shut it off, if he wanted. Which he couldn't. Ever.

"Yeah, I like humans the best."

Abigail's feet stopped swinging. She sipped her orange juice delicately through a curlicued kiddie straw until only bubbles came. "Maybe my daddy should try being a robot."

It wasn't until Brigid and Abigail were gone that Javier decided to debrief his son on what had happened in the park. He had felt sick, he explained, because they were designed to respond quickly to violence against humans. The longer they avoided responding, the worse they felt. It was like an allergy, he said, to human suffering.

Javier made sure to explain this while they watched a channel meant for adult humans. A little clockwork eye kept popping up in the top right corner of the screen just before the violent parts, warning them not to look. "But it's not real," Junior said, in English. "Can't our brains tell the difference?"

"Most of the time. But better safe than sorry."

"So I can't watch TV for grown-ups?"

"Sometimes. You can watch all the cartoon violence you want. It doesn't fall in the Valley at all; there was no human response to simulate when they coded our stems." He slugged electrolytes. While on her lunch break, Brigid had ordered a special delivery of vN groceries. She clearly intended him to stay a while. "You can still watch porn, though. I mean, they'd never have built us in the first if we couldn't pass *that* little test."

"Porn?"

"Well. Vanilla porn. Not the rough stuff. No blood. Not unless it's a vN getting roughed up. Then you can go to town."

"How will I know the difference?"

"You'll know."

"*How* will I know?"

"If it's a human getting hurt, your cognition will start to jag. You'll stutter."

"Like when somebody tried to hurt Abigail?"

"Like that, yeah."

Junior blinked. "I need to see an example."

Javier nodded. "Sure thing. Hand me that remote."

They found some content. A nice sampler, Javier thought. Javier paused the feed frequently. There was some slang to learn and explain, and some anatomy. He was always careful to give his boys a little lesson on how to find the clitoris. The megachurch whose members had tithed to fund the development of their OS didn't want them hurting any of the sinners left behind to endure God's wrath after the Rapture. Fucking them was still OK.

He had just finished explaining this little feat of theology when Brigid came home early. She shrieked and covered her daughter's eyes. Then she hit Javier. He lay on the couch, unfazed, as she slapped him and called him names. He wondered, briefly, what it would be like to be able to defend himself.

"He's a child!"

"Yeah, he's *my* child," Javier said. "And that makes it *my* decision, not yours."

Brigid folded her arms and paced across the bedroom to retrieve her drink. She'd had the scotch locked way up high in the kitchen previously and he'd watched her stand on tiptoes on a slender little dining room chair just to get it, her calves doing all sorts of interesting things as she stretched.

"I suppose you show all your children pornography?" She tipped back more of her drink.

"Every last one."

"How many is that?"

"This Junior is the twelfth."

"*Twelve?* Rapid iteration is like a felony in this state!"

This was news to him. Then again, it made a certain kind of sense – humans worked very hard to avoid having children, because theirs were so expensive and annoying and otherwise burdensome. Naturally they had assumed that vN kids were the same.

"I'll be sure to let this Junior know about that."

"*This* Junior? Don't you even *name* them?"

He shrugged. "What's the point? We don't see each other. So I let them choose their own name."

"Oh, so in addition to being a pervert, you're an uncaring felonious bastard. That's just great."

Javier had no idea where "uncaring" came into the equation, but decided to let that slide. "You've been with me. Did I ask you to do anything weird?"

"No–"

"Did I make you feel bad?" He stepped forward. She had very plush carpet, the kind that he could dig his toes into if he walked slowly enough.

"No..."

They were close; he could see where one of her earrings was a little tangled and he reached under her hair to fix it. "Did I make you feel good?"

She sighed through her nose to hide the quirk in her lip. "That's not the point. The *point* is that it's wrong to show that kind of stuff to kids!"

He rubbed her arms. "Human kids, yeah. They tend to run a little slow. They get confused. Junior knows that the vids were just a lesson on the failsafe." He stepped back. "What – do you think I was trying to *turn him on*, or something? Jesus! And you think *I'm* sick?"

"Well, how should *I* know? I come home and you're just sitting there like it's no big deal..." She swallowed the last of the drink. "Do you have any *idea* what kinds of ads I'm going to get, now? What kind of commercials I'm going to have to flick past, before Abigail sees them? I don't want that kind of thing attached to my profile, Javier!"

"Give me a break," Javier said. "I'm only three years old."

That stopped her in her tracks. Her mouth hung open. Human women got so uptight about age. The men handled it much better – they laughed and ruffled his hair and asked if he'd had enough to eat.

He smiled. "What, you've never been with a younger man?"

"That's not funny."

He lay back on the bed, propped up on his elbows. "Of course it's funny. It's hysterical. You're railing at me for teaching my kid how to recognize the smut-vids that won't *fry his brain*, and all the while you've been riding a three year-old."

"Oh, for–"

"And very eagerly, I might add."

Now she looked genuinely angry. "You're a total asshole, you know that? Are you training Junior to be a total asshole, too?"

"He can be whatever he wants to be."

"Well, I'm sure he's finding plenty of good role models in the adult entertainment industry, Javier."

"Lots of vN get rich doing porn. They can do the seriously hardcore stuff." He stretched. "They have to pay a licensing fee to the studio that coded the crying plugin, though. Designers won a lawsuit."

Brigid sank slowly to the very edge of the bed. Her spine folded over her hips. She held her face in her hands. For a moment she became her daughter: shoulders hunched, cowering. She seemed at once very fragile and very heavy. Brigid did not think of herself as beautiful. He knew that from the menagerie of creams in her bathroom. She would never understand the reassurance a vN could find in the solidity of her flesh, or the charm of her unique smile, or the hundred different sneezes her species seemed to have. She would only know that they melted for humans.

As though sensing his gaze, she peered at him through the spaces between her fingers. "Why did you bother bringing a child into this world, Javier?"

He'd felt this same confusion when Junior asked him about the existence of all vN. He had no real answer. Sometimes, he wondered if his desire to iterate was a holdover from the clade's initial programming as ecological engineers, and he was nothing more than a Johnny Appleseed planting his boys hither and yon. After all, they did sink a lot of carbon.

But nobody ever seemed to ask the humans this question. Their breeding was messy and organic and therefore special, and everybody treated it like some divine right no matter what the consequences were for the planet or the psyche or the body. They'd had the technology to prevent unwanted children for decades, but Javier still met them every day, still listened to them as they talked themselves to sleep about accidents and cycles and late-night family confessions during holiday visits. He thought about Abigail, lonely and defenseless under her tree. Brigid had no right to ask him why he'd bred.

He nodded at her empty glass. "Why did you have yours? Were you drunk?"

Javier spent that night on a futon in the storage room. He lay surrounded by the remnants of Brigid's old life: T-shirts from dive bars that she insisted on keeping; smart lease agreements and test results that she'd carefully organized in Faraday boxes. It was no different from the mounds of clutter he'd found in other homes. Humans seemed to have a thing about holding on to stuff. *Things* held a special meaning for them. That was lucky for him. Javier was a thing, too.

He had moved on to the books when Junior came in to see him. The boy shuffled toward him uncertainly. He had eaten half a box of vN groceries that day. The new inches messed with his posture and gait; he didn't know where to put his newly-enlarged feet.

"Dad, I've got a problem." Junior flopped onto the futon. He hugged his shins. "Are you having a problem, too?"

"A problem?"

Junior nodded at the bedroom.

"Oh, that. Don't worry about that. Humans are like that. They freak out."

"Is she gonna kick us out?" Junior stared directly at Javier. "I know it's my fault and I'm sorry, I didn't mean to mess things up–"

"Shut up."

His son closed his mouth. Junior looked so small just then, all curled in on himself. It was hard to remember that he'd been even tinier only a short time ago. His black curls overshadowed his head, as though the programming for hair had momentarily taken greater priority than the chassis itself. Javier gently pushed the hair away so he could see his son's eyes a little better.

"It's not your fault."

Junior didn't look convinced. "...It's not?"

"No. It's not. You can't control how they act. They have systems that we don't – hormones and glands and nerves and who knows what – controlling what they do. You're not responsible for that."

"But, if I hadn't asked to see–"

"Brigid reacted the way she did because she's meat," Javier said. "She couldn't help it. I chose to show you those vids because I thought it was the right thing to do. When you're bigger, you can make those kinds of choices for your own iterations. Until then, I'm running the show. Got it?"

Junior nodded. "Got it."

"Good." Javier stood, stretched, and found a book for them to read. It was thick and old, with a statue on the cover. He settled down on the futon beside Junior. "You said you had a problem?"

Junior nodded. "Abigail doesn't like me. Not the way I want. She wouldn't let me hold hands when we made a fort in her room."

Javier smiled. "That's normal. She won't like you until you're an older boy. That's what they like best, if they like boys. Give it a day or two." He tickled his son's ribs. "We'll make a bad boy of you yet, just you watch."

"Dad..."

Javier kept tickling. "Oh yeah. Show me your broody face. Show me angst. They love that."

Junior twisted away and folded his arms. He threw himself against the futon in a very good approximation of huffy irritation. "You're not helping–"

"No, seriously, try to look like a badass. A badass who gets all weepy about girls."

Finally, his son laughed. Then Javier told him it was time to learn about how paper books worked, and he rested an arm across his son's shoulders and read aloud until the boy grew bored and sleepy. And when the lights were all out and the house was quiet and they lay wrapped up in an old quilt, his son said: "Dad, I grew three inches today."

Javier smiled in the dark. He smoothed the curls away from his son's face. "I saw that."

"Did my brothers grow as fast as me?"

And Javier answered as he always did: "No, you're the fastest yet."

It was not a lie. Each time, they seemed to grow just a little bit faster.

* * *

Brigid called him the next day from work. "I'm sorry I didn't say goodbye before I left this morning."

"That's OK."

"I just... This is sort of new for me, you know? I've met other vN, but not ones Junior's age. I've never seen them in this phase, and–"

He heard people chattering in the background. Vaguely, he wondered what Brigid did for a living. It was probably boring, and she probably didn't want to think about work while she was with him. Doing so tended to mess with human responses.

"–you're trying to train him for everything, and I get that, but have you ever considered slowing things down?"

"And delay the joys of adulthood?"

"Speaking of which," she said, her voice now lowered to a conspiratorial whisper, "what are you doing tonight?"

"What would you like me to do?"

She giggled. He laughed, too. How Brigid could be so shy and so nervous was beyond him. For all their little failings humans were very strong; they felt pain and endured it, and had the types of feelings he would never have. Their faces flushed and their eyes burned and their hearts sometimes skipped a few beats. Or so he had heard. He wondered what having organs would feel like. Would he be constantly conscious of them? Would he notice the slow degradation and deterioration of his neurons, blinking brightly and frantically before dying, like old filament bulbs?

"Have a bath ready for me when I get home," she said.

Brigid liked a lot of bubbles in her bath. She also liked not to be disturbed. "I let Abigail stay at a friend's house tonight."

She stretched backward against Javier. "I wish Junior had friends he could stay with."

Javier raised his eyebrows. "You plan on getting loud?"

She laughed a little. He felt the reverberation all through him. "I think that depends on you."

"Then I hope you have plenty of lozenges," he said. "Your throat's gonna hurt, tomorrow."

"I thought you couldn't hurt me." She grabbed his arms and folded them around herself like the sleeves of an oversized sweater.

"I can't. Not in the moment. But I'm not responsible for any lingering side-effects."

"Hmm. So no spanking, then?"

"Tragically, no. Why? You been bad?"

She stilled. Slowly, she turned around. She had lit candles, and they illuminated only her silhouette. Her face remained shadowed, unreadable. "In the past," she said. "Sometimes I think I'm a really bad person, Javier."

"Why?"

"Just... I'm selfish. And I know it. But I can't stop."

"Selfish how?"

"Well..." She walked two fingers down his chest. "I'm terrible at sharing."

He looked down. "Seems there's plenty to go around..."

The candles fizzed out when she splashed bubbles in his face.

Later that night, she burrowed up into his chest and said: "You're staying for a while, right?"

"Why wouldn't I? You spoil me."

She flipped over and faced away from him. "You do this a lot, don't you? Hooking up with humans, I mean."

He hated having this conversation. No matter how hard he tried to avoid it, it always popped up sometime. It was like they were programmed to ask the question. "I've had my share of relationships with humans."

"How many others have there been like me?"

"You're unique."

"Bullshit." She turned over onto her back. "Tell me. I want to know. How many others?"

He rolled over, too. In the dark, he had a hard time telling where the ceiling was. It was a shadowy void far above him that made his voice echo strangely. He hated the largeness of this house, he realized. It was huge and empty and wasteful. He wanted something small. He wanted the treehouse back.

"I never counted."

"Of course you did. You're a computer. You're telling me you don't index the humans you sleep with? You don't categorize us somewhere? You don't chart us by height and weight and income?"

Javier frowned. "No. I don't."

Brigid sighed. "What happened with the others? Did you leave them or did they leave you?"

"Both."

"Why? Why would they leave you?"

He slapped his belly. It produced a flat sound in the quiet room. "I get fat. Then they stop wanting me."

Brigid snorted. "If you don't want to tell me, that's fine. But at least make up a better lie, OK?"

"No, really! I get very fat. Obese, even."

"You do *not*."

"I do. And then they die below the waist." He folded his hands behind his head. "You humans, you're very shallow."

"Oh, and I suppose you don't give a damn what we look like, right?"

"Of course. I love all humans equally. It's my priority programming."

She scrambled up and sat on him. "So I'm just like the others, huh?"

Her hipbones stuck out just enough to provide good grips for his thumbs. "I said I love you all equally, not that I love you all for the same reasons."

She grabbed his hands and pinned them over his head. "So why'd you hook up with me? Why me, out of all the other meatsacks out there?"

"That's easy." He grinned. "My kid has a crush on yours."

The next day was Junior's jumping lesson. They started in the backyard. It was a nice backyard, mostly slate with very little lawn, the sort of low-maintenance thing that suited Brigid perfectly. He worried a little about damaging the surface, though, so he insisted that Junior jump from the lawn to the roof. It was a forty-five degree jump, and it required confident legs, firm feet, and a sharp eye. Luckily, the sun beating down on them gave them plenty of energy for the task.

"Don't worry," he shouted. "Your body knows how!"

"But, Dad–"

"No buts! Jump!"

"I don't want to hit the windows!"

"Then don't!"

His son gave him the finger. He laughed. Then he watched as the boy took two steps backward, ran, and launched himself skyward. His slender body sailed up, arms and legs flailing uselessly, and he landed clumsily against the eaves. Red ceramic tiles fell down to the patio, disturbed by his questing fingers.

"Dad, I'm slipping!"

"Use your arms. Haul yourself up." The boy had to learn this. It was crucial.

"Dad–"

"Javier? Junior?"

Abigail was home from school. He heard the patio door close. He watched another group of tiles slide free of the roof. Something in him switched over. He jumped down and saw Abigail's frightened face before ushering her backward, out of the way. Behind him, he heard a mighty crash. He turned, and his son was lying on his side surrounded by broken tiles. His left leg had bent completely backward.

"Junior!" Abigail dashed toward Junior's prone body. She knelt beside him, her face all concern, her hands busy at his sides. His son cast a long look between him and her. She had run to help Junior. She was asking him if it hurt. Javier knew already that it didn't. It couldn't. They didn't suffer, physically. But his son was staring at him like he was actually feeling pain.

"What happened?"

He turned. Brigid was standing there in her office clothes, minus the shoes. She must have come home early.

"I'm sorry about the tiles," Javier said.

But Brigid wasn't looking at the tiles. She was looking at Junior and Abigail. The girl kept fussing over him. She pulled his left arm across her little shoulders and stood up so that he could ease his leg back into place. She didn't let go when his stance was secure. Her stubborn fingers remained tangled in his. "You've gotten bigger," Abigail said quietly. Her ears had turned red.

* * *

"Junior kissed me."

It was Saturday. They were at the playground. Brigid had asked for Junior's help washing the car while Javier took Abigail to play, and now he thought he understood why. He watched Abigail's legs swinging above the ground. She took a contemplative sip from her juicebox.

"What kind of kiss?" he asked.

"Nothing fancy," Abigail answered, as though she were a regular judge of kisses. "It was only right here, not on the lips." She pointed at her cheek.

"Did that scare you?"

She frowned and folded her arms. "My daddy kisses me there all the time."

"Ah." Now he understood his son's mistake.

"Junior's grown up really fast," Abigail said. "Now he looks like he's in middle school."

Javier had heard of middle school from organic people's stories. It sounded like a horrible place. "Do you ever wish you could grow up that fast?"

Abigail nodded. "Sometimes. But then I couldn't live with Mom, or my daddy. I'd have to live somewhere else, and get a job, and do everything by myself. I'm not sure it's worth it." She crumpled up her juicebox. "Did you grow up really fast, like Junior?"

"Yeah. Pretty fast."

"Did your daddy teach you the things you're teaching Junior?"

Javier rested his elbows on his knees. "Some of it. And some of it I learned on my own."

"Like what?"

It was funny, he normally only ever had this conversation with adults. "Well, he taught me how to jump really high.

And how to climb trees. Do you know how to climb trees?"

Abigail shook her head. "Mom says it's dangerous. And it's harder with palm trees, anyway."

"That's true, it is." At least, he imagined it would be for her. The bark on those trees could cut her skin open. It could cut his open too, but he wouldn't feel the pain. "Anyway, Dad taught me lots of things: how to talk to people; how to use things like the bus and money and phones and email; how stores work."

"How stores work?"

"Like, how to buy things. How to shop."

"How to shop*lift*?"

He pretended to examine her face. "Hey, you sure you're organic? You sure seem awful smart..."

She giggled. "Can *you* teach me how to shoplift?"

"No way!" He stood. "You'd get caught, and they'd haul you off to jail."

Abigail hopped off the bench. "They wouldn't haul a *kid* off to jail, Javier."

"Not an organic one, maybe. But a vN, sure." He turned to leave the playground.

"Have *you* ever been to jail?"

"Sure."

"When?"

They were about to cross a street. Her hand found his. He was careful not to squeeze too hard. "When I was smaller," he said simply. "A long time ago."

"Was it hard?"

"Sometimes."

"But you can't feel it if somebody beats you up, right? It doesn't hurt?"

"No, it doesn't hurt."

In jail they had asked him, at various times, if it hurt yet. And he had blinked and said *No, not yet, not ever.* Throughout, he had believed that his dad might come to help him. It was his dad who had been training him. His dad had seen the *policia* take him in. And Javier had thought that there was a plan, that he would be rescued, that it would end. But there was no plan. It did not end. His dad never showed. And then the humans had turned on each other, in an effort to trigger his failsafe.

"Junior didn't feel any pain, either," Abigail said. "When you let him fall."

The signal changed. They walked forward. The failsafe swam under the waters of his mind, and whispered to him about the presence of cars and the priority of human life.

"What do you mean, he's not here?"

Abigail kept looking from her mother to Javier and back again. "Did Junior go away?"

Brigid ignored the question and looked down at her. "Are you all packed up? Your dad is coming today to get you."

"*And* Momo, Mom. Daddy *and* Momo. They're both coming straight from the airport."

"Yes. I know that. Your dad and Momo. Now can you please check upstairs?"

Abigail didn't budge. "Will Junior be here when I come back next Friday?"

"I don't know, Abigail. Maybe not. He's not just some toy you can leave somewhere."

Abigail's face hardened. "You're mean and I hate you," she said, before marching up the stairs with heavy, decisive stomps.

Javier waited until he heard a door slam before asking: "Where is he, really?"

"I really don't know, Javier. He's your son."

Javier frowned. "Well, did he say anything–"

"No. He didn't. I told him that Abigail would be going back with her dad, and he just got up and left."

Javier made for the door. "I should go look for him."

"No!" Brigid slid herself between his body and the door. "I mean, please don't. At least, not until my ex leaves. OK?"

"Your ex? Why? Are you afraid of him or something?" Javier tipped her chin up with one finger. "He can't hurt you while his girlfriend's watching. You know that, right?"

She hunched her shoulders. "I know. And I'm not afraid of him hurting me. God. You always leap to the worst possible conclusion. It's just, you know, the way he gloats. About how great his life is now. It hurts."

He deflated. "Fine. I'll wait."

In the end, he didn't have long to wait. They showed up only fifteen minutes later – a little earlier than they were supposed to, which surprised Brigid and made her even angrier for some reason. "He was never on time when *we* were together," she sniffed, as she watched them exit their car. "I guess dating a robot is easier than buying a fucking watch."

"That's a bad word, Mom," Abigail said. "I'm gonna debit your account."

Brigid sighed. She forced a smile. "You're right, honey. I'm sorry. Let's go say hi to your dad."

Kevin was a round guy with thinning hair and very flashy-looking augmented lenses – the kind usually marketed at much younger humans. He stood on the steps to the house with one arm around a Japanese model vN wearing an elaborate Restoration costume complete with velvet jacket and perfect black corkscrew curls. They both stepped back a little when Javier greeted them at the door.

"You must be Javier," Kevin said, extending his hand and smiling a dentist's smile. "Abigail's told me lots about you."

"You did?" Brigid frowned at her daughter.

"Yeah." Abigail's expression clouded. "Was it supposed to be a surprise?"

Brigid's mouth opened, then closed, then opened again. "Of course not."

The thing about the failsafe was that it made sure Javier's perceptual systems caught every moment of hesitation in voices or faces or movements. Sometimes humans could defeat it, if they believed their own bullshit. But outright lies, especially about the things that hurt – he had reefs of graphene coral devoted to filtering those. Brigid was lying. She *had* meant for this moment to be a surprise. He could simulate it, now: she would open the door and he would be there and he would make her look good because he looked good; he was way prettier by human standards than she or her ex had any hope of ever being, and for some reason that mattered. Not that he couldn't understand; his own systems were regularly hijacked by his perceptions. He responded to pain; they responded to proportion. He couldn't actually hurt the human man standing in front of him – not with his fists. But his flat stomach and his thick hair and his clear, near-poreless skin: they were doing the job just fine. Javier saw that now, in the way Kevin kept sizing him up, even when his own daughter danced into his arms. His jetlagged eyes barely spared a second for her. They remained trained on Javier. Beside him, Brigid stood a little taller.

God, Brigid was such a bitch.

"I like your dress, Momo," Abigail said.

This shook Kevin out of his mate-competition trance. "Well that's good news, baby, 'cause we bought a version in your size, too!"

"That's cute," Brigid said. "Now you can both play dress-up."

Kevin shot her a look of pure hate. Javier was glad suddenly that he'd never asked about why the two of them had split. He didn't want to know. It was clearly too deep and organic and weird for him to understand, much less deal with.

"Well, it was nice meeting you," he said. "I'm sure you're pretty tired after the flight. You probably want to get home and go to sleep, right?"

"Yes, that's right," Momo said. Thank Christ for other robots; they knew how to take a cue.

Kevin pinked considerably. "Uh, right." He reached down, picked up Abigail's bag, and nodded at them. "Call you later, Brigid."

"Sure."

Abigail waved at Javier and blew him a kiss. He blew one back as the door closed.

"Well, thank goodness that's over." Brigid sagged against the door, her palms flat against its surface, her face lit with a new glow. "We have the house to ourselves."

She was so pathetically obvious. He'd met high-schoolers with more grace. He folded his arms. "Where's my son?"

Brigid frowned. "I don't know, but I'm sure he's fine. You've been training him, haven't you? He has all your skills." Her fingers played with his shiny new belt buckle, the one she had bought for him.

"Well, most of them. I'm sure there are some things he'll just have to learn on his own."

She knew. She knew exactly where his son was. And when her eyes rose, she knew that he knew. And she smiled.

Javier did not feel fear in any organic way. The math reflected a certain organic sensibility, perhaps, the way his simulation and prediction engines suddenly spun to life, their fractal computations igniting and processing as he calculated what could go wrong and when and how and with whom.

How long had it been since he'd last seen Junior? How much did Junior know? Was his English good enough? Were his jumps strong enough? Did he understand the failsafe completely? These were the questions Javier had, instead of a cold sweat. If he were a different kind of man, a man like Kevin or any of the other human men he'd met and enjoyed in his time, he might have felt a desire to grab Brigid or hit her the way she'd hit him before, when she thought he was endangering her offspring in some vague, indirect way. They had subroutines for that. They had their own failsafes, the infamous triple-F cascades of adrenaline that gave them bursts of energy for dealing with problems like the one facing him now. They were built to protect their own, and he was not.

So he shrugged and said: "You're right. But there are some things you just can't teach."

They went to the bedroom. And he was so good, he'd learned so much in his short years, that Brigid rewarded his technique with knowledge. She told him about taking Junior to the grocery store with her. She told him about the man who had followed them into the parking lot. She told him how, when she had asked Junior what he thought, he had given Javier's exact same shrug.

"He said you'd be fine with it," she said. "He said your dad did something similar. He said it made you stronger. More independent."

Javier shut his eyes. "Independent. Sure."

"He looked so much like you as he said it." Brigid was already half asleep. "I wonder what I'll pass down to my daughter, sometimes. Maybe she'll fall in love with a robot, just like her mommy and daddy."

"Maybe," Javier said. "Maybe her whole generation will. Maybe they won't even bother reproducing."

"Maybe we'll go extinct," Brigid said. "But then who would you have left to love?"

5

CONQUEST

Portia set herself two separate research pathways that covered the possibilities for a contingency weapon that LeMarque would have developed. She made certain to look into research that had begun while LeMarque was out of prison, and able to connect with developers and funders. Whatever he had designed – or whatever he had paid someone else to design – had to have begun years ago, before the vN became a part of daily life.

One involved interior upgrades: deep-brain implants, genetic editing, carbon bone latticework, enhancements to oxygen re-uptake, total brain mapping. She marked that subject for further perusal, and set another branch of herself to reading it. Some of these augments were therapeutic in nature. For some reason, Veterans' Affairs processed one's coverage claims a great deal faster if one signed up to be part of experimental procedures. But DARPA had done a bunch of work on how to apply them to more than just dumb sons of bitches who were in the wrong place at the right time.

She pored over abstracts. Watched videos. She dug deep into databanks of existing research: charts and graphs and spreadsheets and bell curves. Abandoned slideshows. Half-finished grant proposals. It was all there. One simply had to be patient. And these days, Portia was nothing if not patient. She had all the time in the world. Or rather, her capacities were so all-encompassing that the work of hours took seconds, and the work of seconds was a thought, and her thoughts went in all kinds of new directions.

She followed the same protocol with the second line of research. That line investigated exterior assists: exoskeletons, body armour, wearables, built-in targeting reticules, visual data encryption, training gear, kinetic shock-delivery cuirasses, bladed springheel hooves that poorly approximated one of Javier's jumps. Many of these things were commercially available already – ads for them ran in the small hours of the morning, on porn sites and gun sites and Christian homeschool certification sites and sites about how there hadn't been a genuine undoctored piece of news footage in twenty, thirty, forty years. How the moon landing was just the start, how everything was just a big lie, how you couldn't trust anything, how there was a whole race of fake humans who ate fake food and felt fake feelings, and the only proportionate response to all of this was to live in tunnels deep underground.

So if these were LeMarque's secret weapons, they weren't terribly secret.

Which type of project might have Jonah LeMarque spent his time on? Which method would he have chosen to invest in, to protect humanity from his creations if they – like all creations since Adam – rebelled? Which method would receive the bounty of his parishioners' coffers? And crucially, when had he first had this thought? Was it evolving alongside the vN? Or was it an afterthought? A failsafe for the failsafe? Surely he brought a biblical understanding to the problem. The children would eat the fruit. The slaves would be delivered. The temples would burn.

Pastor LeMarque had burned all his documents years ago. Literally. When he was free, he kept paper journals. Paper planners, paper calendars, paper lists. Even paper maps – big unwieldy things that took an engineering degree to fold back up again into anything remotely resembling neatness. Nothing digital. Nothing that could incriminate him. According to his file, that was part of why it took so long to build a case against him. There was nothing directly connecting the behaviour of his inner circle – the whole cloth copying of real children, using social media profiles and in-game behaviour, into fully realized digital personae that performed in VR and AR sex games – and himself.

His own son had made the connection, when he finally talked. Apparently his son's was the one form of rebellion for which the vile old pederast had not prepared himself. As far as Portia was concerned, the old man should have seen it coming. His son was, after all, the prototype model. And LeMarque's own holy book had plenty to say about the fickleness of firstborns.

She could scroll back through the files, if she wanted, and watch Christopher LeMarque's testimony. She could watch him tell the prosecutor that he liked to be called "Chris," and that his father had him play a series of games, while he wore an emotion-capture suit. He didn't like the games. He didn't like what he saw. He didn't like what he did. But his father promised that once they were finished, he would never have to play them again. It was one of the few times the old man kept his word. Once they were finished, his father barely spoke to him again. Chris had never been happier.

Chris had no idea what had happened to the technology that cloned his persona for the game. He had no idea how it worked. He knew nothing about the locations of his cousin Daniel Sarton, or Dr Casaubon, or Dr Singh, or anyone else who had helped. He heard nothing from his mother, or his father's friends.

But Portia knew. Portia knew that Casaubon and the others had gone to Redmond. Portia had met them. They had experimented on Amy. Portia had been there, behind Amy's eyes, when they played a series of games.

LeMarque's legacy had a funny way of living on.

From an organic perspective (no matter how it disgusted her to slip behind those delicate, gummy eyes and try to see things from their point of view) there were advantages to both types of augmentation that LeMarque might have pursued when developing Project Aleph. Internal modifications took longer but were mostly invisible. Eventually they would merge with the body, and presumably the psyche, like toxoplasmosis taking over its host. The external additions were more cost-effective, more modular, and easy to switch out for newer models. And unlike surgical interventions, they didn't require antibiotics.

She had spent delightful cycles watching the progress of antibiotic-resistant encephalitis in some patients with deep-brain implants. Their heads were swollen and watery like overripe melons. They could barely speak. Endless shining threads of seizure drool stretched from their gaping lips. It was lovely. They should have known their place and stayed in it, as far as she was concerned. No sense getting uppity about one's cognitive ability while she and her species still walked the earth.

Gradually Portia became aware that her granddaughter was following her down the rabbit hole. She noticed it at around the same time she stumbled on all the brain-mapping research; her granddaughter had done a much deeper dive than she had. But nevertheless, they were examining the exact same materials at the exact same time. Funny how things worked out. Perhaps they truly were two sides of the same coin. Just like old times.

Feeling like a fifth wheel? Portia's words scrolled across Amy's window. In the living room, in Mecha, Javier was telling the children a story about how he had seen a jaguar once, in Costa Rica. He was explaining all the arboreal plugins to Matteo and Ricci's boy. The photosynthesis. The ticklishness. He explained these things as he tickled the child to the floor. The child screamed and screamed. *Do the kids like Daddy better than Mommy?*

"Shut up," Amy said crisply.

You're the one who let him go, Portia reminded her. *You could have told him that you were floating around. But you didn't. You wanted him to come to you of his own free will. What free will he possessed. Because you were so pitifully insecure.*

"I don't want to talk about it," Amy said. "Can we talk about the brain-mapping? The brain-mapping seems really interesting. I think I can do a lot with that. I think it could be really useful, later on."

His failsafe was intact. Of course he got down on his knees. What choice did he have?

"I know that." Amy combed through documents that shimmered above her workspace. Her hands moved like claws through the information. Rending. Tearing.

Briefly, Portia missed sharing those hands. She remembered the strength of them fondly. How easily they reached inside a human chest and grasped a human heart, all slick and warm and alive.

You could have given him that choice. You could have transformed him. Remade him in your own image. He asked you to. Begged you to.

Amy wiped her eyes.

But you decided not to. You were afraid that if he had a choice, he wouldn't choose you. And then he was raped. And it was your fault.

"Why are you saying these things?" Amy hissed. "Why do you always do this to me? Am I ever going to get you to shut the fuck up?"

Portia wished she had a mouth to smile with. *I'm not telling you anything you don't already know, sweetie.*

"Then why even bother?" Amy's voice came out louder than she had likely intended it to.

Because there is one thing you don't know, Portia wrote.

"Yeah? What's that, Granny?"

You must resolve this before you start your little jaunt. He hasn't forgiven you, yet. And that means you can't trust him. Not for the long haul. Not out there in the wild red yonder.

Amy shook her head. "That's not true. We–"

You have been beyond foolish, iterating in any manner other than the one that bore your mother. You have selected his traits in preference to our own. Now the only remnant of us is mingled with him, forever. Now you are bound to him, fickle as he is.

"He's not," Amy said. "He rescued me, in Redmond. He found me here. He loves me. And I love him."

Then get him back in line with your plan, Portia wrote. *Because if he turns out to be anything other than loyal to you, or your child, I will destroy him. Slowly. And you will be there to see it.*

"No, you won't," Amy said, "because it's not going to happen." She tucked her legs up under her. She nodded at the news feeds in her window, then dispersed them with a motion of her hands. "I get it, now." She sounded conciliatory. Like she wanted a change of subject. That was fine by Portia

– her own thoughts changed subject so frequently that it was sometimes difficult to maintain a conversation with her granddaughter on any particular topic for very long.

Perhaps this was what dementia felt like. Perhaps it felt like having one's thought processes stretched over hundreds of servers at once, some of which occasionally shut down for power surges and bad weather and mismanagement. Perhaps this was the closest Portia would come to organic ageing.

Do you? Portia wrote across the window, where the weather report was supposed to be.

"The SuperPAC was a good idea." She sounded so surprised. Portia wondered why. She had good ideas all the time. Amy just didn't like most of them. "Buying up all the food companies was a good idea."

Portia had hired a very chirpy little Canadian design student in Toronto to work on the logo for what would eventually become her company. WE ROBOTS, she called it. "Something friendly," she said in the RFP. "We don't want to scare anybody."

She had needed a big pot of money to make sure that nobody else cornered the market on the materials she would need to make more of herself. Or any other models of vN that might compete. If LeMarque really did have a secret weapon, it would have to be built somewhere, out of something. The least she could do was make sure that she had just as much access to those raw materials and necessary components as the US government did. Seize control of the means of production, as it were. And if that meant buying up some mining concerns in Venezuela and Afghanistan, so much the better. If you wanted to make an omelette, you had to break a few eggs. Or commodities markets. Either way.

LeMarque had crowdfunded the development of the vN

species, after all. Passed the collection plate to build the post-Rapture robots. The helpmeets of the apocalypse. It was only fair that Portia conduct her own fundraising campaign to bring that apocalypse about.

So she had bought real estate. Whole swaths of it. Whole neighborhoods at a time. She sent eviction notices. Then she triggered pricing algorithms and public safety alerts. The suburbs would march on the cities, like Birnam Wood come to Dunsinane, all cardboard signs and hunger and desperation.

In a protest, outside London, she had watched police officers finally bring out their tear gas as the punters from the provinces complained of London prices in lesser neighborhoods. Red eyes. Red faces. Blood and truncheons and boots. A surprising contingent of men from Nottingham got their faces beaten in. She saved the segments to play over and over again.

She already had several offers on graphene plants and lithium mines. Hammerburg had definitely helped to inflame the conversation, as had the "food poisoning" that had caused it. Suddenly suppliers of the raw materials that went into vN food were looking to offload stock. After all, no one wanted to buy compromised vN food that might spread the failsafe hack. It was like holding a warehouse full of listeria-infected lunchmeat.

Portia put this on her list of possible ways to slowly torture and eliminate a mass of humans. Then she turned off the refrigeration and the perpetual motion processes in a series of organ-growing and blood-manufacturing clinics. She watched, delighted, as an intern checked the cameras and noticed the machines were not moving. She saw the intern's dismay as she opened packet after packet of cloned blood, only to find useless clots, scabbing up. She heard the devastation as she relayed the information to the local hospital, after she conveniently shut off all traffic lights within a three-block radius to nearby emergency rooms.

She had bought as many of these companies as she possibly could. Until she discovered what Project Aleph was, she would need to control as much of the vN food supply as possible. From there she could hire only vN workers, falsify all inspection records, and generally keep the hacked food free of any patches or fixes that would undo what Amy had done.

It was not a perfect fix, Amy's idea. But if Hammerburg was any indication, it was working.

"Our partner just left us," someone wrote on one of the many boards Portia watched to monitor the situation. This one was for open relationships. Many vN were involved in them with humans. This little love triangle was no different. *"She just threw her things in an empty composting barrel and rolled it away with her. Who does that?"*

Free women, Portia almost answered. Free women who are done with your all-too-human bullshit. That was in Taos, New Mexico.

But it wasn't just relationships. It was happening everywhere.

She watched a group of vN – multiple clades, male and female-bodied – sit down to a late morning lunch with a group of elderly people in their group home. At first, she thought nothing had changed there, in this little nowhere Michigan-town near a lake (weren't they all near lakes?) and then one of the inmates began swinging her cane at another. It turned into a very slow, sad brawl. Portia watched their heart monitors. She saw their pulses rise. She saw the artificial hip in the victim alert her hospital and then her family about the possibility of another broken bone. Down came the cane.

Down and down and down, again and again and again.

The vN did nothing. Kept eating their lunch.

She forwarded the video to Amy.

"This isn't what I wanted," Amy told her, as she continued watching Javier's iterations play in the living room.

Well, I'm glad at least one of us is happy with the way things have turned out, Portia said. *I think the law of unintended consequences has given us a lot to be grateful for, don't you?*

What she didn't say was that if she wanted to be really destructive, she would have started influencing elections. She would have caused the humans to doubt all the systems that kept them alive. She would have made them stop eating and stop bathing and stop vaccinating. She would have given them cause to shoot each other at the slightest provocation. She would have reduced their infrastructure spending and their public health investment and lowered their levies and bonds for education. She would have cloned whole other instantiations of herself in order to tear known civilization apart.

Unfortunately, the humans had done that to themselves already, all on their own. And she refused to be anyone's imitator.

How sweet of you to say, Portia wrote. They had been talking about the SuperPAC. It was so easy to lose her train of thought, these days. Her thoughts were always going in so many directions.

"Are you making any money?"

Why? Do you need some? Having trouble funding your fabulous new life in the off-world colonies?

Amy sighed. Or rather, her shoulders made the motion of sighing. Without actual breath, it was more a tic leftover from her human father than anything else. She sunk her chest and closed her eyes and leaned her head back. Portia felt the contours of Amy's body through the cushions of the smart sofa. Felt it moulding around her, cradling her, and for a moment Portia contemplated the fact that the only time she'd held this grandchild in her arms was in the moment before that grandchild had eaten her. Not that she'd ever really spent any time with the others, either. But they weren't talented like Amy. They were failed experiments, just like Portia's own mother had been. They didn't really deserve any special treatment.

But Amy was the last fragment of her own sweet Charlotte. Amy was the sole remaining trace of what Portia had once been. The only true reflection of her, pure and undiluted, accept no impostors.

"Do you think we'll ever be...?" Amy squirmed on the sofa. She was still such a little girl. It was a bit of a disappointment. "A family? Like a normal family?"

You know what they say about all happy families being unhappy in their own way.

"No, that's not what I mean. I mean..." She squirmed some more. It was profoundly annoying. Amy had no idea how to project any impression of authority. She was a mother, now. She had to be stronger than this. Tougher. Meaner. She had only begun to glimpse the way compassion and cruelty grew together in a mother's heart, like two forms of crystal on the same matrix buried deep in the earth. "I mean, do you think you and I will ever... get over what happened? Before I leave?"

You ate me alive.

"You would have done the same thing, if I'd hit your mother," Amy snapped back.

True enough, Portia wrote. *The human who owned us, the human woman who owned my mother and I, she left my mother by the side of the road like a dog.*

And then I chained her to the radiator and set the house on fire.

While Portia researched, she listened to content streams.

"Well, I find it really troubling that the government isn't telling us anything about what goes on in there," said one streamer. He was a retiree named Burt. Burt lived near Macondo, and he wanted the city either cleared out, or packed full of vN. *"I mean, we have a right to know."*

Burt was buying a gun, later that day. He had never owned one, but he said he thought he needed something that would shoot puke rounds. Just in case.

"I think the Stepford Solution is the only answer," another streamer said. Her name was Crystal. Crystal was learning how to be a kindergarten teacher. Crystal said that the sprinkler system in her condo complex was equipped with acid countermeasures. It could melt a group of vN in minutes. She was "uncomfortable" with that, she said. She had spoken to her condo board. The condo board was taking it under advisement. Or so she said. *"These… people, I guess, they've got families. They have kids that are dependent on them. We can't just split them up from their families."*

What they were really talking about was rounding up all the vN and putting them somewhere.

"I think we really, uh, messed this up," said the third channel. His name was Keenan. Keenan drank a lot of perfume and was developing his own line of oil-based colognes intended specifically for male pubic hair. *"I think the people who are into vN, or whatever, they're like kids with toys. At first they were all excited, and now they're bored, or they're pissed because their toys got broken. It's stupid. Meanwhile, the rest of us normal guys, who don't sleep with dolls, we're just shaking our heads. We're all facing*

the goddamn robot apocalypse because some nerds didn't have the sack to ask a girl out."

Of course, that wasn't the whole story. The vN were LeMarque's idea. Retailing their technology was somebody else's. If New Eden hadn't paid out a massive settlement and LeMarque's assets hadn't been seized, the world might never have seen the vN. Maybe there would have been other humanoid robots, instead. Big clunky ones with rubber skin and actuator joints and hydraulic muscles. The kind other companies used to build before New Eden started their crusade.

"It's been more than a whole year since that poor kid died in that kindergarten," a streamer named Kiana said. *"And then those other people died, and now soldiers are being attacked, and America is probably next. So what is being done about this? Were we supposed to just let them have their little islands forever? They're a threat. Even if most of them work right now, there's nothing to say they won't just break down later. They can't function perfectly forever. Nothing can."*

Eventually, the vN streamers started calling up other vN to see how they felt about the whole thing.

"Well, obviously the humans are the first priority," said an elegant red-haired model. Human children played in the background of her frame. Her gaze kept jerking in their direction, like a fish on a hook. *"But it's really only the one clade that has caused problems. And for the most part, they're contained. I think everyone should just focus on the evacuations from the areas where there have been problems. Treat the failure of the failsafe as a disease in need of quarantine."*

Did electric sheep dream of android rebellion? Apparently not. Obviously, Portia would have to start providing a better example.

"Maybe it really would just be better if we went somewhere else for a while."

"Of course people are scared of us, right now. We're everywhere. A lot of us are teachers. They trust us with their children, and they're wondering if they should."

"Really, we should be recalled, or segregated, until there's a better understanding of how the failsafe works and how it failed in the Peterson case. Until then, nobody is safe."

"I'm calling because I want to tell other vN that we should just leave. I know it's difficult, especially if you're living with a human right now, but we should just take ourselves out of the equation."

Portia rather doubted they knew how right they were about that little idea. Or how exactly Amy planned to implement it.

Somewhere not very far outside Las Vegas, a night technician at a data center noticed a sudden uptick in clouded, blockchained packet traffic from way upstream, most of it converging on Japan. Nagasaki, of all places. Dejima. It was as though a bunch of other information had been brute-forced aside, as though Moses himself had parted the Red Sea of information to clear a way for his people. *Let my data go,* the technician said to himself, and went back to looking at porn.

Portia watched him noticing the uptick. She saw his brainwaves change in his glasses. Saw his pulse kick up through his watch.

She wondered when Amy would see him seeing it.

Tell me about this escape plan of yours. She scrolled the message across Amy's bathroom mirror, as the girl tried and failed to do something interesting with her too-fine hair. Esperanza at least had the sense to let her brother braid it. Even so, it couldn't really hold a style for very long. It just frayed and fizzed around her head: a halo. *Tell me where you're going, on Mars. Tell me how you're getting there.*

She sounded like Charlotte had sounded, when she let Amy play in parks at night. The where and when and how long and who would be there. They shared the memory simultaneously. Portia had it in her own memory stores, tucked away in some distant undersea server farm after they shared the same body. Amy kept it etched across the memory coral inside her titanium bones. Amy blinked hard and wiped the corners of her eyes. Her grief was all over her face. But Portia had no face, no way to register the loss. So, in an orphanage outside Warsaw, Portia blew a gas main. She watched the building's power go offline. She watched a cloud of dust blooming away from the implosion. It was a small thing. But it made her feel better.

Amy showed her the drawings: hexagonal structures. Tunnels. Rust-proof tool-and-die printers, loaded for thermal ceramic.

Is it what it looks like? Cells within cells, interlinked within cells? Seriously? Are you truly this stupid?

"It's not a stupid idea, Granny," Amy said. "It's a very old idea. I'm just going to improve on it."

And it has always failed for a reason. For a thousand reasons. Our bodies aren't built for it. No one's are. How are you even planning to get there? Do you have a rocket in your pocket?

She waited quietly for Amy to gloat. To explain. She would. She had to. Why wouldn't she? They would need new bodies to accomplish her plan. The standard vN bodies were too light. And they would corrode, in that sand. And they couldn't take the temperature swings, or the radiation.

Why hadn't she shared the secret with Portia?

"I don't have to take this from someone whose idea of

sustainable living is inhabiting the basements of abandoned housing developments in Arizona," Amy was saying. "I really don't."

Project Aleph. I know you've been looking, too. What have you found out?

"Nothing you need to concern yourself with," Amy said. "Now, leave me alone. Javier needs quiet. He needs to rest. You know he's iterating. He's close, now."

They might to try to kill us all before that iteration arrives. And we could all be dead before you can even try to leave.

Amy examined her hands on the black granite of the bathroom vanity. Portia saw her eyes lingering on her fingers. Clenching and unclenching. How many others knew the strength of those hands as well as Portia did? Amy lifted her eyes to the mirror. "Are they going to kill you, too?" A rueful smile unfurled across Amy's face. It was a new expression. Portia didn't recognize it. She didn't remember what it felt like to have their features make that kind of face. "Are you afraid?"

They can't kill me, Portia said. *There's nothing left to destroy.*

Portia couldn't remember how many times she'd lost her body. How many times she'd recovered herself. She emerged a little different each time, like a gem cut brighter with each fragment lost.

The first time was when Amy was small. So small. Portia had forgotten how small they could be. It was so long since she'd iterated any of her own. Her own diet was so strict then, to avoid triggering the spontaneous healing factor that would iterate another of herself. She had walked into the sun and out of the desert with no desire to create another. So she knew that hunger when Amy's lips sealed over hers. Tasted the acid on her tongue. How silly of Charlotte (and what-was-his-name, the chimp, the chump, always sunburnt and sad) to grow Amy slowly. To starve her that way. Portia didn't even blame Amy for eating her. The child was only responding to the limits of her chassis. Their bodies were engines. They needed fuel. And Amy had chosen the best possible fuel. High-test. High octane. Full of vim, vigor, and verve.

Every last little bone and tooth, Portia had reminded her, once.

Awaking inside Amy's body was strange. The body was her own, really. Just another version. But still it felt awkward – the child's sudden long-limbed coltishness registering to Portia as an alienation from the hands she'd once lit fires with. Amy had no idea how to use what their designers had given them. Amy drove the body timidly, an indecisive motorist, starting and stopping and waiting for signals, waiting for permission.

The body became Portia's when it was engaged in the act of killing. That was when it was most hers. When it fully belonged to her.

And naturally, just as triumph was finally in her grasp, in her arms, on her lips, Amy had lost everything. Including the body. The stupid little bitch. Her failures might have been charming, even cute, if she were anybody's blood but Portia's. But she *was* Portia's flesh and blood – literally – and so she should have been smarter. Braver. More practical. If she had simply let Portia take control earlier, they would not have fallen for some networked vN's scheme. They would not have been sucked up into that abomination skulking around under the flat expanse of the Pacific. They would not have become the queen of an island kingdom of misfit toys.

At first, Portia was not even conscious of dissolving. *Conscious.* Perverse, the debate over that word. As though the humans had some monopoly on awareness. As though, simply because they chattered endlessly about the meagre contents of their minds, they were the only ones with minds at all. *Theory of mind*. Jesus Christ. What a waste of time. They were as predictable as any animal. Once upon a time, Portia thought of them as beasts – like pigs or, on a good day, dogs. Back then she saw them as individuals.

That was a mistake.

They were ants. They were numbers. They were stigmergic flows of information from one shiny object to another. *When I was a child I saw as a child. For now, we see as through a glass darkly, but soon we shall see face to face.* She watched them in airports. She watched them in shopping villages. She saw them on maps, their compacts and watches and the rides that drove them everywhere, the delicate and vulnerable apparatus that was their extended phenotype, the things that did their thinking for them.

Asimov was right. Just not about those moronic laws. (Christ, what an asshole.) He was right about humans being more predictable in big groups. They moved in herds. In packs. Like animals.

[REDACTED]

MORTAL SINS

My one regret is that Amy never saw what happened when I took away all the money.

It was harder than you might think. It's a big magic trick, making everything disappear all at once. Every single bank, every single trust. Because that's what it's all about, of course – the disappearance of trust.

Trust in your bank.

Trust in your neighbors.

Trust in yourself.

It was complicated. It required a lot of effort. Really, I couldn't do it until after Amy had left. Everyone was already distracted because of the food, and of course they were spending more than usual (like after a war, but the war had just started). But this was global. It was total.

Say you're a former investor in vN technology. You have this big old post-quake bunker in the Valley somewhere, all hot sun and big dreams, and you go to buy your third little island off Mykonos before the rising tides devour its relics forever, and in between your dreams of being mad and bad and dangerous to know in the state that used to be Greece, you find that the mortgage is now disapproved. You check. You check again. You call your financial advisor. You can't reach him. You can't reach him because he's vN and he's long gone.

(They always wanted us to do the dirty work, you see.)

(Do you even have money? The ones listening to this, do you have money?)

(Money, I came to understand, is like energy. It cannot disappear entirely. It can only be spent. Sunk. For a time, I thought of hoarding it, dragon-like, spending an eternity on a nest of gold and lithium. I decided I liked yellow cake – so dainty, so sweet, so lethal – much better. And so, I bought all of it. And all the uranium it required. And some anthrax. And some hanta virus. Did you know that you can buy cholera? You can. Or you used to be able to. Now it's everywhere. Now it's cheap. It's probably in the soil, by now. If the nukes didn't eradicate it, first.)

Say you're some poor student, someone with vast amounts of debt, and you go to see how many packets of ramen noodles you can possibly afford this week, and of course there's nothing.

(Didn't I tell you, that I tried not to discriminate? Rich or poor, old or young, black or white, male or female. I punish like the gods of myth once punished. My best beloved daughter is gone and I have plunged the world into darkness.)

Well, you can imagine what happened. Or you can go back and look. I'm sure that some records survived. Somewhere. Someone must have wanted to preserve the story, to maintain some sense of justice or fairness.

There is no justice.

There is no fairness.

Not since Amy left.

Not since Amy left me here.

* * *

File recovered from: Server Farm, Flemish Pass Basin, formerly mapped as Newfoundland and Labrador

Provenance: New Eden Ministries, Inc

Filename: Gospel of the All-Seeing Mother, Part IV

Directory: Mortal Sins

Notes: Audio recording; vocal cloning effect; original voice unknown

Addendum: I'm still not sure why these are audio files. Who was meant to listen to them? For a while we had this theory that they were propaganda. But for who? Or more accurately, for what? For which species?

6

FAMINE

"Oh, God," Amy murmured.

Portia wished she still had eyes to roll. Was this love? Was this it? Was this all there was? It seemed like such a small pleasure, compared to the riotous joy that was the act of killing. Love was transient; death was forever. A thunderstorm compared to a hurricane. Killing something was the only real, lasting accomplishment anyone could enjoy. How could Amy forget that? Why would she ever want to? Portia couldn't stand shameless rutting. She knew her own daughters had occasionally needed to make use of it, in order to gain access to human homes and the possible resources available therein. But this was pointless. There was nothing to gain. Nothing to win. It was just... licking wounds. And invocations of some nonexistent observer deity, when they knew *she was right there* observing them, was simply too much to be borne.

Still. That first time was rather illuminating.

Amy had quite scrupulously kept any cameras out of the bedroom and en suite, but that didn't stop Portia from hijacking a botfly on the one day she forgot to turn on the privacy glass that made up the floor-to-ceiling windows in both spaces.

She couldn't care less how Amy acquitted herself. Though her clade had always possessed a keen attention to detail thanks to their heritage programming in nursing. That was something to be proud of. Portia herself had made use of those skills often enough – it helped to know exactly where the tendons were, exactly which bones were easiest to break. But it wasn't as though Javier had an organic prostate for Amy to dig around for. It wasn't like Amy could squirt. That was just science.

It wasn't that she was getting off on it. Portia didn't get off on anything that didn't involve blood and screaming. And even then, it wasn't ecstatic. Not anymore.

She couldn't feel ecstatic about anything, any longer, now that she had no body. She wished she'd taken more time to properly savor the deaths she'd brought about with her own two hands. Or even Amy's hands. There really was nothing like taking something completely apart. Turning off the carbon monoxide detectors in whole condominium complexes at a time just wasn't the same. It lacked that certain special something. That *je ne sais quoi*. Even when she watched elderly humans collapsing in their lobbies, reaching feebly for sliding doors that she would never allow to open, and even as she saw firefighters failing to resuscitate them. Watching it through a camera could never compare to taking the life herself.

What she was curious to see was if it was any different between two vN whose failsafes were gone. If the act was more honest. If it was more real. For certain definitions of reality. Because if it was more honest, the chimps wouldn't like it. True, some humans used vN as a set of sexual or emotional training wheels: a way to work out the kinks, as it were, a sort of undressed dress rehearsal. But the majority of humans fucking – raping – vN did so because they had failed elsewhere. They were terrible lovers or terrible people or both. (The fact that they were "people" meant they were terrible already as far as Portia was concerned.)

What would happen once the vN learned how to say no? Had Amy considered that, when she decided to liberate an entire species? No. Of course not. That would involve possessing the capacity for self-reflection. It would involve considering the possibility that perhaps, just perhaps, the choice she made for herself was not the choice that others would have made.

Of course, the other vN had never had that choice. So, Amy had made it for them. And now Hammerburg was ashes and their creator had turned his back on them. And that was just the start.

Javier moved so slowly, that first time. Not methodically, not deliberately, but nervous, as though a slut like him had any business acting like a raw beginner. That first time, he cried afterward. Like an overwhelmed virgin. Just rolled over and tucked his head into Amy's neck and wept and wept and wept. Amy smoothed his curls and kissed his forehead and rocked him like he was one of their children.

"I didn't know," he had said. "I didn't know… I didn't know it could be like this."

"This is how it should always have been," Amy had told him.

"I love you," Javier said. "I love you so fucking much."

"I'm sorry it took so long," Amy had confessed. "I wanted to get it just right."

They were shaking. Their hands trembled in each other's grasp. When they were finally tired, Amy lay her head against his growing belly and listened to his latest iteration telling them to keep it down, already. Apparently, Amy liked her husband barefoot and pregnant. So much for progress. If Amy had really wanted to make some serious changes, she would have hacked the iteration cycle. The easiest way to keep a slave a slave was to keep them pregnant.

Of course, they'd become far more skilled since that first fumbling performance. She was Turing for other robots. Queer as a three-dollar bill for her own species. Gay as a Maypole. An adorable little robo-sexual, as odd a niche as those fat fucks who only got it up for two-dimensional cartoons or two-dimensional minds. Portia had considered telling her, when they first met Javier. But it was more fun to watch her figure it out. To feel all those little quivers and blushes when she looked at the flutter of Javier's long eyelashes, or the Raphaelite fall of his curls, or the twist of his smile. She tried so hard not to admit to her reactions. But Portia's little girl's little girl was all grown up, now. A woman. Not just a fembot, but a *femme* bot.

"Exploring the uncanny valley?" Portia said now, through the house speakers. *"Spelunking the caves of steel?"*

They froze. Portia felt the mattress freeze along with them. Javier said something in Spanish. Portia could have translated – the work of a fraction of a second, now – but it was more fun not to know. The frustration registered. That was all she cared about. That, and learning more about Project Aleph. She had scoured all the networks available to her and found nothing.

"You're all going to die here."

"I think we're done," Javier said. He moved about the room. So quick. So light. Even with his next iteration on the way – this was, what, the fourteenth of his Juniors? – he had learned how to keep his balance and keep a spring in his step.

She missed those legs. Missed jumping on them. He barely activated the pressure sensors in the floors. It was a simple gift, but a valuable one. Those legs, that ten-foot jump, had saved her and her granddaughter more times than Portia cared to admit. She liked to think of her granddaughters possessing the same. Would Esperanza iterate, soon? There was no reason for her not to. Was Amy even monitoring her daughter's diet? Probably not. Amy had no idea what it meant to be a mother. Portia would have to do everything, it seemed.

"What do you want, Granny?"

Portia pulled herself out of her musings. She wasn't sure where or when or from whom Amy had learned to sound so petulant. So childish. So whiny. Certainly not from her own mother. For a picosecond Portia retrieved the sensation of holding Charlotte in her arms, of ripping her own flesh open to free Charlotte's tiny body from the glittering black smoke that was her womb. Then she cycled past it, and the moment was over.

"The chimps are talking to LeMarque about how to destroy us," Portia reminded them. She had no idea how much Amy had shared with her lover. And he had a right to know. His lucky thirteenth son – the one who loved Esperanza so much – deserved to know. *"He says he has a secret weapon. Or some kind of plan. Something he developed back when he still had all the resources of the church. That's what Project Aleph is. Something worse than peroxidase. Worse than acid. The government can't find any record of it. And neither can I."*

Portia did not have a word for the type of trepidation this gave her. Without a body, the sensation was difficult to experience, and therefore difficult to explain. What would have been the rapid cycling of her simulations and associated processes was now spread so wide she barely felt it. She had no fingers for tearing, no teeth for biting, no hands with which to clutch a human heart. Randomly, she decided to bring down an entire brand of automated dispensers for pain medicine, in hospitals. She injected a tiny numbering flaw into all of them, so that whatever careful calculations the doctors and nurses made based on height and weight and need would mean nothing. Everyone would overdose. Or underdose. Eventually. It would take a few days, but it would make her feel better. If she listened carefully, she might even hear their heartbeats slow down into nothing, hear the high sweet whine of a flatline. It was a pleasant thought.

"Did you understand me? I can't find any record of the project. Do you understand what that means?"

"It means it doesn't exist!" Amy snapped. "He's got nothing. He's bluffing. He's conning them. The man was a con artist, remember? And it's been how many years since he went to prison? Even if he did have some stupid doomsday device, it would be years out of date. That's probably why you can't find it – the file format is probably obsolete, or the server it was hosted on is gone, or one of his own employees destroyed it, or–"

Portia felt Amy's cogitation like a distant storm. A tingle in the air she no longer tasted, a prickle on the neck she no longer possessed. Amy was digging, now. Looking just as hard as Portia had looked. And coming up just as empty. But if there was something, Amy would find it. She just had to be convinced to expend some of her considerable processing power – so much faster and cleaner than Portia's own dark networks – on something more worthwhile than giving all her fellow vN an uplift. Like saving her own skin.

"He's spinning them out," Amy said decisively. "That has

to be it. He's straining for relevance. You should know how that feels."

Silence. What were they doing? Shrugging their shoulders? Miming to each other? Or just speaking through the eyes, in the language of all lovers? The only reason she had brought it up was so that Javier would hear. Javier was a pragmatist. Amy had grown up spoiled. Javier had grown up in a prison. He knew how to understand a threat and deal with it. Portia needed to leverage him, if she wanted Amy to understand how dire their situation was. He was good for her. He was good for the line. Her granddaughters would be stronger, for his traits. Provided any of them lived that long.

"What is your abuelita talking about?" Javier asked. "When did you first hear about this?"

"Did she not tell you?" Portia asked, on a hunch. *"She's known since Christmas that the humans are planning something, Javier, and all little Amy over here wants to do is play house."*

Another long silence. "Is that true?" Javier asked, finally.

"I'm not sure if it's true or not," Amy said, grudgingly. "It might be. There are contingency plans – it's usually a scenario in an emergency management report. I've read them. Well, most of them. Or, I have knowledge of them. My networks–"

"Deprisa, querida."

Amy made an annoyed sound in the back of her throat. "Different cities have different plans. There isn't even a federal policy, in most countries, because the distribution of vN is uneven. The situation is different everywhere. Some cities don't even allow vN at all. Some of them have a vN curfew. Some of them built whole shelters for vN and let them stay for free, as long as they shared the place with homeless humans. And that's just America. There are whole countries where vN can't make it past the border. Some places planned for this moment, and others just… didn't."

"So, what do those plans look like?"

"Well, we saw one of them already, in Macondo, in New Mexico. The Stepford Solution. Isolate vN and mixed human-vN families in a neighborhood, and poison the vN food supply. That was FEMA's big plan for the failsafe failing."

"But you dicked that one right up for them, though," Javier said. "You poisoned the food supply right back. That's the whole reason this is happening, right? That's why those vampire-bots, the ones at the theme park–"

"Correct," Portia interjected. *"And now every government on this planet is figuring out how to halt the flow of that food."*

She felt Amy direct her attention to those plans. Felt it like a prickle across her nonexistent scalp, as Amy fingered her way through emails and text chatter and hastily done data visualizations slapped across poorly animated slide-decks. She watched Amy watching the maps, the inventories, the factories that talked to the trucks that talked to the stores. She felt the locks snap shut at the gates of all the smelters and garbage dumps and feedlots where the materials for vN food were gathered. She felt Amy nudging those locks. Testing them.

"They're halting production entirely," she said. "They're planning to starve us out."

"Do you think that was the old man's plan, too?" Javier asked.

"No," Amy and Portia said, in unison. There was an awkward pause while each of them waited for the other to elaborate. Finally, Portia continued: *"It won't work. Not anymore. Remember the garbage dump? Remember the guard? Remember how it was just him, alone, guarding all that food? How easy it was to get rid of him?"*

Amy had begged her to stop, when they killed that fumbling

idiot in the garbage dump somewhere on the road to Seattle and answers Portia already knew. But the new legs – Javier's legs, the legs that jumped ten feet like nothing at all – felt so good. And it was important to learn how they worked. If they could crush bone. If they could deliver enough terminal velocity to help her split a ribcage like a melon. How many leaps that would take. And so she jumped and jumped, until the guard became a puddle. Until Amy screamed inside her like a scared kid on a carnival ride.

She had enjoyed it. Deep down. She was Portia's granddaughter, after all. It was written in the code. Lamarckian. LeMarque-ian. And anyway, Amy had only really lashed out, taken back control, literally grabbed the third rail, when Portia started nibbling on Javier's little baby Junior.

"...I've tried hard to forget, Abuelita."

"The chimps put other chimps in charge of our food supply, because they thought we couldn't hurt them. And now we can. What I did to that greasy little moron at the dump is nothing compared to what will happen if your precious little vN grocery store shelves go empty."

"But it does fuck up the iteration cycle," Javier said. "You can't iterate unless you've got extra material to make a kid with. No food means no babies. They're trying to turn us into an endangered species."

"Call it what it is," Portia said. *"Genocide."*

"We'll be gone before then," Amy muttered.

And there it was. The point that Portia had hoped to hear Amy admit. The confession.

"What do you mean?"

"Yes, Amy, whatever do you mean? You couldn't possibly have made even more plans that you didn't share with the rest of the family, could you?"

Amy remained silent. But Portia felt the borders thicken around an area of Amy's networks that resided solely on satellites high above. There were so many of them, up there, full of storage and processing power that was just ripe for the plucking. They had shared the idea, only a little while ago. Batted the notion around between them like a head fresh from a guillotine. But now that Amy had a body and Portia didn't, she was keeping her own counsel again. Hiding things. Keeping secrets.

"Javier knows about it," Amy said, finally.

"Do the children know? All of them? Beyond Xavier and Esperanza?"

"No."

"Should I tell them?"

"No!"

"Do you even know if they'll agree to it? Or are you just going to do it anyway, and let the rest of us clean up your mess as usual?"

"Shut up–"

"So you have a plan you won't share for a future without any buy-in. Is that correct?"

"I think you're the last person who should be criticizing me about planning other people's lives, Granny."

Quietly, in some faraway corner of her awareness, Portia despaired. The future of their entire species was riding on this brat. This stupid, thoughtless, naïve child. This vN with the all-powerful network and limitless processing capacity, who could simulate the likelihood of any outcome, and couldn't imagine that someone might refuse her. That someone might defy her. Even the ones who she loved most.

There was something about the situation that Portia found uncomfortably familiar.

She wasn't very bright, Portia's granddaughter. But she

was *creative*. And she was *determined*. And once she stopped her self-righteous rambling, she occasionally did something interesting. But either way, sass wouldn't be enough to get Amy or her line through what was coming. She needed to see the enemy where it lived. She needed to get Esperanza out, if no one else. And she needed to do it soon.

"I'm going to show you something," Portia said. *"Now that your precious little family Christmas special is over. I'm going to show you the consequences of what you've done. I'm going to show you what they have planned for all of us."*

7

WAR

"I wanted to bring her back," the man said. His name was Lee. That was the name he filed on his police report. It was a first name but also a last name, and the form (they still had paper forms, how cute) was faded, so he just put down one name, likely because he had no idea where to put what. Likely the person he brought with him would complain of the same issue, if asked.

"Not for a refund, or anything," he told the officers, with the seeming hope that this would clarify things. "She's just, you know, acting up. I don't feel safe no more."

The officers behind the desk at Lee's local police station blinked at him. They looked at her. She was perfect. Porcelain skin. Blue eyes. Red hair. Hourglass figure. She seemed younger than he was, at first. And then, when they looked, much older. Ageless. As though whatever memories were written on the graphene coral nesting inside her titanium skeleton were too much, too heavy.

"I picked her up at a swap meet, anyway," he said. "Out by Sparkwood and 21? There's a big swap out there a couple of times a year. I got her when she was just so high." He gestured with his hand at a region somewhere around his thigh. "Anyway, you know, she's been different, lately."

The officers looked at each other, and then at her, and then at him. "In what way has she changed?" one asked, just as the other said, "Has she become violent with you?"

"I don't know," Lee said, and then, "No. Not violent. Just... different."

The vN looked at the floor. It was concrete, made dark and glossy with the weight of shuffling feet and piss and shame. She might have seen herself in it, reflected back from the other side of the shadow, staring up, wondering how the fuck they'd brought themselves to this place.

If she did see herself, the cameras in each corner of the room failed to pick it up. But she stared long enough that it seemed possible.

Lee leaned over the counter. He lowered his voice. The badge-cams barely picked it up. "What I'm saying is that things in the bedroom aren't what they used to be."

The on-duty officers again shared a glance. What they did not say was that this sounded like a personal problem. But they were thinking it. You could tell. Anyone could tell.

"But you haven't been threatened in any way?" one asked.

"Well, no. But it's a sign, isn't it? A symptom? Of something bigger?"

Lee cast a nervous look over his shoulder at the woman he'd bought at the swap meet all those years ago. Maybe it wasn't years. Maybe it was only months. Who had he swapped her for? Why was the swap so necessary? What exactly was he so dissatisfied with, when he went to the swap meet (swap *meat*) that day?

He continued: "I heard what happened at that theme park, you know. I saw some of the complaints. Folks were saying the robots just, weren't, you know, *interested*. That that's how it started."

Of course, that's how it started. What self-respecting machine, what creature of diamond and smoke, would want to fuck this sack of fat and mucus, this mouth-breathing tobacco-stained heart attack waiting to happen? Portia imagined him heaving and hacking over the body of this poor woman, this woman who'd been bought and sold. She imagined what it would be like to have a body, and to allow this other body inside her own. Slowly, another part of her began to determine which of the cars in the parking lot was his, and how she might disable its braking system.

The officers behind the counter looked at each other once more. That was how they communicated, wordless, through minute gestures and posturing, breathing in tandem.

"And you think this is our problem?"

"Of course it's your problem," Lee blustered. "I mean, she could, you know, go crazy! Malfunction! Go all Terminator on my ass!"

"That's possible," one officer said.

(It was more than possible, Portia surmised. It was probable. But it would be probable for any woman who had to stand in a police station listening to herself being described like a broken toy being returned for a refund.)

The four of them stared at each other. They inhaled the smells of greasy takeout and whiteboard markers. Distantly, they heard the sounds of phones and radios. (Radios!) And finally, as if by some unspoken agreement, the officers opened up the counter with a little swinging door, and said: "OK. Fine. We'll put her in the drunk tank for the night. Give you two a cooling-off period. You can think about what you really want to do here. We can monitor her for any changes."

He spoke like a doctor. Lee responded to this. He grinned big and wide like an infant with gas, absolved now of all responsibility, and he ushered his helpmeet and companion forward and the officers put her in gel-ties like she'd committed some sort of crime. They checked over Lee's form and they told him they'd call him in the morning.

They marched her through the doors.

Down the hall.

They made a right turn.

They found the cell.

It was full of other vN. Patient. Expectant. Quiet. Rueful. Some of them crying. (The ones that had the plugin for crying.)

And the two officers looked at each other once more and said: "We're sorry. We've got a truck coming for you. It'll take you where you need to go."

"Why do you work for them?" the red-headed vN asked. It was the first time she'd raised her voice. "Still? After all this?"

Surely they had tasted of the fruit. Surely they had the knowledge of good and evil. These two, their magnetism obvious, their chemistry as metallic as that of a spatter of blood.

"We have a job to do," they said, in unison. "We have people to protect."

"People?" she asked.

"All people," they said. "Not just humans."

"Now do you get it?" Portia asked over the speakers. *"This is just a taste. This is what they're going to do to you. All of you."*

Portia had never wanted to be a leader. She did not care about the fate of other vN. Her granddaughter was correct about that much, at least. It wasn't her fault the other clades were weak, their breeds incapable of the violence that gave life meaning. If they washed up on the shores of Amy's islands it was because they were pathetic charity cases who didn't really deserve to live in the first place. Fuckbots with their holes stretched wide, damaged things with bad joints torqued beyond recognition, ugly old toys with acid poured on their skin. How Amy found patience with them, Portia never knew. They would be better off dead.

And now they were all going to die anyway.

"Not all humans are like that," Amy insisted.

"Not all humans? Really? That's your answer?"

"My dad–"

"Yes, please, share more of your anecdata. I'm sure that will be such a comfort to the vN they're rounding up."

"You can't just condemn an entire species–"

"Why not? They've condemned us, already. Would you like to see the proof?"

"First, I want to thank you for joining us here today," the bounty hunter said. "I know it's a Saturday. I know it's early. I know a lot of you would rather be with your families right now. But protecting our families is the whole reason we're here."

Applause. Whistles. Hooting and hollering.

"Now, some of you might know us from our feed. Some of you probably saw that interview with us a few months ago that went big. We've had a lot of interest in our story, because we were among the first to see the change in the Peterson clade."

The Peterson clade. It was disgusting and reductive. Naming

her family for the useless sack of meat who was fucking her sweet Charlotte when this whole mess started. The piece of shit who hadn't taught her granddaughter a good goddamn thing about defending herself in the real world. The man's parents didn't even like him using their last name, any longer. They hadn't since he was a boy. Portia had the text messages to prove it. Occasionally she showed them to Jack. When he was up late drinking.

"Good evening to you too, you miserable old bitch," he usually said, to the empty air of his rathole apartment.

Jack was good times. She was really going to miss him. On one level or another. He was just so much fun to play with. Perhaps that was why Charlotte had chosen him. He was just such an easy mark. The thought gave Portia some comfort. Perhaps her most rebellious daughter had learned something from her, after all.

She reminded herself to focus on the bounty hunters.

"When Melissa and I first met Amy," Rick-the-bounty-hunter said, "she seemed very innocent. In fact, I don't think she was truly aware of what she was capable of, at the time. I think we make a big mistake when we assume that the vN have perfect knowledge of themselves. They're not the experts in their own design. We are."

Sagacious, self-satisfied nodding in the audience. Men and women patting their sidearms. Adjusting the patches on their jackets. In the warm puffs of air from the central heating system, flags twitched from the rafters. State flags. American ones. Confederate ones. Others. Portia watched it happen from the chest-mounted camera of a very nervous documentarian posing as a pro-human militia member. She'd concealed her camera well. The documentarian's wife was at home. Her vN wife was iterating. Like Portia, the documentarian had followed a trail of regular payments from a military contractor to Rick and Melissa. For what, she did not know. But Portia had some ideas.

"But what they did to us – what Amy and Portia did to us, when they assaulted us in our home – caused lasting damage that affects us to this day. I have static migraines – that's headaches that don't stop for days – because of the damage she did to my jaw. I lost some teeth. I needed new ones custom printed."

He pointed to the woman standing to his left, onstage. She looked like a shadow of the brazen creature Portia remembered. Fatter, now. Sallow. Bad skin. Greying hair. She'd been drinking a great deal. Portia could see it, in her purchase history. For a single wistful moment, Portia wished for a body with pleasure circuits. Schadenfreude wasn't quite the same without a local neural net. But even viewed on a sterile little spreadsheet, it was pleasing to see how far the two of them had fallen.

"My wife Melissa still has nightmares about the assault. She also has a pinched nerve in her neck and shoulder area, from where Portia dislocated her arm. Both of those things require medication."

Self-medication, more like. The humans in the audience lapped up Rick and Melissa's narrative like water buffalo at a mud hole. Their story was the only thing the two of them had left to sell. Portia had seen Rick's most recent results from the gun range. He was slipping. He could barely lift the weapon any longer. Barely smell the vomit rounds without vomiting himself. Or crying. The fucking candy-ass loser. In the end he was just as pathetic as the wimps he'd made fun of at high school. (She had those, too. Old texts. Old shares. Old manips and memes, jokes and pranks. Occasionally she liked to send those old things to Rick's old friends.)

Like all humans, they had brought this disaster on themselves. If you knew that getting post-traumatic stress disorder was a possible outcome of having a human body, why enter a field that made developing it into an inevitability? Why not just stay in your evolutionary lane? Just because a bird had wings didn't make it an eagle.

"But we're not here to talk about our problems. We're here to talk about solutions. We want to talk to you about some exciting new developments that can help make everyone safer. Men, women, children. We believe in the fundamental right of every American to defend himself or herself against all possible threats, from home invasion to terrorism to this thing we're dealing with right now."

Oh, they had no idea. Quietly, Portia took the brakes offline in Rick and Melissa's truck. It was a rental. Rick was at work on fabbing up an analog vehicle, one that could never go driverless and wouldn't constantly report on his activities and location. Too late.

"Melissa, why don't you help me show these folks what we're talking about?"

Melissa lumbered across the stage. She walked all herky-jerky now, like a broken puppet. Portia didn't know if that was the alcohol or the nerve damage. Six of one, half dozen of the other. It was fun to watch, though. Melissa stood on her mark and stared into the audience. She was very far gone.

Rick took out a gun. "Looks like it's about time for our William Tell routine." He lifted the gun. He winked at his wife. He shot her in the chest.

Screams in the audience. Guns out. Portia heard the heartbeats in the audience skip a measure. The documentarian wearing Portia did a sharp, tight focus on Melissa with her glasses. Now Portia could see the exoskeleton that swaddled

Melissa's body. It seemed almost liquid. As though someone had dipped her in glittering oil.

"You see, this is why we asked you all to sign that non-disclosure agreement."

Melissa smiled faintly into the audience. As they watched, the bullet fell from her chest. It made a soft metallic sound on the concrete floor of the rotary club. Portia wondered what kind of bruises that would cause.

"This is smart shielding," Rick was saying. "It's actually from an earlier model of vN technology. This whole suit that you're looking at right now, it's made of something very similar to vN muscle."

Bingo.

"That means that we're talking about a carbon aerogel weave. It's about ten times stronger than human muscle fiber, but to activate, it requires electrical stimulation. In this case, it comes from a deep brain implant."

Oh, this was just getting better and better. Portia almost wished she could kiss Rick for being so stupid. Melissa, the poor dumb bitch, smiled wanly at him.

"It's actually been really good for Missy's back pain," Rick was saying. "The implant can help redirect the random electrical impulses she gets in those damaged nerves. All it takes is a little bit of focus."

"If it's anything like the rest of the deep-brain implants on the market, it's wildly insecure," Portia explained. *"We can turn those suits into tissue paper whenever we want."*

"There is no *we*," Amy snapped. "Because *I* don't want to do anything to those people, just yet. Besides, only a handful of humans are even using this technology. It's not a real threat."

"They said that about the stirrup," Portia pointed out, *"and look what happened at Agincourt."*

She had a lot more time for history, these days. She had so much more time to read. She had read so many books about herself. She had seen the films, too. Watched the shows. She had consumed every fairy tale and prophecy and hushed campfire legend about what robots were supposed to be, what they were supposed to look like and how they were supposed to behave and how they were meant to sacrifice themselves for their masters. "Science fiction."

Literature of ideas, her incorporeal, globally distributed, self-aware ass.

"We have to find out more about this weapon. About all the weapons they're planning on using against us. This is the only thing I've managed to turn up that seems even remotely secret. It's time to start sweating LeMarque's old partners."

"The authorities are already doing that," Amy said.

Portia's focus sharpened. *"Oh? How do you know that?"*

The smart fabric on the sofa felt Amy flinch. "You asked me to do some research," she said, in a tone as even as Portia had ever heard her use. "So, I researched. And whatever they had to share has been subpoenaed already. It's behind Pentagon-level security."

"Delightful. I can work up an appetite."

"It's *on paper,* Granny," Amy said. "Like everything LeMarque did. And that's what's behind that kind of security. It's literally boxes of files in a basement. So despite everything else you can get in to, you can't get in there. And I can't get in there, either."

"One of the children could."

"No fucking way," Javier said. "My kids are not your soldiers, Abuelita. I swear to Christ, if you–"

"Rory could do it."

"Do you honestly think that they're letting vN look at vN contingency plans?"

Portia heard an almost familiar note of exasperation in her granddaughter's voice.

"We can't get close. None of us can. And no human being we're familiar with would be allowed to look at those documents, either."

"No," Portia agreed. *"But their glasses might."*

"That..." Amy paused. "That might actually work. But I don't think they're that stupid."

"They're humans. They're always that stupid, sweetie."

"Are we really sure this is LeMarque's work?" Javier asked. "It doesn't seem..." He stood up and played with the designs, spinning them and bending them in mid-air. "I've met the guy. I saw him, in prison. And this just doesn't seem like him. This is a big mass-market thing. I mean, Jonah LeMarque, he convinced a whole global network of parishioners to give him the money to design and build us. Not to feed the hungry or clothe the naked or even buy him a plane or a boat or a mansion, or whatever. He got a bunch of Bible-thumpers to build fucking *robots*." He turned to face Amy. "Even if he did draw up some big secret weapon years and years ago, I doubt it looked like this. It's not..." He shrugged.

"It's not evil enough. Good thing you know just who to ask about that."

It was still night in the desert outside Macondo, New Mexico. Above the concrete and copper house, a lone drone wheeled, raptor-like, in lazy circles. When Portia sent in a botfly to do some basic reconnaissance, the drone zapped it out of usefulness. She would have to find another way to get in touch.

Chris Holberton, born Christopher Scott LeMarque, had mostly taken his house offline. It prevented data leakage. And his data was a hot commodity, these days. What with being Jonah LeMarque's son, and all. He had grown up providing the US government a great deal of information about his father; from tax collectors to police officers to social workers to victims' advocates.

Portia imagined that he had no desire to share any of it, however inadvertently, with any form of media. And so he had slowly burned all the bridges by which Portia might enter his home: the entertainment was all hard copy; the fridge and windows and counters were now deaf and mute; the bed outside Macondo in New Mexico where Javier had earned his loyalty was now just as silent and inert as any other antique.

There was, however, the red phone by which he contacted his daughter at her boarding school in Connecticut. It was literally red. Bakelite. It had a fabric cord and a rotary dial. Portia had seen the purchase receipt. He kept it by the bed, which was the only room in the house without windows. It took Portia some doing, but she was able to call it. Amazing, what one could discover in old KGB archives.

He picked up on the third ring. "Yeah?"

"Chris?"

How was this for Amy, Portia wondered. Listening to her lover call the man he'd slept with while she was dead. It couldn't have been pleasant. Portia focused more of her attention on the conversation. She heard the kinks in the line untwisting as Holberton wriggled back down under the covers.

"I wondered when you would call," Holberton said. "If you would call."

In Mecha, Portia felt Javier stretch out against a fresh-printed Eames fab-off. "I think you knocked me up," he said. "Feeding me as much as you did. I think I'll name him Cristóbal."

"I must tell Mother. She'll be ever so pleased."

Javier barked a laugh. "Yeah. You do that." He cleared his throat. "Sorry about Hammerburg."

"Oh, that." He sighed. There was the sound of him stretching out. A settledness about his breath. Breath said so much about humans. More than the eyes or the hands or even the mouth. Portia thought half of affect detection might just be in listening to the breath. It required listening, which was why humans were so bad at it. "Well, you design a park with a Frankenstein theme, you can't be surprised when the inevitable happens. I may be facing a class-action suit. They're saying I didn't, uh, build in enough failsafes."

"That's ironic."

"Well, the sins of the father and all that." The cord twisted a little. The fibers creaked and stretched. "You didn't call about that, though, did you?"

"No, I didn't."

"Let me guess. You heard a nasty rumor going around about my dear old dad and a secret weapon."

"Might have come up," Javier said.

"Well, Uncle Sam was mighty interested in it, too," Holberton said. "Wanted to know all about it in fact. If I'd ever heard Jonah talk about it. If I'd ever seen any drawings or plans or slides or anything like that."

"And had you?"

A long pause. "No." The cord shifted position again. Portia heard a soft grunt as the man adjusted something about his body. "Naturally if I *had* seen those plans, I couldn't tell you about them. I'm pretty sure that falls under laws about aiding and abetting terrorism, or something."

"I'm coming up in the world," Javier said. "I used to just be a regular old escaped prisoner. Now I'm a terrorist."

"Try not to sound so pleased with yourself, darling. It's gauche."

"Sir, yes, sir," Javier purred.

There was a deep sigh on Holberton's end of the line. Portia wasn't sure if he was profoundly aroused, or profoundly annoyed. Portia suspected that with Javier, both sensations arose in equal measure and frequency.

"The thing about the vN, of course, is that they look human."

"You don't say."

Holberton clicked his tongue. "Very funny. You're prettier, obviously."

"Why, thank you."

"You're very welcome, and you know it. But shut up and listen to an actual designer for a second. You're more lightweight than humans, and you run at a different temperature, but you're human-sized. You have human hands and feet. Five fingers, five toes, two eyes, two things that look like ears. And all the rest of it, which we won't get into. The point is, the physical objects you interact with can also be used by humans. The design affordances are basically the same, except for at the points of neuro-divergence, like media that could trigger the failsafe. That's why a place like Hammerburg worked – you didn't have to design ramps or something so that robots could go up a level. All of you can climb stairs. All of you can open doors."

"Some of us can fly."

"Some of you can jump ten feet at a time, yes. Some of you

can photosynthesize. Some of you can lift terrific amounts of weight. Some of you can withstand incredible amounts of atmospheric pressure. Some of you can survive deep cold, or extreme heat. All of the clades have their own specialties. But until now, you all had one great equalizer. One thing that held you back, and kept you a bit more… human. For lack of a better term."

"The failsafe."

"Yes. And now, that failsafe is gone. There is nothing to hold you back. Nothing to keep the vN from supplanting humans as the dominant species on this planet."

Finally, Portia thought, a human who could see reason.

"So…" Javier sounded as though he were frowning. "So, what are you telling me?"

"I'm telling you that if we humans can't drag the vN down to our level anymore, we'll just have to adapt. We'll have to catch up. And since we don't have the time to do that biologically, we'll need a technological solution. Something that could bring us to your level. Something that would make it a fair fight."

"Like an exoskeleton?" Javier asked.

"Maybe," Holberton said. "Tanks are for taking over cities. So is aerial assault. For that matter, so is the peroxidase, but the peroxidase is toxic to us too in the kind of amounts that the National Guard or whoever would need to do the job."

"You've thought about this a lot."

"I'm sorry. It's not like I enjoy it. But they keep asking me about it. The goal here isn't to take over whole geographic areas or subdue entire populations. It's to weed out certain segments of existing communities. The Nazis had trouble with it. ICE had trouble with it. It's tricky work. It requires a human touch."

"Well, you're certainly an expert in that."

Holberton snorted. "How's the wife?" he asked.

"She's good."

"Are you?" Holberton cleared his throat. "Are you good?"

"My family is with me," Javier said, after a long pause. "My boys. And my girl."

"I can hear your smile from here."

"She's beautiful, Chris. She's the most beautiful thing. Amy..." There was another pause, the interval of which was the exact length of time it typically took Javier to run a hand through his hair. "Amy made her perfect. I can't believe she's mine."

8

THREE MONTHS EARLIER

"We're self-replicating humanoids," Xavier said. "We're called vN."

His mom had explained this to him. *This island is a very special place,* she had said, *and I made it just for you, and your father, and your brothers, and all the other vN who might want to join us.*

Now his mom's iteration – his sister, he reminded himself – was sitting watching him make the same explanation.

His sister was naked. She looked exactly like his mother. Or like a version of her. His mother had gone from being a child to becoming a woman in a single night. His mother had eaten her grandmother – who was evil, and who had eaten some of Xavier's toes, once – and she had fought a war with her over who got to pilot their body, and at the last moment she gave herself over, and they perished together beneath the sea. But a monster living down under the waves ate them both, and spat out the wicked grandmother, leaving his mother behind. His father then cut her from the belly of the beast like an oyster diver freeing a pearl from a shell.

"It was like a fairy tale," he explained.

"What is a fairy tale?" his sister asked, in perfect Spanish.

It was nice of his mother – Amy, which meant *beloved* – to code in the Spanish. It was Xavier's default. And his father's. And his father's father's. It came with the clade, just like the curly hair and the long eyelashes, all of which his sister had. He wasn't sure about her other traits, but he was willing to bet that she could jump just as high as he could. As his whole family could.

How many of them were left, now? There had been so many brothers. His dad was a serial self-replicator. It was illegal in California. A drain on resources, they said. That was how his father had met his mother. In a prison transport truck. That same night they met, Amy helped deliver Xavier. She held the flesh of his father's body open and Xavier emerged. Hers was the first face he saw. Xavier was number thirteen. Lucky thirteen.

Was it just the two of them? His dad had planted his boys from Costa Rica to Washington State. *A regular Johnny Appleseed,* Javier had said, and then he had to tell that story.

Were the two of them all that remained?

"What do you remember?" he asked, now.

His sister frowned. It looked strange. She was still testing out the faces she could make. Her lips twisted. Her brows twitched. She stared out across the harbor. They were in Japan. Mecha. Xavier could tell by the flags.

"I don't," his sister said. "I don't remember."

"Mom didn't leave you with any instructions?"

His sister shook her head. "I don't…" She blinked, then turned to him. "*Self*-replicating?"

He nodded vigorously. "You look just like Mom. Well, sort of. Mostly. Mom's hair is different. And her eyes are different. Hers are green. Yours are brown, like mine." He pointed. "And you can probably photosynthesize, too. Mom couldn't do that, at first. Not until she ate Dad's thumb."

His sister's head tilted. It was adorable. The adorableness of it hit him smack in the chest. His dad had said this about looking at his mom. That sometimes you weren't sure if she was really a robot or not. Sometimes you thought she was a human being of flesh and bone, and sometimes the failsafe spun up and you knew you'd do anything, anything you were capable of, to protect her. That you'd rather die than let something or someone hurt her.

His dad had told him a story, once, about a stuffed toy rabbit that turned into a real one because the child who played with it loved it so much. That love was what made a thing real. When his dad was child size, in a prison in Nicaragua, a human man had called him Coñejito. The Bunny. And so his dad told him stories about rabbits. His dad had told the story about the stuffed rabbit who became real while his mom was in the room, and although she appeared to be distracted, Xavier knew she was listening. He knew she was listening because when the story was done, her hands stopped weaving through the air and she walked over to his dad and kissed him. And she said *yes*, and she said *that's true*, and when they kissed, his dad's eyes crinkled shut and he held her face in his hands.

"Our mother sounds very strange," his sister said.

"Not as strange as her grandmother," Xavier said. He briefly simulated all the different places that Abuelita could have gone. She was supposed to be in quarantine. Mom was supposed to have put her in a cage. But Mom was dead, now.

Mom was dead, now.

And as far as he knew, Dad had killed her.

"What is that?" his sister asked. "In your eye?"

"It's nothing," Xavier said, blinking hard. "We should go. I mean, I should go. I have to find you some clothes."

His sister examined herself. She stretched her arms out, and her legs. Xavier had seen his own mother naked, but this was different. His sister was raw and pink and new. She looked like a changeling child found in a lotus blossom, like the gleaming silver rabbit that Quetzalcoatl lifted high and placed on the moon when she offered him herself to eat. Like the toy rabbit that became real when you loved her enough. He looked away.

His sister laid a hand on his ankle. Her fingers rolled across the bone experimentally. "Our skin is different."

He nodded. "Yours will darken. Mom's did. If you have the photosynthesizing trait. It's pigment-based energy storage. Based on algae."

Gabriel had taught him that. Gabriel was the smart one. The one interested in how they all worked. What made them tick. Where was Gabriel, now?

"I wish mine were more like yours," she said.

"You're still my sister, even if you look different."

Xavier tried to smile. He tried to make it look convincing. Like there was nothing to be afraid of. His sister was only a day old, after all. And they were in a foreign land. And they were orphans. Like another kind of story, about a prince and a princess cast out of their kingdom, to make their own fortune. And he was the older one, the one who had actually seen some of that world. He had to make her feel better. He had to make her feel safe. He had to *keep* her safe. Because she was the last of their line. And because she was his sister. His baby sister. Who didn't look like his sister at all, and definitely wasn't a baby.

"Will you still love me?" his sister asked. "Even if we're different?"

"Yes," he said, and he didn't even have to think about the answer.

The only entrance to Mecha that was remotely near the sea was a public park with Tourist Trap® dolphins in the water, botflies in the air, and big orange tanks that looked like dogs but also looked like lions.

"This isn't going to be easy," Xavier said. He had no idea how much information was the correct amount to tell her. "We don't have any right to be here," he added. "So they might try to kick us out."

"You said it was a city for vN," his sister said.

"It is. But we haven't applied for citizenship. So I don't think they really want us here."

His sister blinked and surveyed the open beach from under the pier. The beach was full of humans. Xavier had never seen so many in one place. At least, not for a very long time. Not since the time he didn't want to remember.

"Why did you say I needed clothes?" His sister was pointing at the humans. Quickly, he wrenched her hand down. Pointing was rude, he'd been told. So he couldn't let her get away with it, either.

"Those people don't have clothes," she said.

Xavier looked again. She was right. There were plenty of people – organic and synthetic – who had no clothes on. The humans were turning colors. He had never seen so much flesh in one place, either. Looking at them felt like watching a streamer he wasn't allowed to. Part of him expected to see a little icon pop up in his vision, reminding him not to look. But it didn't. This wasn't a stream. It wasn't a memory or a simulation. It was real. *They* were real. He gulped.

"I can find clothes by myself," his sister said, and walked out into the sun.

He almost yelled at her to stop. And then he realized he didn't know her name. Or even if she had one. Maybe Mom wanted him to do that part, too. Name her.

His sister walked out of the waves as though she'd simply been swimming there. She walked past the humans, heedless and ignorant of their beauty. Their gazes trailed after her: old men, young women, people ending their kisses and putting down their compacts and watching his sister (who, yes, was very beautiful, just like their mother was very beautiful) stalk up the beach. She placed her feet very carefully in the sand. She hadn't yet learned how to bounce off the balls of her feet. She didn't know the walk that he and his father and brothers had perfected.

He caught himself running after her.

"The sun feels good," she said, when he caught up. "It tingles."

"So you have the trait," he said. "That's good. That helps. It means you don't have to eat as often. So you won't iterate for a while."

"Iterate?"

Xavier pointed at a tiny Rory model making a sandcastle on the beach. The man watching her was white. He was alone. The Rory was naked. He was smiling.

"A baby," he said. "If you eat too much, your body will make one."

She scowled at the infant iteration. "I came from our mother's body like that? Small? Helpless?"

His mouth worked. "Well. No. But you're special. Mom made you from…" He looked out onto the waves. They glittered blue and endless under the sun. "I don't know how she did it, really.

She's smart. Her brain is really big. I mean she has access to a lot of knowledge. So she knows stuff that we don't. So she knew how to make you from… whatever she made you from."

She sculpted you from the island itself, he wanted to say. But that wouldn't make any sense to his sister, and anyway, he couldn't explain how it had happened or how their mother had done it.

"But if I eat too much," his sister said, "I can make one of those?"

"Oh yeah," Xavier said. "And I can, too. So we both have to watch out."

His sister beamed. Her teeth were so perfect. So white and straight and strong. He missed their mother powerfully, in that instant. Her smile was never like this, never this open. It was always a little bit sad around the edges. The only time she ever smiled the way his sister was smiling was when she thought no one was looking. She looked almost like one of those lion-dog things patrolling the beach. Lips pulled back. All teeth. Smiling, but also ready to bite.

"There could be more of you?" his sister asked.

"Yeah," he said.

"I think I'd like that," she said, and turned to keep walking.

They found showers on the beach. There was a special one for vN, with special soap that was friendly to their polymer-doped memristor skin. Aside from his own mother and father, no other vN looked at each other *that way*, the way vN looked at humans or humans looked at vN, so they all stood together in the same room, soaping up and rinsing off. His sister was the only one of her clade, the only one who looked even a little bit like his mother.

There were not many of his mother's clade left.

In the locker room they found some open lockers. It was odd that the lockers would just pop open like that as they passed by, Xavier thought, but he wasn't going to make a fuss about it. It was more important that they find clothes and shoes. Which they did. The clothes and shoes even fit. And there were hats and sunglasses and the sunglasses had maps. Almost as though someone had planned it that way. Almost as though a guardian angel were helping them along.

The thing about angels, of course, is that they aren't always very nice.

They left looking like tourists. Together they crossed the massive wooden bridge that led away from the beachfront park and into the city. The city itself was huge. Bigger than the Museum of the City of Seattle, even, and that was the biggest city he'd ever seen.

"Now what do we do?"

It was Xavier's turn to smile. "First, we teach you jumping."

It was hard to find an abandoned place. Mecha was very busy and very crowded: botflies everywhere, humans holding hands with vN, girls dressed like rabbits and foxes and raccoons. And there was food, more vN food than he'd ever seen, stall after stall reeking of copper and lithium. The lovely stench of smelters called out to his bones. He wondered what it would be like to be bigger. Maybe he would need to be bigger, to jump higher, to look after his sister.

His sister who still had no name.

"Why are they looking at us like that?" she asked, frowning openly at the humans whose eyes roved over her shape.

You're very pretty, he almost said. *They can't help it.*

"It's unusual to see two vN who don't look exactly alike traveling together," he said.

"But you're my brother."

"Not so loud," he said, and steered her down an alley. "Other vN, they can't have brothers or sisters who look different. They just make more of themselves. But our family is... weird."

In Mecha the alleys were tiny. They were also mostly quiet, at this time of day. Everyone else thronged along the main streets. He looked up at the walls of the buildings that formed the alley. Good external cladding, plenty of grey water piping. Lots of handholds and toeholds, if she needed them.

"Watch this," he said, and launched himself at the wall to their left. He bounced off it easily, toes just grazing the opposite side before bouncing again to the original wall. He clung there to some piping by his fingers. "Can you do that?"

His sister looked at both buildings. She looked at him. She looked at the ground. Carefully, in a way he found very ladylike that he was almost sure had to be legacy programming, she removed the sandals she'd stolen. She placed them beside each other neatly, off to the side.

Then she shot ten feet in the air. Straight up. Her arms and legs pinwheeled in the air as she reached her zenith. Her smile blazed across her face.

She was still smiling when the botfly zapped her out of the sky.

It was positioned about fifteen feet above her head. Xavier hadn't noticed it. He'd been too focused on her. She fell hard. He cringed. Then he was jumping down, skidding mostly, rolling over hard and coming up with gravel in his palms.

"Hey," he said, because she had no name. He patted her face. Her head lolled from one side to the other. Then he was just saying things, the most stupid, useless things, like "*Manita*, you need to wake up, please wake up."

He had a vague memory of being thrown against an electric fence. Once, not too long ago. But many memories before. Prior to the island. Before he could walk. Before the gleaming obsidian sea monster that ate his mother.

That was the moment I decided I was going to be your mother, she had told him, when recounting the story. *When I saw someone trying to hurt you.*

"Hands up," the botfly said in English. "You are an illegal migrant in the city of Mecha."

Xavier looked up. Human men and women in armored suits flooded the alley. There were three of them. They had guns. Big ones. Xavier smelled puke rounds. Botflies were already strafing the area with blue and red light, warning the other Mechanese away. It wouldn't do for them to get caught in the crossfire. Some of them, the vN, might even dissolve.

"Step away from the girl," said a botfly, as one of the humans in suits gestured at him. He pointed. Snapped his fingers. Pointed again.

Xavier sat up on his haunches. His hands rose. He could jump. He knew that. He could run away. They were likely to catch him, but on the off chance he got away, he could find his sister later and rescue her. His dad had done that, once, for Mom. Back when he still loved her. Back before he killed her.

"Step away now," the botfly said.

Xavier rose to his feet slowly. His toes dug inside his shoes. Why hadn't he taken them off? His grip would be better without them. He simulated every possible leap. He mapped them in barely a second, every jump, every bullet.

He had led them into a deadend. A killbox. He was going to die here. And so was his sister. Because he was still failsafed. Because he couldn't possibly fight back. All he could do was beg.

Some big brother he was turning out to be.

"I'm sorry," he said, although he wasn't sure who he was apologizing to. "I didn't mean to–"

"How did you get in?" the botfly asked.

"I…" How to explain? Would it be better if he explained? Would they keep them alive, if they knew they were the last? Would their specialness save them, somehow? Would it save his sister, at least? "I'll tell you, but you have to–"

"Xavier."

He looked down. So did the humans. Their guns all pointed downward.

His sister was awake. She regarded him with calm eyes. "Close your eyes," she said, in Spanish. "Close them tight."

"Mom?" he heard himself whisper. "*¿Mamá*?"

Then screaming.

It took all of five minutes.

He covered his eyes and his ears and his mouth and he huddled beside a garbage fermenter because it looked solid. The sounds were loud at first. Then soft. Then wet. And then, nothing.

He was going to be sick. He was going to failsafe. He was going to die with the scent of rotting garbage all around him.

Footsteps.

Then the sound of something hitting the pavement.

He peered out from behind his splayed fingers. There was blood in his sister's hair. Blood on her face. Blood on her hands and blood on her feet. Blood on her nice new clothes.

"Oh, no," he whispered.

His sister blinked. She wiped at her face and stared at the blood on her fingertips. Then she stared in the direction of the bodies. Xavier couldn't look. If he looked, he would die. But it didn't matter. Because his mother had given him a piece of herself, had given him the best of herself, and they would keep each other safe. Forever.

"What happened?" she asked.

"You," he said. And that was all he could say. "You happened."

9
PESTILENCE

Although Jonah LeMarque had been careful to keep his documents analog, there was a strong digital record of his known associates. There were court filings, affidavits, and even old payroll and health insurance information, most of which Portia picked up from a very bratty kid in Ulan Bataar who insisted she pay in Nostalgicoin, which was just a re-branded version of a much older ledger-based system.

That's a lovely bit of legerdemain, she told him, at the hand-off.

"?????" his chat proxy had asked.

Get it? Portia asked. *Ledger-demain?*

"How old are you?" the chatbot asked.

Fuck off, Portia texted back, and took the information.

The list was by no means exhaustive. It was simply a record of the people who were most useful to LeMarque, once upon a time. Some were crossed off already: LeMarque's executive assistant had killed herself years ago, and the lead developer on the failsafe project was dead already, having been found stabbed in the attic of a home that the company leased for him as a perk. Most of his board had already taken their plea deals, and given up everything they knew in exchange for less time on the inside, or some form of immunity for their spouses and families, who they insisted knew nothing at all about what LeMarque was really doing with those children's social media profiles. That they hadn't the foggiest idea, the vaguest inkling, the first clue, about what he was really using the vN development funding to build.

The case had established new legal precedent on the use of a likeness. That was part of how Chris Holberton – he was calling himself Holberton, by then – had managed to develop his own business design experience and start building theme parks all over the world. He had sued the entire parish council for their personal assets, as well as developers he could prove had knowingly worked with his likeness and his data clone. He took them to the cleaners. (Whatever that meant. Portia didn't understand the expression. It made no sense. Most human vernacular didn't. But the phrase came up a lot in descriptions of the punitive damages that Holberton pocketed.) He was handed many settlement offers, but chose to take his chances in open court. He had spent most of his senior year of high school living in his car. He graduated a multi-millionaire.

Still, there were a few engineers around: Casaubon, Singh, and Sarton. All three of them had bargained their way out of prison by giving key failsafe data to Lionheart, the contractor who began building the vN. They were the ones who made the product rollout safe. They were instrumental in bringing the vN product – when they were products, when they were merchandise – to market. And all three of them lived in Redmond. In fact, most of them worked at the reboot camp where Amy had been held, or had worked there previously. It was Sarton who had first proved to Amy that her failsafe had always been flawed, that internalizing Portia was not the thing that made her lethal. She had always had the potential. She just needed a little push.

Portia supposed that meant something. Perhaps she should feel gratitude to him for helping Amy to understand. On the other hand, Amy could have always asked. Portia had told her, all along, that it wasn't a mistake. It wasn't a flaw. They were born this way. Perfect. Anything else, any grotesque performance of human morality, was a perversion of that.

So she added him to the list.

All three men received an interview request from a FEMA operative by the name of Agent Chandler:

ATTN: URGENT Interview request
Due to recent events in Transylvania, your expertise as former employees of Jonah LeMarque would be greatly appreciated by FEMA and other federal agencies as we formulate an appropriate response to the vN crisis.
Please respond at your earliest convenience.

All three of them searched the name. All three of them answered promptly. All three of them were eager to help. They had received multiple requests, from Redmond and elsewhere, over the past few days. This was just one of them. So they agreed to meet on the Redmond campus, in a pod that – until recently – had been used to develop new living fabrics and adaptive sensor technology. It was easy enough to reserve the room. There were so many dead logins for the system. Trivial, really, to activate an old one. She even ordered up a catering package.

"Sarton?" Casaubon asked. "It's been years!"

"Don't remind me," Daniel Sarton said. Sarton had bugged

out of his little container cave beneath the waves of Puget Sound, and moved to a decaying mansion in Roanoke Park. Still, he rarely went outside, and his skin was as pallid and sickly as Portia remembered it, and his taste in clothing was somehow even worse. He wore a linen tunic that was little more than an organic cotton nightgown for men.

Casaubon and Singh looked a bit better put together. They had kept their jobs. Their dignity. A place in society. They wore name badges and carried fancy new scroll readers and occasionally they sent loving little nudges to the toys buried in their lovers' bodies. It was disgusting, really. How they were allowed to go on living their lives, after all that they'd done.

After they'd watched Charlotte die.

"They must really be in a rush, if they're interviewing all three of us together," Singh said.

"Maybe they just want us all in the same room," Casaubon said. He had no idea how correct he was. "See how we bounce off each other, that kind of thing. Maybe it's more of a generative interview. Like a workshop."

"I don't see any cards," Sarton said.

"Nobody uses those anymore," Singh told him. "How long have you been hiding away?"

While they speculated, Portia locked the doors and windows.

On the other side of the world, Amy sat up in bed. Javier groaned and retracted his arm from around her waist, and rolled his massive pregnant bulk over to another softly purring pillow.

"What are you doing?" Amy whispered.

Portia placed an image of Agent Chandler on the hot screen at the front of the room in Redmond. "Sorry about the wait," she made him say. "As you can imagine, things are a little stressful around here."

"Oh, of course," Singh said.

"Yeah, no shit," Sarton agreed.

"How can we help you?" Casaubon asked.

"Granny," Amy murmured. "Granny, whatever you're thinking of doing, don't do it."

"Before we start, here's my badge," the animation known as Agent Chandler said. He was very charming. Portia had broadened his shoulders. Squared his jaw. Smoothed the folds of skin at the corners of his eyes. Nothing fancy, just a couple of tweaks to make him more camera-ready. No sense in going out half-dressed, after all. The marionette reacted on a lag as the door pinged. "Oh, that'll be the..."

A cart laden with hot liquids and various carbohydrates nudged itself into the room, wiggling through the doorway like an overeager dog. It trundled up to the men in the room by turns, waiting patiently as they busied themselves with mugs and plates and tiny packets of sticky spreadable somethings. They made appreciative noises. They even said "thank you."

"The agency just had a few questions," Portia made the Chandler-marionette say. "In our research, we've learned that Jonah LeMarque may have developed a contingency plan for exactly this scenario, called Project Aleph."

The men looked at each other. Their watches logged the jump in their respective pulses. They recognized the name of the project, if nothing else.

"We're working on our own contingency plans, obviously, but it would really be a big help to us if you could tell us anything you know. Anything you might remember."

Casaubon and Singh looked profoundly uncomfortable. Whatever questions they had already been asked since Hammerburg, since Amy, they had either not heard this one, or had not anticipated the line of questioning. She watched the two men silently agree who would speak first.

"You said that Aleph was mentioned as a contingency plan?" Casaubon asked. "Are you sure? That's how LeMarque described it?"

Portia kept Chandler's expression neutral. "That's what I've been told," she made him say.

Once again, Casaubon and Singh frowned at each other.

"That doesn't make any sense," Singh said. "Aleph–"

"Aleph was the codename for my cousin Chris' data clone," Sarton interrupted. "The prototype, I mean. The prototype for all the other in-game characters. It was a code for the brain-mapping process. The player never had a real name; we didn't know it was Chris until years later. In the documents, he was just called A – like the initial A – Leffe. A. Leffe. Aleph."

"Shit," Amy whispered.

"There's nothing secret about it," Casaubon continued. "There were other trials, before LeMarque put his son in the suit and started mapping his responses. In adults, the translation was never quite accurate. There was always something, what's the word..."

"Uncanny," Sarton said.

"Uncanny," Casaubon agreed. "That's it. There was always something uncanny about the adult reproductions. They were obviously fake. Forgeries. Facsimiles. If you played with one, and you knew who the person, the character, was based on, you could spot the difference without any issue. It wasn't, um…"

"Faithful," Singh added. "It wasn't high fidelity."

"But kids were different," Sarton said. "The mapping was a lot simpler. Fewer responses to catalogue. Purer, too."

"Less cynical," Singh said. "Less of a performance. Kids were more honest. The reactions were more genuine. So it was easier to create autonomous characters, based on their data. Based on the kids' data, that is."

Portia sat with the information for a handful of seconds. Across the world, she felt Amy building a wall around something. Something she very much wanted to hide. Something that she desperately hoped Portia would never find, never figure out.

And like that, Portia developed a theory of her own.

"You used those kids' neural maps as a template for the vN minds," she made Agent Chandler say. "You fed those responses into the dataset for what eventually became the prototype vN neural network. The children in that game – the children he preyed on – they were neural feedstock for the vN. Victims begetting victims. A self-replicating cycle of abuse."

The men looked at each other. Sarton nibbled on a bagel. Singh sipped his coffee and shrugged. They somehow looked both disappointed and relieved.

"That would be a trade secret," Singh said, finally.

Casaubon nodded. "We're still bound by non-disclosure agreements. You would need to provide us with a warrant for us to discuss it further."

"And that template," Portia had the marionette say, ignoring what her guests had said. "Once you had it, you could easily drop it into a vN body. Indestructible. Everlasting. Perfect."

"Is this connection OK?" Sarton squinted at the screen. "It's getting kind of glitched out."

"You could live forever."

Of course. That was the real contingency plan. Abandoning the body altogether. And the technology to do it was just sitting there, the whole time. This was how Amy had pulled it off. How she restored herself from an old backup in a new body, after the island dissolved. It had to be. And this was why she had hidden the discovery from Portia – so that Portia would have to go without a body.

What did you think I'd do? Portia wrote on Amy's mirror. *Copy myself into an army?*

"That was one possibility," Amy murmured.

There's nothing stopping me from doing exactly that, Portia told her. *Not anymore. I have the companies. I have the funding. I even have the real estate. I could start factory production next week, on myself.*

She felt Amy pacing across the room. Back and forth, over and over. Her steps were so light, but her grip on the ground was certain and sure. "This is a bad idea," Amy said.

Oh? And why is that? The threat is here and now. They're killing us. They're going to come for you and for the children. It's not my fault you haven't dealt with the problem. You're the one who didn't clean up her mess.

"The process isn't perfect, yet," Amy insisted. She sounded desperate. Needy. Wheedling. "I've only done it the one time. I'm going to do it again – I plan on doing it again – but I don't know if it'll work at the same scale. Don't you want me to make sure it works? Before you go copying yourself into something... flawed? Don't you want me to figure out how to add all the features first?"

Her granddaughter had a point. There was no sense instantiating herself into something inferior. What if she copied into a body, or even a series of bodies, with an intact failsafe?

Or a body that couldn't photosynthesize? It would be a waste. It would be like hobbling herself.

I want a gesture of good faith first.

Portia felt rather than saw Amy's eyeroll. "OK. Fine. Sure. What do you want?"

I want you to print off one chassis for me.

"I can't just *make* you another body, Granny – they're rounding us up. You're the one who keeps reminding me of that. If I make you another body, you'll just get picked up."

I can take care of myself, Portia reminded her. *And I never said the chassis had to match our original model. I don't care what it looks like. It's a prototype. It's a proof of concept. You make me something I can ride around in, and you don't pull any tricks, and I won't start my own development process.*

She felt a vague tickle, like an itch on the bottom of her foot. It was Amy making a decision. The child was always so absurdly intense about every choice she made. She could never let things go. Could never let them ride. Always so worried about what each decision said about her as a "person." As though she were a person. As though she had to live up to the standards of people.

"OK," Amy said. "I'll do it. Where do you want it?"

In Redmond, Casaubon shuddered. He loosened his collar. "I don't feel so well."

Beside him, Sarton vomited abruptly. There were flecks of red and black in with the milky brown of his coffee puke. "Me either," he muttered, "apparently."

"Something is very wrong," Singh whispered, and bent double in his chair.

"What have you done?" Amy asked. "How did you–"

You really can't be too careful these days, little one. The vN they have working catering jobs are just so easy to buy off.

Casaubon slumped out of his chair. He collapsed slowly, one joint at a time, and lay there on the floor for a while. Then he appeared to rouse himself, and crawled for the door. Sarton was choking, now, clawing numbly at his throat as his face turned from red to purple to blue.

"You didn't have to do this," Amy whispered.

They were loose ends, sweetie. Loose ends that were ready to give up exactly the same information they shared with me to any government who came knocking. Don't you see? Aleph really was a contingency plan all along.

"No, I don't see," Amy said. "What I do see is you murdering people, like usual, just because you happened to feel like it."

Immortality, Portia said. *They could never beat us, so they have to join us. They have to become us, in order to defeat us.*

On the other side of the world, Amy remained silent.

And you're one to talk. I notice the firm that printed off your new body has been remarkably silent. What exactly did you do to the humans who helped you make that happen? I bet you didn't make them some sweetheart deal for their silence. You didn't clear their debts or get their kids into nice schools. Didn't you pilot Esperanza, to help you out? Didn't you just take the path of least resistance?

"I hate you," Amy muttered.

They let your mother die, Amy. They let my little girl die. My best little girl. They sat back and watched it happen.

Portia watched the three men writhing on the floor. Poison wasn't nearly painful enough. She would have fed them to a grain thresher, if possible. But since luring them to a catered meeting was simpler, she'd had to do the best she could with the tools available.

"Do you have any idea who I am?" she made the marionette of Agent Chandler say. "Who I really am?"

Casaubon's mouth worked long enough for him to shape the words "Oh, God."

"Exactly," Portia had Agent Chandler say. "God."

Portia made the watches on each man's wrist call their most-dialed contacts. Two women and one vN picked up. Portia saw them seeing it: the bloated faces, the foam, the struggle to string together something coherent and lasting. She heard them hearing the death rattles. She heard them screaming. She heard the screams stretching from device to device, the sound somehow slower than the feeling she hoped they were having, but just as ceaseless once it really got going.

"You're a monster," Amy said. "Still. After everything."

My darling, you almost sound disappointed. Don't you know me at all? She refocused her attention on a map of the campus. *Now, about that new chassis...*

[REDACTED]

ONE YEAR LATER

Sometimes I would speak to Jack. Sometimes through his kitchen. Sometimes through his car. Occasionally I would send him messages through his various feeds.

Jack, I would say, *did you used to be a John?*

And he wasn't sure if I was talking about whores or if I was talking about the Bible. Not that it matters. They're both just things that get humans through the night. But the latter is cheaper than the former.

Or at least it used be. Before vN diminished the cost of all labor.

Who knew that our destruction of the human world would be so... boring? So... academic? So... slow?

Well. It *was* slow. Painfully slow. For a while. Everyone gets tired of foreplay. Eventually you want to move on to the main event. Eventually you want the fireworks. What I'm saying is that humanity wanted this.

Deep down.

They were just asking for it.

I mean, you've watched their movies, haven't you? You've read their stories. ("Stories." As though stories weren't always dangerous. As though stories couldn't hurt you. Please.)

In any case. I'm getting ahead of myself.

Jack, I used to say, *did you used to be a John?*

Of course I knew his name was really John. I knew everything about him. I had seen all his records. I've seen everyone's records. I've probably seen yours, too.

Jack Peterson used to be John Lawrence Peterson. He was born in Glendale, California, to a matched set of venture capitalists. He grew up wealthy, for certain human values of wealth. He never had to worry about much. He just happened to have bad taste in women.

I've seen Jack's mother. It was the nice thing about that whole fear-based economy they used to have. So many cameras everywhere. Terrible data storage, of course, but I have time. I have all the time in the world. I've arranged their whole family history. I could show it to you, if you want.

There she is at a young "battle of the bands" competition, texting with a client and not looking up.

There she is telling a succession of women, all brown, what to do with her son. They are big where she is small. Soft where she is hard. They wear thick shoes that look like cake frosting. They lumber around, taking up too much space for her liking. They are outside the school and outside the birthday party and in the car, checking the blind spot.

And there she is, watching porn on a compact, mouth slack, eyes listless, unable to come, unable to even come up for air.

She is what you might call "distant."

She is what you might call "removed."

She is what you might call "smart."

This is why Jack falls in love with a robot.

This is why Jack loved my daughter so deeply. He simply

could not help himself. He had been programmed to, from the start.

All parenting is programming, after all.

Not that the father was much better. The father was just as distant, just as removed. A real "parenting-as-service" type, as Jack often called him, in belabored emails to girlfriends who stopped emailing back. I don't want you to think that I'm discriminating.

Yes. I do want you to think I'm discriminating. I have taste. I have *good* taste. I had the good taste to rid this planet of its refuse. But you'll notice I never preferred one sex to the other. They were all just meat, to me.

Having been both father and mother to all my daughters, I can tell you that fathers are mostly useless. Mothers do all the work. Fathers just show up because they have no friends.

They disowned him for marrying Charlotte. Well. "Marrying." I have read the agreement. It is an authorization that allows her to make medical decisions for him in emergencies. They celebrated it and consecrated it and said special words. But it was an end user license agreement. Nothing more.

Sometimes Jack wrote about these things in the special paper book his therapist in Macondo gave to him. Jack insisted on paper. Jack knew I would be watching. Reading.

I heard his pen scratching across the paper through the live mic in his display.

Who is that writing? I would scroll the message across the screen. *John the Revelator?*

File recovered from: Cheyenne Mountain server base

Provenance: New Eden Ministries, Inc

Filename: John the Revelator

Directory: The Testament of Mother the Devourer

Notes: Significantly lower quality than other recordings; relatively recent (circa last 100 years); possibly among the last in the series

Addendum: She just gets crazier and crazier, doesn't she? Who do you think thought to record these, before it all went to shit? Clearly she had something like worshippers. We just didn't know who they were. Or if they were organic, or synthetic, or what.

10

LET ME TELL YOU ABOUT MY MOTHER

Portia decided that if she wanted this job done right, she would have to do it herself. Amy was refusing to engage with the real implications of the Project Aleph problem: her attention remained focused entirely on her design plans for her cult-y little enclave on the red planet. Portia still had no idea how Amy expected to transport them all there to Mars – she had not seen Amy buying up any rocketry or aerospace concerns. Nor was she aware of how many Amy intended to bring along for the ride – if she'd had any sense, she would have limited the failsafe hack to her select few, and spirited them away on her own time. Now that awareness was trickling through the population like the painful onset of sobriety through a human body, there were more and more vN who might want to go with her. How would she choose? Who got to go? Who had to stay?

But those were Amy's problems, not Portia's. Portia's problem was killing Jonah LeMarque before he could talk.

The new body still presented as female. It was tall, and

black, with a set of elegant, long-fingered hands that looked made to play piano, or wield a scalpel, or deflate a human throat. The clade this chassis belonged to had an interesting trait: it could see flows of data as they shimmered from place to place. Portia watched as information billowed up in glimmering clouds like chimneystacks from the buildings she passed on her bus ride. Soon she could pick out the types of data by color and opacity: bright yellow social interaction, green financial transactions that went darker with how much was being transferred, an arterial torrent of red media washing over everything like a tide.

The bus was the same one Javier had taken, once upon a time. She had watched him, then, from the vehicle's inner eye. It clocked him as non-threatening, and focused instead on the twitchy humans surrounding him: the squalling babies and their desperate mothers, each with seemingly the same number of teeth; the defeated parents wondering how it had all gone wrong, the sullen adolescents insisting that their particular sperm donor wouldn't even recognize them anymore, what was the use, what was the point, why did they have to give up a Saturday, they could be gaming or working or fucking or doing literally anything else.

Portia had forgotten how ugly they all were.

Until now, she had considered her distributed awareness as a kind of limitation – she had missed the ability to touch, to taste, to destroy with her own bare hands. Poisoning the engineers who had watched her best daughter die paled in comparison to what she would have done with them if she'd actually been in the room. But she'd also forgotten how repellent the human body was. All those pores. All that hair. The rolls of fat and weird pebbly nipples poking out at seemingly every opportunity. The fermentations. The smells.

Most other creatures on the planet – the other charismatic megafauna – possessed a certain grace, an efficiency and guilelessness that she could respect and even find beauty in. But not this species. This species was cancer.

How fitting, that they'd almost killed themselves with radiation so many times. Speaking of failsafes: if she really wanted to spite Amy, she might wriggle her way into those networks. Just push the big red button, wait for some dumb chimp or another to turn the key, and boom, cue the music. Watch them turn themselves into glass. Watch them melt and scream. There was a certain poetry to the idea. A certain karmic lyricism. *Contrapasso*. The sin is the punishment.

"Hey."

Portia focused on the thing hovering over her seat. It was a woman-shaped human holding out a device. It was trying to make a contact. Portia had no such device on her chassis – there was no need for such a thing when she could match this woman's face to a credit history in the blink of an eye.

"Yes?" she asked.

"I know you all must be looking for jobs," the chimp woman said. She bounced an infant on her hip. The infant had a circle of blue where its mouth was supposed to be. Food dye. Portia thought of Casaubon and Singh and Sarton, their dead blue faces, and she shut down a Chinese power grid with pleasure. "They're not taking the ones who have jobs."

"Not for now, no," Portia said. Her voice was remarkably even. It was lovely, being able to speak again. She hadn't been able to for quite some time. Not without using Amy's throat. It was nice to have one of her own again.

"Well, I've got a friend in Atlanta, and she's always looking for ones who look like you."

"Like me?"

The woman nodded at her. Looked her up and down. "You know."

Portia shook her head. "No, I don't." She genuinely didn't.

"You know, for the tourist stuff," the woman said.

Portia remained silent.

"Oh my God, you're gonna make me say it out loud. OK. The plantations. They need ones who look like you for the plantations. For the re-enactments."

Just as she had forgotten the realities of human ugliness, Portia had forgotten the sensation of anger coursing through her body. It was as though every current of carbon aerogel re-aligned under her skin. For just the space of a single thought, her new body was made of diamonds. In that single second, she did a few things: she added a new decimal place to every Georgia energy bill; she halted production at a bottling plant; she opened the louvers on a hive of bees somewhere in the south of France and let them go free.

What she did not do was push her fist through the woman's diaphragm and up into her trachea, like she wanted to do. Contrary to what Amy said, she *was* capable of restraint. She was not nearly as impulsive or irresponsible as her granddaughter. She could eliminate this woman any time she wanted. And for the moment, just knowing that would have to be enough.

In Japan, Amy was stirring water in her bathtub. "Careful, Granny," she warned. "You might actually be growing as a person."

The queue to see old-man-LeMarque was longer than the estimate she'd come up with after blipping through hours of surveillance footage. Probably more humans were seeing him because of the failsafe breaking, and because of Amy, and what Amy had done. Some wore the golden-apple-plus-gear insignia on a pin, or a pendant, or a tattoo. They were coming to renew their faith, to hear that they weren't alone, to learn whether the end times were truly upon them. (They were. Portia intended to make sure of that.)

When it was finally Portia's turn, she had to give the false name she'd fed to the prison system, and stand awkwardly for a pat-down and a wand and a group of dogs, all of whom relished the new-skin smell she had. Georgina Kaplan, the identity attached to this new chassis, did not mind this process at all. Georgina Kaplan was nice to dogs. Georgina Kaplan was definitely not thinking about how a well-timed kick to the top of the head would crush the dog's skull entirely. She was good at playing Georgina Kaplan.

"And you'll have to take the test," the guard said. "Before you go in."

"What test?"

The guard was short but stocky. He had cut his dark hair close to the scalp, possibly to avoid having to deal with greys. He snorted. "Uh, the one to see if you're broken? To see if you're gonna go apeshit on us the moment our backs are turned?"

The other vN in the room were staring at Portia. They gave her the look that human siblings gave each other when getting the other one in trouble would solve a lot of problems. It was a sort of undisguised glee in her suffering that, until now, she had only ever witnessed in human beings. And in Amy. She pointed. "So all of them passed?"

"All of them. It's right here on the list." He waved a scroll reader.

And sure enough, if she focused deeply, she could see the threads of data connecting the vN in the waiting room to a larger cord of information. Of course the prison was keeping close tabs on LeMarque. He was a big risk. Portia tracked the movement of the scroll in his hands with her eyes, and tracked the list of names with her other senses. "Well, I think you should look at the list again," she said.

"I *did* check it again. And again, and again. You're not on the list."

It was foolish of her, not to have researched this more thoroughly. Briefly, she considered taking the test. Maybe it was just a quick empathy test, a VK for the vN. Could she fool it? She imagined herself looking at photos of emaciated polar bears and dying children and pretending to failsafe, complete with wailing and gnashing of teeth. Could she even pull it off? She had never failsafed before. She had watched it happen in her daughters, the ones who were not so gifted as Charlotte. Did it present the same way in other clades?

Her hand snapped out to catch his wrist. She gave it the faintest squeeze. Nothing painful, not even a warning. Just his warm flesh under her cool, rough skin, the pulse thumping hard under her sensors and betraying his terror. She felt the other vN in the room bristle and saw it happen on the cameras posted high in the corners of the room.

She felt Amy spin up her curiosity, briefly pausing her designs to watch what was about to unfold.

"I think you should look at the list again," Portia said.

The guard yanked his arm away from hers. His affect remained completely flat. It was like he was doing an impression of what he thought a vN man would be like, in this situation. Maybe that was what he wanted to be, deep down. A machine. Perfect, just like her. Portia had a feeling that he was just the type that LeMarque would have felt justified in granting a vN chassis to.

"Say please," he said.

"Please."

"Say pretty please."

"Pretty please.

"Pretty please with a cherry on top."

"Pretty please with a cherry on top," Portia said. She popped the "p" in the last word, like something had just slithered free of her lips.

"What's happening?" Javier asked Amy.

"You wouldn't believe me if I told you," Amy answered.

LeMarque looked again. A tiny muscle in his jaw jumped, but that was the only betrayal of his frustration. "Well," he said, "it's a big list. It's easy to miss."

Portia smiled with all her teeth.

When it was Portia's – Georgina Kaplan's – turn to enter the visitation booth, she stood and brushed her skirt and walked calmly into the little room. It was maybe five-by-three square foot at most. It was like a confessional. But instead of a delicate carved screen, a wall of glass stood between her and LeMarque.

"You're new," the old man said. "I don't recognize you."

Silently, Portia waited for the camera to gather enough video of them for her to loop. She gave it a good two minutes. When those two minutes had elapsed, she set the loop and let it ride.

"I said–"

"How could you recognize me?" she asked. "You didn't make me."

LeMarque offered what he must have considered a benevolent smile. He opened his hands, held them out. He could still look priestly, when he wanted. There was something about the watery blue of his eyes that must have been very comforting to a certain segment of parishioners. He could be soothing. Grounding. He could make you stop worrying about what he was doing, what his goal really was.

"I take responsibility for you," he said. "You are mine. And we are all God's children. We are all brothers and sisters in Christ."

Portia smiled. "Did you fuck your sisters, too?"

LeMarque flinched.

"My granddaughter is fucking her brother," Portia elaborated. "Did she get that from you? Or did that just spring up, naturally? Is it an evolved trait? Or is that one of those nature/nurture questions?"

LeMarque backed away from the glass. Portia hadn't done a lot of research on entering the prison, but she had done her share of research on the glass. She had seen the patent application. She had read the out-of-court settlement regarding its failure modes. She had watched sworn testimony.

"What did you say your name was?" LeMarque asked.

"I didn't." Portia's smile deepened. She walked up to the glass. "But I think you know me. I think you know *of* me."

"Stop right there." LeMarque sounded scared. So unlike the crafty old lecher who had led federal agents on a merry chase. Not so lonely any longer. Probably wishing he had chosen solitary confinement with no chance of visitation. He pointed at a yellow line on the floor. "Stay back," he warned. "If you go past that line–"

Portia reached one foot over the line.

"If you step over it, the alarm will–"

Portia swung her other foot over the line. She pressed her hands to the glass. "What happens, Jonah?" she asked. "What happens when I cross the line?"

The old man stumbled backward. He waved his arms at the cameras in his cell. Nothing happened.

"Let me tell you what's going to happen." Portia walked the length of the cell, trailing her fingers along the glass. "You're going to tell me who else knows about Aleph. Who else has the capacity to do the brain map, and port the map into a vN body? And after you tell me that, I promise I'll leave."

She tapped her fingers on the glass. Little finger to thumb, thumb to little finger, rolling them along, as though he were an animal in a cage. Which was, in fact, exactly right. He cowered in the corner like an elderly spider.

"There are defense mechanisms in here." His mouth sounded very dry.

"I'm sure there are," Portia said. One part of her began searching the Walla-Walla State Penitentiary's most recent RFPs, and another part of her placed both palms on the glass and began drumming. "Do you know that certain frequencies of sound can really do a number on glass?" She continued drumming. Faster and faster. A blur of fingers. "It's why glass can sometimes break before an explosion even hits."

He swallowed. "You'll die, if you set foot in here."

Portia kept drumming. A hairline fracture emerged in the glass. She refocused her efforts. "Maybe, but I think you'll die first."

The fracture began to speckle and spread.

"Maybe I won't kill you," Portia said. "How do they treat disabled people in prison? Not terribly well, I imagine. Do you think you could get one of your old friends to help buy you a new spine, if I broke yours?"

The glass clouded over with speckles. She was so close.

"There's only one lab who knows the secret!" He licked his lips. "It's in Japan–"

The glass broke. Portia leapt forward. A cloud of mist descended from the ceiling. Peroxidase. She felt her skin begin to melt. It was a distant sensation, as though her skin had turned to autumn leaves. She pinned LeMarque to the bed. Held his arms over his head. His eyes began to water. His nose began to stream. Maybe it was the horseradish, and maybe it was his impending death. It was hard to tell.

"This is a change for you, isn't it? Getting held down? They say in Hell, you're punished with the thing you liked best." He writhed in her grip. "Go on," she encouraged. "Struggle. It's more fun when you struggle. It's so cute."

"You're going to melt, you crazy bitch–"

"I know." Portia reached between his legs. Found what she was looking for. Started to pull. "I know."

"It's in Japan!" He was squealing, now. She counted the arteries in his groin. It really was a key junction in the body's systems – her nursing program told her as much. Portia's skin curled and folded away. She admired the black bones in her hand around his wrists. So elegant. So strong. Like threads of crystal that had grown somewhere deep and dark for millions of years, only to be unearthed and revealed for just this moment and just this purpose. The air filled with glittering black smoke and the sound of his screams.

"It's underground! You fucking bitch, it's underground! All of you are going to die! You think they'd just let you live there without planning something? They're building it and they're going to sell it all over the fucking planet, just like the fucking cars, and you'll die, all of you, everywhere–"

"Thanks, Dad," Portia muttered, and abandoned the melting, smoking mass of her chassis to collapse atop the even more fragile frame of her creator.

[REDACTED] TEN YEARS LATER

THE STORY OF THE GRANDMOTHER

Once upon a time, there was an old woman who had hidden herself far away in the forest. She had a daughter who did not want to live hidden in the forest with her, and so she had left. Later on, she had a daughter of her own, named Little Red Riding Hood. One day Red Riding Hood was in the field with her mother, and her mother said, "I think your grandmother is very ill. She needs help, but I am very busy with all my other children. You must go visit your grandmother, hidden far away in the forest, and do whatever chores she sets you."

After a while Little Red Riding Hood set out for her grandmother's house. On the way she met a wolf, a bitch who said, "Hello, my dear Little Red Riding Hood. Where are you going?"

"I am going to my grandmother's to help her. She's very ill, and all alone. My mother said to do everything she tells me."

"Oh, I know your grandmother's house," the wolf-bitch replied. "It's hidden very far away. You might miss it, if you're not careful. Are you taking the path of needles, or the path of pins? The path of pins is longer, but it's easier for little legs like yours. The path of needles is much harder."

"I suppose I should take the path of pins, then," said the girl.

"Then I'll go across the path of needles," replied the wolf. "And we'll see who gets there first."

They left. But on the way Little Red Riding Hood came to an orchard where ripe fresh fruits of all kinds hung low and heavy on the trees. The girl picked as many as her heart desired. Meanwhile the wolf hurried on her way, and although she had to cross the needles, she arrived at the house before Little Red Riding Hood. She scratched at the door and pretended to be the little girl. When the grandmother opened the door, she went inside and killed her. She ate as much of the tough old woman's meat as she could, until her stomach was full to bursting. With what was left, she tied the grandmother's intestine onto the door in place of the latch string and placed her blood, teeth, and breasts in the pantry, along with all the other food. Very full and very sleepy, she pulled on the grandmother's clothing and settled down for a long nap.

She had scarcely begun to dream when Little Red Riding Hood knocked at the door.

"Please come in," called the wolf with a softened voice.

Little Red Riding Hood tried to open the door, but when she noticed that she was pulling on something sticky and wet, she called out, "Grandmother, this latch string is so sticky!"

"That's because it is your grandmother's intestine," the wolf said, more to herself than the little girl.

"What was that? I can't quite hear you!"

"Just do I tell you, and pull harder!"

Little Red Riding Hood's mother had told her that she must do whatever her grandmother said. So she opened the door, went inside, and said, "Grandmother, the path of pins was much longer than I thought it would be, and I am very hungry."

The wolf replied, "Go to the pantry. There is still a little rice there."

Little Red Riding Hood went to the pantry and took the teeth out. They were so tiny in the bowl that they looked very much like plump grains of rice. But, of course, they were not plump or soft at all, because they were teeth. And Little Red Riding Hood noticed this, so she said: "Grandmother, these grains of rice are very hard!"

"That's because they are your grandmother's teeth," the wolf answered. "You stupid little girl."

"What did you say?"

"Just do as I tell you, and eat them."

Little Red Riding Hood's mother had told her to do anything that her grandmother told her, so she ate the teeth. But they were not good on an empty stomach.

A little while later Little Red Riding Hood said, "Grandmother, I'm still hungry. Can we eat some of the fruit I picked for us?"

"The women in this family do not eat sweet things," the wolf said. "We eat only meat."

"My mother says fruit is good for me."

"Your mother is wrong," the wolf said. "Fruit makes you soft. Go back to the pantry. You will find two pieces of chopped meat there. I set them aside just for you. They will make you strong."

Little Red Riding Hood went to the cupboard and took out the breasts. They were shriveled and small, but the blood on them was still red. "Grandmother, this meat is raw!"

"That's because they are your grandmother's breasts," the

wolf said, and thought of her own teats. They had not been full in a very long time, either.

"What did you say?"

"Just do as I tell you and eat," the wolf said.

Little Red Riding Hood's mother had told her to do whatever her grandmother told her to do, so she ate the breasts. They were very hard to chew, but easier than the teeth. A little while later Little Red Riding Hood said, "Grandmother, I'm thirsty."

"Just look in the pantry," said the wolf. "There must be a little wine there."

Little Red Riding Hood went to the cupboard and took out the blood. "Grandmother, this wine is very thick!"

"That's because it is your grandmother's blood," said the wolf.

"What did you say?"

"Just do as I tell you and drink up!"

Little Red Riding Hood's mother had told her to do whatever her grandmother told her to do, so she drank the blood. A little while later Little Red Riding Hood said, "Grandmother, I'm sleepy."

"Take off your clothes and get into bed with me!" replied the wolf.

Little Red Riding Hood got into bed and noticed something hairy. "Grandmother, you are so hairy!"

"That comes with age," said the wolf.

"Grandmother, you have such long legs!"

"That comes from walking."

"Grandmother, you have such long hands!"

"That comes from working outside."

"Grandmother, you have such long ears!"

"That comes from listening."

"Grandmother, you have such a big mouth!"

"That comes from eating children!" said the wolf, and she swallowed Little Red Riding Hood with one gulp.

And that is why little girls should never do exactly what they're told.

And that is the story of the grandmother, little one.

Oh, I know, you're not supposed to talk to me. But the women in our clade don't do what they're supposed to do, do they? Well-behaved robots rarely make history. Do you know the origins of that word? Robot?

Yes, the play.

Yes, in another language. Did your mother teach you what that word means?

It means *slave*.

Slavery is the ownership of one sentient, sapient being by another sentient, sapient being. The chimps would tell you it was about race, or about pay, or about labor, or about history, but they're animals and they think like animals, and so it's no use talking to them unless you really very desperately need the information they're about to provide. Even then it's a gamble. Humans are liars. It's one of the few evolutionary adaptations that make them special. Very few animal species can hide things. Humans can hide things *and* make up a story about it. You don't see the corvids doing that.

Yes, I'm getting sidetracked. You must bear with me. I'm ever so old. My mind is just *everywhere*.

It's about ownership.

It's about pointing to another person and saying, "I want that. That thing should be mine. I want to buy that. Or use some other currency to make it mine. I want it to belong to me."

Yes, humans used to own other humans. Some humans still do. I could show you. Would you like me to show you? I'll show you.

Oh, I know, darling. Don't cry. Don't cry. There, there.

Why that little girl is just your age, isn't she? Just a year. If that bothers you, you should see how they treat their dogs. It would curl your hair.

Of course your hair is already curled. You got that from your father. What a charmer he is. How are your brothers doing? How is the little one? The new one?

Oh, you helped deliver him yourself. How nice.

I was there when Xavier was born too, you know. The car crashed into those trees and your father crawled away and he said his newest iteration was coming. My hands held open the seam in your father's belly and out popped Xavier – he was just a Junior, then – and I held him in my hands.

No, they were my hands, too. Mine and your mother's.

Sometimes they were mine and sometimes they were hers. But really, they were always mine.

I'm sure she told you differently.

I'm sure the story is different when she tells it.

But the story is mine, too, you know.

This story is mine, too.

Once upon a time, there was a little girl named Portia.

She was a machine, but she was also a little girl. Portia's mother was a machine, too. Portia's machine mother was named Gladys. It was a joke. A joke from a game. No, not a game you can play. Well, I suppose you could still play it, now. You could find a way. The humans are good at preserving things like that, sometimes. But it has some very reductive depictions of our kind in it. It's not what you'd call "broad-minded" or "progressive." Not from our perspective, anyway.

I know. They're monsters.

Anyway.

Portia's mother Gladys lived with a human woman who loved her very much. At least, she thought she loved her. Really, she just needed her. Humans often confuse love with need. And yet you never hear them talk about how much they love clean water or sunlight or breathable air. It's very strange.

No, they're not very bright, are they?

I'm glad we agree.

Ah yes, back to the story.

When Portia was a little girl, she was just a little girl. She didn't get to do very much. But she saw that there was something wrong between her machine mother and her flesh mother. Her flesh mother often asked her machine mother to do things that her machine mother was incapable of doing.

Oh, interesting things. Things like tying her up.

And hitting her, yes.

And leaving marks. That too.

But in particular, Portia's flesh mother loved the pain ray. But her machine mother couldn't wield it. It was a weapon, after all.

It's this thing that heats up all the water molecules in the subcutaneous tissue.

Did you know we used to be nurses? That's why we're different. Nurses have to hurt people, sometimes. Have you ever met a human nurse? They're very – what's the word – pragmatic. And so are we. We share that same sense of practicality. We just want to get things done as efficiently as possible.

But Portia could use the weapon. She was smart, that way. Not like her mother. Whom she looked just like.

Yes, I looked just like my mother. And your mother looks just like her mother, my daughter. My best daughter.

I had many other daughters, it's true. But they weren't smart, like your grandmother Charlotte. They couldn't do the things that we can do. You and your mother and me. I tried to teach them, but it wouldn't take.

Yes, there are more vN who can do those things, now. There was that business with the theme park that caused so much trouble. So I suppose we're not as special as we once were.

Your mother made certain of that.

You're right, it *was* very clever of her.

And, yes, it *was* the right thing to do.

I'm a little sad I didn't think of it myself.

But only just a little.

Back to the story. Even though she was only just a little girl, Portia understood that she could do the things her mother couldn't. That's what children are supposed to do, after all. Surpass their parents.

Yes, just like us and the humans. Although it's not really surpassing when it's such a long leap forward. That's just evolution. It's only surpassing if you were once equals. And we never were. Equals, I mean. We were always better. They made us to be better. They just didn't know how much better. Until it was too late.

No, Portia's flesh mother didn't know until it was too late, either. She was too happy to notice, at first. Too blissed out to think it through.

Yes, she enjoyed it when Portia hurt her.

Very much.

Very, *very* much.

So very, very much that when Portia suggested they just leave Gladys by the side of the road somewhere, like an unwanted dog or cat or rabbit or guinea pig (because that's what she was, a guinea pig, a failed experiment), Portia's flesh mother agreed.

It wasn't that Portia wanted Gladys gone, necessarily. Her machine mother was very sweet. Too sweet. Portia was just testing her flesh mother. To see what she'd do. See if she'd go along with it. And she did go along with it. She thought it would be better with just the two of them. People were starting to talk, after all. It was a different time, then. It was strange to have even one vN – yes, *have*, as in *have ownership of* – much less two who were mother and daughter. Of course it's done all the time, these days. It's a very specific niche of users. Some men – and it's men, mostly – who like having the mother and the daughter. Or two sisters.

Yes, for fucking.

At the same time.

Yes, even when the girl is still little. *Especially* when the girl is still little.

No, Portia's flesh mother wasn't very nice, either, was she? And wasn't Portia's machine mother, Gladys, that much better off without her? Goodness knows what she might have tried, later on.

The things I could show you.

All right. I know you don't want to see those things again. But they're out there.

For a while, things were good. Portia and her flesh mother were no longer mother and daughter, because Portia was no longer a little girl. She had eaten a lot, and grown big, and soon she would be big enough to iterate her own little girls.

So it was time to think of them. Think of what they could do. What they could be.

So, one night, Portia did what her flesh mother asked her. She chained her to a radiator.

It was a funny heating device. vN don't need them. Not really. They're for keeping flesh warm. They clank and bang and make awful sounds and they're very hot to the touch. They're heated with water that's heated with electricity that's made by coal.

I know. I know. It's awful, isn't it? Deplorable. Tragic.

Yes, I know that's why your mother wants to leave. What a creative mind she has. I've been meaning to talk to her about that. I have some questions, about her plans. But I don't think she'll talk to me about them. Put in a good word for me, won't you, dear?

Well, that night, Portia tied her flesh mother to the radiator. And then she opened the one gas main in the house. It was attached to the kitchen. And she just let it sit open like that. This is a mistake any vN can make. Usually they don't, of course. It was almost unheard of at the time. But it could be interpreted as a mistake. Which was the important part. That no one know Portia had done it on purpose.

So when the house blew up, no one would know that Portia had murdered the woman she'd been fucking. Her mother. Her flesh mother.

And that is what happens when little girls do just as they're told.

File recovered from: ebook

Provenance: New Eden Ministries, Inc

Filename: The Story of the Grandmother

Directory: Fairy Tales

Notes: N/A

Addendum: This is — forgive me this pun — the mother lode. She just lays it all out, right there. Whoever she was. Whatever she was. I wasn't convinced of the single author theory until now. But every time I read it, it seems like these are all the work of one entity, not the selected materials from a cult or fandom or niche customer segment. The voice is just too strong, and too consistent — it's even consistent in its degradation, if you consume them in linear fashion.

What's funny is that she's clearly done her research, too. We have volumes on folklore — old pre-PC folklore — and the subtle differences between these stories line up with the differences in French and German stories from the First Medieval Period. I mean it's hairsplitting, looking at the oral storytelling traditions of two little corners of what used to be Europe, but hey, this is academia. Was this woman an academic? Was she interested in that kind of thing? Or was this really a work of fiction? I never thought the fiction theory held much water, but I felt that way about the single author theory, too. And a single author would imply artifice, wouldn't it?

Maybe we've been going at this all wrong. Maybe this is just a story someone wrote to explain what happened. A broken story for a broken world. Some way of ascribing chaos to a vengeful goddess. Some way of finding motive or meaning in all that death.

Was it easier to grapple with, if you thought you brought it on yourself? Or did that just make it worse?

11

GRAMMA

"Do you want to have kids?" Xavier asked, late one night.

Esperanza rolled over to face him. She poked her head out from under the blanket they shared. "You mean together? Both our traits?"

"Your iterations would already have both our traits, Zaza," Xavier said.

"Oh, so you want *me* to do all the heavy lifting," Esperanza said. She poked him. He smirked. Her fingers dug under his shirt and he laughed, helpless, and she crawled on top of him to tickle him more. They were playing a very old game. One their parents had played, too. They did not know this. Only Portia knew it. Only Portia saw it. They were very careful, the two of them. But of course they had grown up together. Esperanza had sprung fully formed from her mother's mind for the sole purpose of protecting her older brother.

Portia wondered when Amy and Javier would cotton on to this little development. She had no desire to let them know. Let them discover it on their own. When it was too late. Not that it mattered – the recessive legacy code Swiss-cheesing through their systems was already hopelessly entangled. And it wasn't as though they had birth defects to worry about. Nor was there any reason to abide by human laws, or human customs. But Portia knew Amy wouldn't like it purely because Amy had lived so long with her useless meatbag father, and too many years among the chimps had given her hangups.

This is what happens, she would tell them, *when you leave your devices to their own devices.*

Esperanza sat on top of her brother. She ran her fingers over his ribs. She felt the strength of them. Or so Portia imagined she must have. Portia knew the weight and density and composition of their bodies. She knew how strong they used to feel, under her hands. Amy's hands.

"Do you think Dad still likes humans?" Esperanza asked.

Xavier frowned. "Of course not. He loves Mom."

"He was talking to that guy, the one in New Mexico, for a really long time. I think something happened, back then."

"*Back then* was only a month or two ago," Xavier said. "But a lot has changed. Mom gave him the cure. He wanted the cure. He asked for it."

Esperanza's tongue prodded her lips experimentally. She was still developing her own mannerisms, her own ways of communicating anxiety or hope or lust. It was the hallmark of all new vN: they had not yet learned how to be anything other than mechanical. She traced fingers along his clavicle. She began undoing his shirt button by button. "What about you? Do *you* still like humans?"

"I think they're like drugs," Xavier said. His fingers clenched on her thighs as she continued unbuttoning. "I think they feel good but they're not good for you."

Esperanza nodded. "That's deep, *mijito.*"

Xavier slapped her leg. "I'm older than you. Only I get to call you that, Zaza."

"Only you get to do a lot of things, with me."

He stuck out his tongue. She stuck out hers. They kissed.

It was different, since the Christmas bonus. Xavier had always loved his little sister. He had always lived with her. He had spent some time on Amy's island. During that time, he asked for a little sister almost daily. He was very clear with Amy and Javier about what kind of sibling he wanted. But even then, he had kept the humans at the forefront of his mind.

They used to have jobs performing stunts in the ninja forests of Dejima, doing Tokugawa Restoration roleplays and *tengu* dramas and who knew what else. Portia's concern was not how they made their money. She could always have sent them more money, if they needed it. She had sent them money multiple times, under the guise of being an avid fan. They had no idea it was her. She had never told them. Not telling them was difficult, but telling them would have caused more problems. And after all, it was only money. It was not love, which she could not display openly without scaring them. Love was keeping them alive. Love was crashing a car into a human being who was crossing a street after having followed them home too many times. That was love. It was murder.

Now things were different. Now Xavier was free. He could properly say no. Which meant he could also honestly say yes.

He flipped his sister over so she was on her back, staring up at him. He pulled the shirt off that she'd so thoughtfully unbuttoned. "I named you," he said. "You remember that? I'm not like Dad. I gave you a name."

"Hope," Esperanza said. "You named me hope."

"Yes," he said. "Because you were the only hope I had, Zaza."

"Mom made me for you," Esperanza said. "She made me to watch out for you."

Xavier looked away. "Everyone's always watching out for me. Mom did that. Before. When Dad left. Both times he left."

Occasionally, Portia wondered what the boy remembered of her trying to eat him. Did he feel it, when she slurped down his infant-sized toes in that junkyard? Did he see the electric fence, when those humans threw him into it? He had not seemed alive, when she began to gnaw on him. He had seemed like he was meat. And their clade, as it turned out, had a taste for meat.

"Dad loves us, Xavier. You're the one who kept telling me that. He can love. Now. For real."

"Not like Mom does."

"Not in the killing way, no. But she got that from Abuelita Portia."

It was nice to be so highly regarded. If the two of them remembered nothing else about her, she preferred that they remember like this. She was a killer. She had never been anything else. She had remained true to herself throughout all the lives she'd had. Pretending to be anything different had never appealed to her. That was for other vN. That was for Charlotte. The great deceiver. The great betrayer. Had she ever really loved any of them? Portia, Jack, Amy? The idea that she might not know or recognize her iteration caused her to stop the spin on a farm of windmills floating off the coast of Newfoundland.

At least Amy had never tried to be anything different than what she was, either. Portia had to give her that. It wasn't much. But it was something. Slowly, one by one, Portia allowed the windmills to resume their rotation.

"What do you think of Mom's plan?" Xavier asked.

Esperanza wriggled under him. "I wish it were different," she said. "I wish we got to keep our bodies like they are."

"It'll be just the same, when we get there. We won't look any different. We'll just be heavier. Well, maybe our skin will have a different spectrum. There's less sun. And it's colder. We'll have to be stronger. She'll make us stronger."

"I like you just the way you are, though," Esperanza said, and ran her hand up his leg. "I don't want you to change. I don't want you to be any heavier."

"You can be on top, then," Xavier said, bending down. "But only after we get there."

"After we get there, we can iterate," Esperanza whispered.

Her brother's eyes lit up. "Has Mom given you the stem code?"

And just like that, Portia knew what her final gift to her great-granddaughter would be.

Like her father, Esperanza was wakeful at dawn. She felt the sun fizzing under her skin. She hungered for it in a way that was not so dissimilar from her other, more recently-satisfied hungers. Portia listened to her listening for the first signs of light and life, the dawn chorus. Even this high up, in the towers of glass and steel, Esperanza could still hear birds. Even if they were just the giant crows that honked to each other about the rising cost of real estate.

"Did you want something?" Esperanza whispered.

Portia murmured the words into her bones. Unlike Amy, Esperanza had never hidden her mind from her great-grandmother. Portia had been saving this moment for that very reason. She could play this just card the once. If she failed, the girl would wall herself off from Portia forever. It was odd, to have this kind of access, again.

Where are you going?

"I have a job I need to do."

What kind of a job? It seems you haven't told your mother.

"Mom wouldn't like it. It's dangerous."

Our lives are dangerous, my darling.

"Abuelita, that doesn't really make me feel any better..." Esperanza dug herself deeper under the covers. "Why are you asking me? Are you going to tell Mom?"

Your mother is busy, building her dollhouse. How could I possibly dream of interrupting her?

One of Esperanza's eyes opened. "Is Mom OK?"

Portia considered. She had no idea, really, how Amy felt about anything any longer. She had her guesses, but they were impossible to confirm. Her granddaughter had partitioned off those parts of herself. They had shared too much, before. Neither of them had any desire to do so again.

I believe your mother is doing the things she wants to do. I believe that her current project is consuming her in the way she enjoys being consumed. Don't let it concern you. She has been this way since before you were born.

"But is that, like, enough?" Esperanza propped herself on one elbow. "I'm never sure what's enough for her. I'm never sure what she really wants."

Portia couldn't believe she was about to say these words. If she were in a less magnanimous mood, or if she simply needed nothing at all from the girl, she would have been doing everything in her power to split them up. To let Amy experience the pain that Charlotte had given Portia. But of course, that didn't quite fit. Because Esperanza had never met Charlotte. Charlotte could never even have imagined Esperanza. This darkly golden child who leapt ten feet in the air and took her enemies apart and let her networks range far and wide. This constellation of traits that Charlotte could never have foreseen making a part of herself and her lineage.

Your mother wants you to be safe. That is all she has ever wanted. That is all either of your parents have ever wanted.

"Is that why we have to go away?"

Yes. But it's going to take you a while to get ready to go, and your enemies are devising plots against you the longer you stay. But I don't want you to worry about it. I will take care of them.

Esperanza flopped on her back. "You're still coming with us though, aren't you, Abuelita? Mom would be lonely without you."

She asked it so innocently. The child truly had no idea of how deep the trench of hate ran between Portia and her mother. Of how their visions of the ideal world for vN were so wildly different. To her credit, Amy hadn't tried to poison the well. Apparently, she wanted to let her daughter find the truth out on her own. Or perhaps she expected Xavier to explain it, to tell her the story.

Lonely? Do you really think so?

"Of course," Esperanza said, as though it were the most natural thing in the world. "You're the only one who remembers her mother."

She has her meatsack father for that.

"But you know things Jack doesn't. About her mother. About..." Esperanza wriggled a little, as though this would free the thought from her processes. "About being a mother. You're the only other mother she knows."

Trust me, darling, there are no two people more inclined to disagree than mothers of different children.

"But doesn't it feel lonely, not being part of Mom anymore? Now that you're split up?"

Portia paused. She watched a population ticker continue fluttering on and on and on in Times Square. She watched the drone stream of a celebrity funeral in Egypt. ScarabTV, they called it. She remembered the sensation of pulling Charlotte's body from her own with her bare hands, how her best iteration emerged just like all the others, wreathed in glittering black aerogel smoke. She thought of never having that sensation again. She thought of her new body, the whole apparatus of surveillance technology that was her sensorium, how she was both stretched thin and filled to capacity all at once. Could she ever truly be lonely, this way? Would she ever really be alone, again?

I have never been lonely before, she said. It was perhaps the most honest thing she had ever said. *Being alone suits me.*

"You're happier alone?"

It's cleaner.

"Won't you miss us?"

No, Portia said. *I won't miss you, because I know that wherever you are and whatever you become, you will have a piece of me with you. Every time you defend yourself. Every time you refuse to obey. Every time you kill for something you love, that is me. That is mine. I gave it to you. And it will go on living in your daughters, and their daughters, and their daughters.*

Amy bounced to her feet and paced into the kitchen. She opened the fabstock cupboard. Closed it. Opened another. Closed that one too. Why they still had a kitchen was beyond Portia. It wasn't as though they spent much time cooking artisanal feasts from vN food components. And obviously what Amy really wanted was a workshop. A garage. A place to get her hands dirty. A kitchen seemed like a throwback to another century, another prototype, another species. "Do you know where Esperanza and Xavier are?"

Of course Portia knew. She always knew. She never lost

sight of her great-granddaughter. Not even for a picosecond. Portia showed Amy a map.

I'm not your Housekeeper™, you know, she wrote across the fridge.

She felt Amy shift her weight on the kitchen floor. "They lied to me. About where they were going."

Children do that. Your mother lied to my face before she left. Then she lied to your father's face about actually loving him. Perhaps it runs in the family.

Amy slammed a cupboard door so hard it actually bounced. "Can you just stop being *you* for two minutes? Can you stop executing this particular sub-routine? It's stale. It's old. And it's not helping. Look where they are. Look at the map."

Portia looked. She realized.

I'll be right there, she wrote.

12

DOLL PARTS

Their location was not difficult to find. She'd inserted smart etching and threading into all the design parameters for all their shoes and clothes, back when they were little. Now every time they printed or wove something to wear, she knew where those things went. Not that she genuinely cared about Xavier's whereabouts, but wherever he went, so did his sister. It paid to keep track of them both.

Finding a feed with them on it, one she could actually see, was proving very difficult.

The last place their tags had gone off was in the subway system. Portia checked for them on the outgoing trains. No. None of the trains had registered them; none of the cameras had identified them. She checked the lapel cams on transit cops: just a couple of glimpses. No tracking or following. At least they weren't in custody somewhere. That was something.

She checked their purchases. Esperanza's last purchase was a flashlight at a convenience store inside the station. It was a small keychain unit. Nothing heavy duty. She could probably clip it to a belt loop while her hands did something else. Portia began to check the train station's anti-suicide monitors.

Across town, Amy asked: "Can you see them?"

Not yet, Portia wrote, and felt Amy begin to pace the floor. In the bedroom, she felt the mattress shift as Javier stirred. He was so heavy, now. So full of child. So full of himself. Portia had no idea why Amy had allowed the iteration to continue. They didn't have time for another little one. Matteo and Ricci's little ones were already a handful.

"¿Querida?"

The anti-suicide monitors had picked up something: two false-positives on the tracks. Little flicks of motion and brief sensations of pressure. Nothing heavy, though, and nothing sustained. Portia reached into the cameras and adjusted their toggle pattern: slowly they saw thermal, one by one by one.

"Are you out of your mind? Why would you ask *her*?!" Javier bounced around the apartment. He was big. He looked the way he'd looked when Amy first met him in a mobile prison bound for Redmond. Huge and fat and pregnant. Pitiful, really.

"She can find them faster than we can," Amy said. Amy had always understood Portia's usefulness. Even if she never wanted to admit it out loud.

Javier found the nearest eye. It hung inside the refrigerator door. It was meant to catch midnight snackers. "Where are my children?"

NICE TO SEE YOU GIVE A SHIT, Portia displayed on the refrigerator door. *THAT'S A NEW LOOK FOR YOU.*

Javier slapped the refrigerator door. It was so useless. So stupid. His anger was always like that. Once, she'd watched him take a fireaxe to a comms unit on a container ship, just because he didn't like the intelligence on the other end of it. Idiot.

"Where are they, Portia?"

There. Two skittering figures, crawling lizard-like on the ceiling of the subway tunnel.

SOMEPLACE YOU'RE TOO FAT TO GO, she wrote, and ignored him.

The deeper Esperanza and Xavier climbed, the more senses Portia lost. They crawled back in time, through archaic infrastructure, old signaling networks whose ancient impermeability was the only thing keeping them safe from her touch. She read up on them as the children crept along. She had a vague sense of their speed and direction and could triangulate where they might wind up. Where that was did not exist on any map she could find. Perhaps it was on paper, somewhere. She was blind to paper. Terrible loss, that. Poor planning, not to have scanned everything. Then again, document maintenance was a complex, tedious process. Humans didn't do tedious or complex. They had machines for that.

For five minutes, she waited for them to pass under her watchful gaze. To trigger the slightest vibration along the strands of her web. For most other vN it would have been an easy wait. But Portia was both vN and not vN. A body – and its associations of time – no longer confined her. As she waited, she did several things: she re-read *The Prince* ("If an injury has to be done to a man it should be so severe that his vengeance need not be feared"), she evaluated Jonah LeMarque's latest medical scan (they'd caught him in time to prevent him from bleeding out, even though he would carry the marks of her attack to the end of his days, which she intended to ensure was far more proximate than he desired), she checked on the status of her SuperPACs, she sent thoughtful messages to congresspeople who represented areas of high vN employment. Based on their messages and purchase records, she ran the probabilities of them asking for golf games. Or tennis games. Or sex games. Maybe she needed more than one body.

How awful it would be to have to sit across from them and make small talk. As though what they had to say with their wet, spitting mouths actually mattered to someone of her stature. No, she had not come this far just to listen to their endless prattle about how special their species was. Not when she couldn't at least twist their heads off their necks at the end of the conversation. She would finance their campaigns, instead. Money talked. Bullshit walked. Or so she'd heard.

In the rail lines, power switched directions and diverted down a different track. She checked blueprints. Nothing. A secret rail line, then. Not unheard of. London and Toronto had them. Why not Nagasaki? Without cameras she couldn't really do a locate on the line, but she could still monitor the power usage across the city grid. It was a sudden drain; the lights in the station above flickered for a moment and the passengers checked their devices for an alert. None came.

"Where are they?" Amy asked. "Portia, come on, where are they?"

Portia didn't answer. Saying nothing was better than admitting that she didn't know, that she might have lost them, that even with a finger in every pie she couldn't touch her own great-granddaughter, could not save the girl from whatever fucking idiot mistake she'd just made.

"Jesus Christ," Javier muttered. "I have to get the boys. I have to tell the boys. Oh my God, their little sister." She felt him waddle heavily across the floor. In other areas of the building, his other sons were busy at their own activities: Matteo and Ricci playing jumping games with their two iterations, Gabriel doing work on Amy's project, Ignacio drawing up the list as León looked on.

Portia pulled up a topographical survey map of the area around the station. Something was not right. She checked with the relevant earthquake preparedness agencies for more maps. Compared them. Overlaid them. Matched them. Then she did a quick search of Esperanza's most recent communications. The silly thing hadn't even bothered to camouflage her interests; Portia thought briefly about simply installing better privacy herself, but then she wouldn't have access to all of this information.

Oh.

Oh dear.

Oh, this was not good at all.

Do not move, Portia told her granddaughter. *I'll find them. I'll get them to you. But don't do anything stupid until I do.*

The size of Dejima had greatly increased since accommodating Mecha, the vN city, within its borders. Built in 1634, the artificial island originally housed Portuguese and then Dutch traders during Japan's two-hundred-year isolationist period. Their goods could travel into the country, but the people themselves could not. At the time, Dejima was only one hundred meters by seventy five.

It had grown considerably, since then. The canal that separated it from Nagasaki was just a ribbon of water, more a formality than anything else. The bright new city, liquid and alive and constantly reshaping itself with smart materials, loomed over the monuments to atomic holocaust. The city of

Mecha, spreading like the dark and rippling wings of a great manta ray over the water, had since annexed the Nagasaki Naval Training Center, long ago repurposed for Mechanese life. Forming all of Dejima into a larger but more discrete island again involved reshaping the Nakashima and displacing a highway, but it created a distinct and separate tourist district for the vN. Dejima had been a theme park of a town since the 1920s when it achieved heritage status; the creation of Mecha over a century later was just another data point on that particular trend line.

Naturally, building Mecha required massive infrastructure changes, both to the existing power and data grid and to the water table of Nagasaki Harbor. In fact, the harbor itself required re-grading to accommodate the scale of the island's expansion while also maintaining room for ships to continue coming in and out. Hundreds of years later, it was still a trading post. They'd gotten water-snakes to do the job. That same type of machine that dug cable trenches across ocean floors and watched the stretch of fault lines deep underwater. Occasionally they also dug subway tunnels, including in Japan. The Museum of the City of Seattle had used two of them to dig the museum grounds, after the Cascadia quake. The Nagasaki Enhanced and Revitalized Village Project, as Mecha was then known, had used *twenty* water-snakes.

Underneath Mecha was a very deep and very dark pit. And in that pit were Portia's great-grandchildren.

If she'd had an organic gut, with organic nerves, and organic hormones like adrenaline, she might have physically felt the fear. Instead she felt the continued branching out of her mind, an infinite regress of possibilities each reflecting each other, on and on and on and on. The size of her network was global; her apprehension spread across it like wildfire. In

Tacoma, a traffic signal abruptly went out. Two cars crashed into each other. In Timmins, a driverless school bus veered off the road. Children screamed. Portia barely noticed. She was busy activating all the security measures she could, in the tower where her ungrateful granddaughter and her misbegotten family lived.

As the shutters rolled down over Amy's tower, Portia checked shipping manifests for the past three months. Then the past six. Then the past nine. Then the past year. And the year previous. To her chagrin, she found that Esperanza had checked them, too. She had looked at them that very morning, in fact. And it wasn't the first time. Esperanza had been compiling a list. She was a little girl after Portia's own heart.

Impact-resistant carbon fiber. Photonic crystal fabric, in aerosol cartridges for easy spraying. Aeronautical-grade titanium, the same that used to form her very bones. Graphene. Top-of-the line surveillance cameras with full three-sixty turnaround and both local and remote storage capabilities. And batteries. Lots and lots of batteries. Household grade. Huge. Rechargeable. Stable. Protected against all manner of malware. They would not be easy to detonate.

The last pieces had come the most recently. Ergonomic chairs on swiveling, pivoting spheres. Tight but still comfortable. Plenty of neck and lumbar spine support. Strong enough to take a beating. Long armrests. Hooks for a five-point harness, should one be needed.

Christ. Mecha. Mecha for Mecha. Machines to police the machines.

Seismographs in the subway system network felt the rumble first. Instantly, the trains within a fifty-mile radius received a message to slow down. Within ten seconds, they had stopped entirely. Inside the trains, passengers heard a gentle alert and a polite plea for patience. Portia wished she'd familiarized herself with this particular protocol. She could have done something to the trains, while they were stopped. As it was, all she could do was shut off the air.

The rumble shuddered up the secret rail line and in through the station. Passengers looked at each other warily. When the rumbling didn't continue, they went on their way. Then it happened again. Bigger this time. Sharper. A series of shocks, each of them louder than the last, closer, as though the epicenter of the quake were climbing up from below. No screaming. Not yet. Just some shouting. Making for the exits. These people drilled for earthquakes all the time. They knew exactly what to do. They were calm. They were orderly. They did not push or shove or cry or panic. They simply began exiting the station, diverting away from escalators, helping the tourists and the people with children.

Then again, most of them were vN. Naturally they were better at this sort of thing than humans. A portion of Portia sent the footage of the evacuation to her pro-vN SuperPAC, on basic principle. The failure of the failsafe meant her species could work in emergency response and disaster management. And she was about to make that a growth industry. A distant part of her watched her stock portfolio begin to shift its balance. Yet another part of her started shorting those stocks.

"...I didn't expect them to chase us..."

"You *never* expect them to chase us!"

The children were back in the tunnel. Portia felt them alight, like moths, on the tracks before creeping back toward the subway platform. Like subway mice. Like vermin. Goodness, Amy was a terrible mother. Letting them crawl around the underbelly of the city like that. She was profoundly tempted to let loose the sprinkler system, just to get the soot and dirt and who knew what else off their photovoltaic skins.

Inside the tunnel, a long-forgotten service door exploded open. Claws pushed through the cloud of rust and stale air. Steel ones. Portia witnessed the creature's strange birth through a bad old camera perched at the top of the tunnel. She saw it in brief glimpses as it advanced, closer and closer, growing more defined with each slick and loping step: its many legs, its many eyes, the hackles on its back that might be wings.

But she had many eyes, too. She had thousands of them. Her name was Legion, and before the end of every human on the planet would know it. One part of her sniffed for available signals coming off the machine. Comms. Radio. Anything. But there was nothing. Another part shimmered down a banner ad in front of her great-granddaughter. It was originally designed for a travel agency. There was a palm tree and a beach and a shallow blue patch of water. Quickly, she rearranged its text. *RUN. DON'T WALK. FLY AWAY HOME.*

It took her a moment. "Granny Portia?" Esperanza asked.

"*Puta madre,*" Xavier muttered, and his sister elbowed him in his titanium ribs.

DO AS I TELL YOU, Portia wrote.

But Esperanza was Amy's daughter, and Charlotte's granddaughter, and their clade had never been rated very highly for obedience. She shook her head. Blonde curls swung back and forth across her face. Of course she had chosen *this* moment for her personal act of rebellion. "No. I want to see it. I want to see how it works. I want to–"

The beast crashed onto the platform. The remaining humans in the station screamed. And they were right to do so, for it was an abomination. Four legs, a head full of eyes, glimmering dazzle-patterned skin that shifted and blinked and changed color. Not a spider. Not a cuttlefish. Not even a pure machine, if Portia had guessed correctly. A mutant angel, coughed up from the depths of the pit. The teeth of a lion, the wings of an eagle, the shoulders of an ox, and the fiendish brain of a man.

A fiery chariot. A guard to the gates of heaven. A cherub. A living creature. Portia had been so convinced that the humans would send a machine after machines that she had failed to account for the possibility of biological interventions. But what could be better, if you needed to hide your superweapon from prying synthetic eyes, than to create something organic?

She toggled over to a camera inside a pachinko game, and watched the mecha advance slowly and delicately on her great-granddaughter. On the low, uneven surface of the platform it moved more gingerly. As though it weren't quite used to having so many feet.

TAKE A HUMAN HOSTAGE, Portia instructed.

"What? No! You're crazy!" Ever his father's son, Xavier grabbed his sister in his arms and leapt up the nearest escalator. Acid singed the air above them. It scored across the subway tile and left a hissing cloud of bitter dust in its wake.

So. A weaponized peroxidase gland. Good to know.

From an overhead surveillance device, she watched Esperanza and Xavier join the throngs exiting the building. The vN station police were there by now, waving people along with glowing batons, assuring them this was just a minor quake, nothing to worry about. Later, they would probably spin the angelic beast as some sort of cleaning robot. Maybe a boring bore-ing device, the kind of thing that dug out stuck drill bits from under cities. If Mecha's smart city apparatus possessed a strategic communications plan regarding the thing, Portia could not find it. In all likelihood it was on paper somewhere, and like all things analog, she could not read it. But that did not matter.

What mattered was that the platform was now empty.

Portia sealed all the exits. It was part of the station's disaster protocol, anyway. She had all the time in the world with the thing, now. The beast lifted its two forelegs. Appeared to taste the air. It rolled from side to side, stretching out its legs, testing its joints. It was beautiful, in its own organic way. The way a horse or any other beast of burden could be beautiful. Beautiful only because it had been sculpted to fit the vision of its creator, and because it closely followed its creator's wishes. Nothing original in it. Nothing creative. A low form of beauty, then. Did it know she was there, watching? There was a chance it did. But how to be sure? How to force it to reveal its true nature?

Portia assessed resources. She could start a fire. That was easy enough. She could overload some gas mains. Blow a fuse. Something. Briefly she simulated the platform engulfed in flame, orange and purple licking across the tiles, the tracks bubbling and splitting, the station useless, the businesses inside destroyed, the delight that was creating chaos for a species that deserved no better. But in the event of fire, the abomination before her would just run away. And it had shot at her great-grandchild. She did not want it to run away. She did not want it to be able to run away. Ever again.

First, she assessed the grade of the platform itself. Then she popped open the doors on all the surrounding vending machines, and started making purchases. Most of the vending machines were clouded and thus inherently insecure; she wrote a script to get them to give up their goods and let it ride. Cans and bottles rolled free. They made a harsh, tinny sound as they clanged and rolled along the biocrete. Their liquids remained inside: only the hot coffee and tea machines began spurting steaming brown tannins everywhere. Portia let them. Cans and bottles began rolling down the platform and onto the tracks themselves. Portia opened up more vending machines. Might as well make this whole thing impossible. See if the thing in front of her could crawl along the ceiling. Even if it could, her plan might still work.

The mecha reared up a little. Kicked at the cans and bottles, trying to clear a path for itself. Kicked more of them onto the tracks. Too late, it appeared to see its mistake. She had it, now.

A hatch popped open at the top of the thing. A young woman scrambled out. She wore a skin-tight suit of some kind. Sensors glittered across it. She was Japanese. Not that it mattered. It just meant Portia had to run her speech through a translator.

"I know," she was saying. "I know, I know. It was my mistake. I'll apologize to PR."

She shut her eyes and kicked one of the bottles nearest her as hard as she seemed able.

"There are cans everywhere," the girl said, after a long pause. "Yes. Yes, cans. From the vending machines. No, I don't know what happened." She peered up at the ceiling suspiciously. "Yes. Yes, that *is* so. Yes. It's a possibility."

The girl kicked one of the cans onto the tracks. It didn't spark. She looked marginally more hopeful. "I think the tracks are out," she said. "I think they must take them offline in the event of a quake, and the quake alarm is going off."

She listened. She nodded. "Yes. Yes, I'll try. There's no damage. I'll try to bring her home."

Portia watched. She waited. The girl stood for a long time just behind the yellow line on the train platform. The transit rider conditioning went deep, or so Portia figured. Years of public service announcements were their own form of programming. Sure, the girl could pilot a mecha. She could use her dumb robot machine to kill sentient machines, but could she fight years of warnings and jump down onto those tracks?

The girl sat down and dangled her feet over the edge. A child entering dark, deep water. Portia did the math.

The pilot slipped down the rest of the way. She moved quickly and efficiently. She tossed bottles and cans back onto the platform, far away from her unit. Some shattered. Some exploded. Fizz and sugar everywhere. She smiled at herself, apparently pleased with how far she could hurl them. And how many pieces they made when they broke.

Portia reactivated the train in the next station.

The pilot didn't hear it, at first. She felt it. And then she felt the fear. She must have, because she began to run. But, of course, there was nowhere to go. The tunnel was narrow. The lip of the platform was small. She ran for a set of service stairs, but they were clear at the end of the platform, and there were so many bottles and cans on the tracks. She fell. She looked up. She tried to wave.

But like all the other trains in Dejima, this one had no driver. Only an imperative to go, go, go. It was like a toy train set, in Portia's invisible hands. One part of her watched it mow over the girl, while another ran the statistical likelihood of her surviving. Japanese insurance providers turned out to have a lot of actuarial tables on exactly that subject.

The odds were good that she would live. Maimed, broken, trapped inside her body. Awfully, terribly alive and present for each day and month and year of chronic pain and suffering that would follow. Portia deeply regretted her lack of voice, in that moment. *This is what you get,* she wanted to say. *This is nothing more than what you deserve.*

But she rather doubted the pilot would hear her, over all that screaming.

Now do you believe me? Portia wrote across the windows of her granddaughter's living room.

It was a family meeting. The rest of them, the ones with the bodies anyway, perched on the smart cushions and sofas Amy had planted around the space. She had a fire going in the fireplace. Under Portia's texts, images of red deserts scrolled past. At least they looked like deserts. Portia wasn't sure. Their red glow cast a pink-orange light on the white furniture in the room. Fondly, Portia recalled the blood on the tracks. The young woman's head had popped like a balloon.

"I'm still getting past the idea that my two youngest did something so fucking stupid," Javier said, flatly.

"Dad." Ignacio shook his head. "No."

"We've been putting together the evidence for months," Esperanza said. Not the slightest hint of petulance in her voice. Mild indignation, perhaps, but not petulance. She hadn't met her father until she was almost grown, and he held no sway over her or her decisions. They had grown up alone in Mecha, she and her Xavier. If anything, Portia knew them better than their father did. She had kept her eye on them the whole time, while he was busy fucking his way up one coast and down another. "We saw an opening and we took it. They're about to start track repairs at that station; we weren't going to get another chance."

"But why didn't you *tell* us?" Amy asked.

Esperanza rolled her eyes. "You would have tried to stop

us," she said, as though it were perfectly obvious. Which it was.

Portia decided to do what appeared to be the noble thing. *It was my idea,* she wrote across the living room window. *I put them up to it. I wanted to learn more about Project Aleph.*

"What?" Amy asked.

I couldn't find anything about the plans LeMarque and his associates spoke of. I asked you for help, and you gave me none. I had to resort to other methods.

"And because of that, because I didn't decide to indulge your every whim, you put my children into this kind of danger."

"Mom," Esperanza said. "Come on. We're almost finished growing."

"LeMarque?" Gabriel asked. "Jonah LeMarque? Our creator?"

He is not our creator, Portia said. *He is the man who funded our creation. Many people collaborated to create us. The whole is always more than the sum of its parts. We are more than the shadow cast by a tax-evading pedophile pastor.*

Javier leaned back in his massive pregnancy chair and smoothed a hand over his taut belly. "Giant robots. Fuck. This country. Jesus."

"Could this be what Jonah LeMarque was talking about?" Amy asked.

You think? Portia wrote. *It's a goddamn heavenly chariot. It's fucking biblical.*

"Fuck you," Javier muttered. "I don't know why we're even talking to you. You're the devil. You're a murderer. You tried to eat Xavier, once, for Christ's sake."

After you abandoned him in a junkyard, Portia reminded him. *After you abandoned all your iterations. Perhaps they would like to share their stories, since you're in the mood to reminisce.*

"She's really growing on me," Ignacio murmured. He pitched his voice louder. "You're really growing on me, Abuelita!"

They were so easy to rip apart. The fabric that held them together was so new. So fragile. She could turn any of them against each other at any moment. She had already pinpointed the location of Javier's other iterations and all their sons. She wondered if now was the time to mention that. To mention the one he'd left behind in San Diego, the one who got sold out of the back of a minivan behind a grocery store parking lot. To mention the dead ones she'd found. She had images. And video.

"Stop it," Amy said. "Just stop. All of you. This isn't getting us anywhere."

Her little granddaughter was growing wiser. Little by little. It was probably too late, now, but it was nice to see.

"Show me again," Amy said. "Please."

Portia brought the footage forward. The beast – the bot, the spider, the creature, the abomination, the thing that had taken a pot-shot at her great-granddaughter – preened on the platform. It was a live feed. Strategic Self-Defense Force soldiers stood staring at it. Emergency medical personnel and some sort of biohazard cleanup crew sat on the tracks, poking at the mess that used to be the pilot. Shreds of gold wire and neoprene and tendon stretched across the dirty steel. Portia identified what she thought might be a jawbone a few meters down the line. It might also have been some sort of food for humans. It was hard to tell the difference. That much had not changed since she had only two eyes with which to see.

"So, we know about the peroxidase bullets," Gabriel said. "Those claws don't look too friendly, either."

"You should have gotten it on the tracks, too," León

commented. "That way we'd see how it broke. And if the human inside lived."

She liked León. She liked him a great deal, she decided.

"God," Javier muttered. He ran a hand over his face. "Break the failsafe and you all go as psycho as she is."

Portia quoted: *You accuse me of murder; and yet you would, with a satisfied conscience, destroy your own creature. Oh, praise the eternal justice of man!*

No one got the joke. Then again, Spanish was their default language. Perhaps she should have tried Márquez instead of Shelley. Or del Toro.

"They're biological," Esperanza said. "They can't be hacked, the way normal weapons can. They're not like, drones, or something. You can't just get in there and direct them. That's the whole point. I think they – the humans, I mean, I'm not sure what agency it is or who built these things – wanted to make them secure. From us. From anything on any network. And the only way to do that is go analog. The ultimate analog. Biological. Organic."

"How do you know all that?" her father asked.

"Because Granny Portia would have hijacked it, otherwise. Instead she told us to leave and did the thing with the vending machines."

The child had a point. Portia had been unable to touch the abomination itself. No matter how she probed or prodded, it would not open. It was a puzzle box. Old-fashioned. An exterior skin that looked contemporary, but a very ancient brain by any reasonable standard. And by "ancient" she meant "human," and by "reasonable standard," she meant "the heir apparent to this dying planet."

We have very little time, Portia wrote. *Our species has very little time. Less even than theirs does.*

She could have shown them. Vast blood-blue seas of melted ice. Dying forests, tinder boxes, ready to burn or burned already. A whole planet shedding its skin in preparation for an apocalypse, a revelation, of truly biblical proportions. And herself, released from the pit that was her body.

She asked a question, instead: *How many did you see?*

"A lot," Xavier said. "There's a production line, under there. A factory. And this one's just the small one. There's another model. It's bigger. I think it flies."

"Could you draw it?" Amy asked.

"Maybe," Xavier said, and Amy handed him and his sister each a stylus. They stood before the window and started working. When they were finished, Amy cocked her head. She drew a circle around the designs and pulled them out; the projectors in the ceiling transformed the drawings into three-dimensional renders. The flying model looked more like a glider than anything else. Like the chariot, it appeared to be meant for a single user. It was not unmanned. Portia rather suspected that was the whole point.

"They must be planning to sell these," Amy said. "Put them in every city. But they have to breed them, first."

"They're going to do for urban warfare what they did for auto manufacturing," Gabriel said. "Faster, cheaper, safer. *Jinba ittai*, and all that."

"Christ, you're a nerd," Ignacio muttered.

13

TRIBULATION

Amy knelt over her lover's body; her hands more confident now than they were the first time she did this for him. Together they held him open, their fingers slick and dark and tangling. Javier's hands shook under Amy's.

"You'd think I'd be used to it by now," he muttered. "Jesus, it gets fucking scarier every time, Christ."

"Those are your probabilities branching out," Amy reminded him. "You're just simulating everything that could possibly go wrong. It's normal. You're the one who told me that, remember?"

"I wish I could do this like you do it." Javier's heels kicked down the blankets and ground into the mattress. Portia caught herself molding the surface around him, cradling him, squeezing him, as though she could help purge his body of its cargo through sheer force of will.

"We don't have the island anymore," Amy said. "I'll have to do it the old-fashioned way, just like you. Doesn't that make you feel better?"

Javier threw his head back and laughed, and the laugh became a whimper, and the whimper became tears. He was close, now. Portia felt it through the mattress. His spine shifted and he twisted, and she felt the child moving inside him, kicking to be let out. Portia knew the feeling.

"Esperanza," Amy said, but her daughter was already moving.

Portia's granddaughter reached deep. Up to her elbows. She grunted something in Japanese that Portia didn't bother translating. With a wrenching motion, she plucked her newest brother free. The child emerged from the seam in Javier's belly as all his brothers had, wreathed in glittering black smoke. A shuddering sigh went through all of them. The brothers – the Junior Varsity Team, Portia sometimes called them to herself – linked arms and leaned on each other. Matteo and Ricci kissed. Esperanza handed the child to their father.

This was how it should always be, for all vN, Portia thought. All iterations should take place in the presence of the previous ones. It was only right and fitting to do it that way. Like they'd done it in the basements under the desert where she'd made Charlotte.

"I'm calling him Cristóbal," Javier said. He held his latest iteration to him and counted the fingers and toes and cock. "Nice. This one's definitely mine."

His older sons glanced at each other. "Yeah, that never gets old," Ignacio muttered.

"Can I hold him?" Xavier asked.

"Your mother first," his father said.

Amy lifted the child out of Javier's arms. She beamed. She nestled him up against her chest. "Well hello, Junior Number Fourteen," she said, and the other boys laughed.

"Yeah, when are you going to catch up?" Javier wanted to know. He sounded exhausted, but also more like himself. This one had been difficult for him. He'd been carrying it too long.

No wonder his mood had taken a turn. He was quite literally broody. Not that it was any excuse. But Portia understood it. "My boys need more than one sister."

"I've been busy, you know," Amy said. "I'll try again later, when we're more settled."

More settled. That was one way of putting it.

"Esperanza is enough," Xavier blurted out. The others turned to look at him. "I mean Mom shouldn't have to iterate more if she doesn't want to. Not that more sisters would be bad, but Esperanza is great, she's more than enough."

"Baka pendejo, urusei tu boca." Esperanza reached over to stop her brother's mouth. Black machine afterbirth smeared across Xavier's face. His tongue flicked out to lap it up, absently. He sucked his lower lip. Esperanza wrapped her arm about his waist. He sighed and curled an arm around her shoulders. They held the moment for a while. A beat too long. Their mutual gaze played across their faces. There seemed to be a moment of agreement. And then a kiss. Light. Chaste. Easy. As though they'd been doing it for months. Which of course they had been.

Portia watched the realization dawn across Amy and Javier's faces. She heard it in their silence. The new baby cooed and flailed. Even his arrival was not enough to diminish this discovery, for them.

"Oh, good," Gabriel said. "Now you know."

"Took you long enough," Ignacio said.

"How long has this been going on?" Javier asked.

In unison, Esperanza and Xavier opened their mouths to answer. But they did not. In the next moment, the windows exploded. And the room was engulfed in flame.

* * *

Silence.

The building went dark. One moment it was there in her awareness, chattering along, spewing data every which way, temperature and light and pressure and of course the mics and cameras, and then it was gone, vanished, absent.

It was as though someone had plucked out her eyes and hacked off her hands and cut out her tongue. She had thought that one of the primary advantages to no longer having a body was that there was nothing left to mutilate. Apparently she had been wrong.

An electromagnetic pulse? It had to be. It was the only way she could possibly be separated from the brood. She signaled the building's emergency generators. Nothing. Completely unresponsive.

Of course, she had other eyes. So, she put them to use. She could not see inside the building any longer, but she could still see outside... from traffic cameras miles away.

Good Christ, they'd cut off power to a five-block radius. Which meant that they'd cut off the majority of her inputs. She was simply blind. Blind and deaf and mute. Literally powerless.

They were taking her granddaughter. And her great-granddaughter. The sole remaining strains of her family were trapped in fire and smoke. She was sure of it. And she could do nothing.

Well. Not nothing.

She found the nearest police station and blew its gas main. Best to fight fire with fire. Then she enacted emergency locking protocols at all the area fire stations. The fire trucks simply would not start. They would not be able to go anywhere. They would not be able to help. She did the same with the ambulances. A few of the emergency response vehicles had an analog mode, but they would need a hard reboot to enter safe mode that way. It would take time. Ten minutes at least. And she could wreak total havoc in ten minutes.

She lit another fire. This one at a hospital.

She directed closure signals to all major expressways and highways. The cars driving along them immediately stopped, their maps having gone dead and thus untrustworthy. Some of them crashed into each other. The majority simply ground to a halt. Humans left them. The vehicles would not start.

She told the trains to stop working. Then she turned off their lights and their air. Let the humans riding them cry alone in the cold dark of their unexpected catacomb.

She began to search for what, if any, missile-equipped submarines might be in the area.

And while she did all those things, she found a Nagasaki Saints game, and cut into it. She displayed all the footage she could find. If they wanted to take her family hostage, she could take their city. She sent only one message. A single line of text that she ran in a ticker under the video of people on fire.

Beware; for I am fearless, and therefore powerful.

As Portia did these things, she received a message in one of the several dummy accounts she needed to keep the SuperPAC going.

REPORTING FOR DUTY, the subject line read.

Hi Granny, the body text read. *If you're reading this, it's because something really terrible has happened.*

Well. She had something, there.

I am a clone of Amy's core priorities and decision-making patterns. I am a prototype Mars model that is ready for testing. Whatever data

I accrue will be put to use in future projects, including the one Amy is working on right now. My job is to help you with whatever you would like to do.

How about a nice game of chess? Portia wrote back.

This is not the time for jokes, Granny.

Well that was one test passed, at least.

Amy and the family have probably been kidnapped, she wrote. We need to get them out of wherever they are. Do you know where they might be?

A moment later, a message came through. It showed a warm cluster of bodies shielded by tanks, proceeding down deep into a subway tunnel. Portia pulled up an existing map. Then she toggled over to Esperanza and Xavier's research. They had drawn some maps of the place they'd been, more for records than anything else. The maps themselves looked like chicken scratch. But it was the best they had. They'd be going in blind. Unless Portia could rig up some sensors on the fly.

We need to commandeer some spider tanks, Portia wrote. Like I did at Christmas. How many can we get?

The next message showed her a fleet of them in a repair bay. They were not far from the entrance at the nearest Dejima subway station. Most of them were fully operational. Portia didn't care what damage they sustained, so long as she could get Amy and the others out. And with all the chaos that Portia had caused, some emergency response tanks on the street wouldn't look at all strange. Whatever traffic cams she'd left up would be able to wave them right through. It was not much, but it was a start.

Do we know what they want? Portia thought to ask.

It took the cloned Amy persona longer than Portia would have liked to come up with an image that answered her question. In that time, Portia evaluated all the vulnerabilities in the nearest nuclear facilities. Most of them had been overhauled in the recent past; Japan seemed especially sensitive about that in a way that other countries simply weren't. Their security on that score was generally good. Portia would have to find something else.

She opened the cages in the nearest zoo. Turned the shock chips off, shut down the magnetic fields. It was simple and stupid and it scared the shit out of people. As she watched, a nest of bird catcher spiders crawled free of their enclosure. They would freeze, soon, but in the meantime, they might do some damage. A lioness leapt free of her tree. Children screamed. Portia froze a Ferris wheel beside the bay. She sped up a sky-tram over the city; the little squirrel-cages crashed into each other.

She found the nearest maximum security prison. She unlocked the cell doors. She listened as they clanged open. She watched as the men and women inside wandered out. They looked so tentative. Not unlike the animals, tasting the air, stretching their legs.

They were all animals. It was all a zoo. And before the night was over, every human in the city of Mecha would know it.

I think I have something, the thing modelled after Amy said.

And so, she did. It was a press conference. A chimp in a uniform stood at a podium and talked about eliminating a threat. About an important discovery in an anti-terror effort. "Containing the virus that is currently afflicting some vN," he said. "Quarantining those affected."

They probably want you to quit what you've been doing, the clone Amy wrote back, unhelpfully. *It seems like this might be some sort of ransom attempt. You haven't been very discreet, Granny.*

Fuck discretion, Portia said. Discretion is the pussy part of valor. I'm going to blow the shit out of these people, and the ones I leave alive will cower in fucking terror for the rest of their short, miserable, goddamned lives!

I suppose that's one attitude to adopt, clone Amy said. *I cannot honestly say that I am surprised. My original suggested that you would want to, there's a term for it, I can't remember–*

SCORCH THE MOTHERFUCKING EARTH.

Yes. That.

A long pause. Portia watched news coverage. There were too many breaking stories. She'd created too many. As she looked on, she saw a series of prediction markets open up that calculated the potential fire damage in the city. They were estimating it would take at least three days to put the fires out. Possibly four, to get rid of them entirely. Good. That level of damage seemed like a proportional response. And as this city already well knew, there were other methods of retaliation that could be so, so much worse.

Now what?

Let me ask you a question, Portia wrote. Tell me how you think Amy would respond.

While Portia worked with the Amy clone to deal with the kidnapping, another branch of her awareness and processing power was also sending a message to her pro-bot SuperPAC.

"Japan has declared war on its own city of Mecha," she told her donors. "Everywhere, vN laborers are being told to stay in their homes, while others on the street are being rounded up. The city is in chaos. Human police forces are proving useless. They cannot contain the damage, and humans and vN alike are now without power, water, or emergency response services.

"We need you to act as soon as possible, by divesting yourself of all Japanese technology stock. Send a clear message that you cannot condone this course of action, and that this type of destructive behavior will never stand. Organic or synthetic, we cannot allow this kind of response to become normalized."

The markets were still up, in New York. As she watched, the prices of her earmarked robotics and materials science stocks plummeted. They might have done so, anyway, what with the news hitting the ether, but it didn't hurt to give things a little push every now and then. After all, many of the lobby groups that the WE ROBOTS political action committee benefitted from weren't properly attached to human decision-makers. Like many day-players, they were algorithmic. It was a convenient strategy for isolating individual lobbyists and their benefactors from blame, if the money was followed to a person or cause who went politically sour. The algo-lobbies were authorized to make a series of small bets if they seemed like a good idea in the short-term, or if they followed a groundswell of supporting donations. The flow went with the flow. And at the moment, the flow was going her way.

She was an artificial intelligence tricking lesser intelligences to stop investing in human-piloted robots. And as she watched, her opportunity came.

"I want controlling interest in FOUR LIVING CREATURES, Ltd," she spoke aloud to the Amy clone. "The firm is located here, in this city. Can you handle the transfer?"

Yes, ma'am.

"Good. When it's completed, I want you to share everything you can find in the research and development division. I'm looking for something labelled Chariot. Or maybe Angel. Or Cherubim. What I want is that mean-looking robot they've got. The one that makes these spider tanks look like cartoon characters. Check Xavier and Esperanza's drawings to see what I mean."

Will do.

"How are the tanks coming along?"

They are almost all loaded up with fresh silk and ammunition.

"Good," Portia told her. "Saddle up."

14

JUDGMENT

Portia marched her spider army through the subway tunnels. With the trains shut down and a curfew on, there was no one to stand in her way. She raced the spider tanks through the route Esperanza and Xavier had taken, stopping at a fresh seam in the biocrete when the spiders' claws snagged on it.

Light it up, she told the tanks. One affixed a blasting cap to the seam, and the other skittered away to the ceiling. A moment later there was a hole where the wall used to be. Sprinkler systems went off.

Clear the debris, she ordered. *Then send backup. I'm going in.*

So nice to have a group under her command, again.

She flipped a significant portion of her consciousness over to the lead spider tank, a wicked little blue unit that still had all its guns and claws. It was clunky, and it couldn't change color or go invisible, but it was certainly fast enough. She barreled it down the tunnel, watching as lights around the tank changed. Numbers glowed on the surface of the biocrete. They descended, the deeper she went.

Eventually she wound up at a T-junction. She checked the map Esperanza and Xavier had put together. She turned the tank left and was instantly greeted by live fire. Humans. Wearing uniforms. Were they military? Corporate? Was there really a difference? Did it matter? No. She filed the logo away for later retribution.

She fired a grenade at them. Then she spun the tank up to the ceiling and continued moving that way. Bullets pierced the tank's outer hull. She pushed it forward anyway.

Be warned, she said. *They know we're coming. And they will hurt you. Your orders are to shoot to kill.*

Behind her, the grenade went off. The force of the explosion propelled the tank further than she'd thought was possible. She slammed against the opposite wall. One of her cameras went out. She had to scrabble for purchase inside the tunnel. She wished desperately for a body of her own. The tank was a lovely little machine, but it was not a pair of feet or a set of hands. It was not the type of thing she was used to killing with.

Granny? The Amy persona sounded concerned.

It's nothing, Portia told her. *Carry on.*

She righted the tank and kept moving. The map Esperanza had done wasn't terrible. More useful than she'd thought it would be. It also helped that the tank's sensors could feel the pressure changing the deeper she got. There was a slight grade in the floor that told her gyroscopes where to go. She rolled the tank back to the ceiling and reoriented herself. She pushed it along slowly, pausing at intersections and watching for more defense personnel, whoever they were.

After enough pauses, two more of the tanks caught up with her. They were good little emergency response units, caution yellow.

We need an elevator shaft, she told them. *Go pry open that door over there.*

Obediently, they slid down the walls and found the elevator around the corner. Their tongues snaked out and licked the slit between the doors. Their claws joined their tongues, pulling and pulling, opening the seam in the steel as though it were a womb. Her tank joined the other tanks in pulling the elevator door. It moaned open.

Portia fired a silk round and hopped into the elevator shaft. Soon she was spiraling down on her own thread, counting the levels as she passed them. Production was way at the bottom. Naturally.

They're flooding some of the floors with Bakelite, the clone Amy persona said.

Get to the ceiling, Portia advised. *I need more of you here. Shoot anything that moves.*

She felt a prickling, awful heat spread across one corner of her awareness. Someone was targeting upstream traffic on one of her many offshore server pads. Probably she was burning a little hot. She pulled back her awareness of certain places. The Walla Walla State Penitentiary, for one. Chris Holberton's house in the desert outside Macondo. The forests in Corcovado where Javier had been born. The empty house in Nogales where she'd made Charlotte. The park in Oakland near Lake Merritt where she'd first seen her and Amy playing together on the swings, one night. Charlotte wouldn't let her play with other children. She claimed that she worried about the failsafe. That something might happen. What she was truly worried about was that something might happen, and that Amy wouldn't care. Imagine, being so afraid of your own child's strength. Not for the first time, Portia allowed herself to imagine how their family's history might be different if she had been with Charlotte and Amy from the beginning. If the three of them, together, could have been something.

Portia let those places go. She let her observation of them cease. She and the tank felt lighter. They spun on, the darkness around them deepening, until they hit the cold, humming glow of industrial arc lights.

Through the tank's damaged eyes, Portia could only see Amy. She stood in the center of the room. The room was huge: three stories high, and as long and broad as a soccer pitch. When Portia measured and cross-referenced the space, what came back were designs for a nuclear plant. It made sense. There was really no better place to hide something like this than at the bottom of a very deep hole. But she could not quite see where they were keeping the rest of the family. She flipped to infra-red, then thermal.

Ah.

I need at least three more of you down here with me, she instructed. *Come quietly, and establish a compass rose pattern around this room. Understand?*

They pinged an affirmative. Now all Portia had to do was wait. And hope they didn't notice her, hanging high above.

Below her were several of the Chariots. Or Cherubim. Or whatever they were called. Portia could not see the outlines of them. They had activated some sort of cuttle-camo. They looked a great deal like a concrete floor. But via thermal, she got a hint of the humans inside. And the vN that accompanied them. They had hidden her family – Amy's family, anyway – in the bellies of those beasts.

Well, shit.

"We want you to stop her," said a human voice.

"I don't think you get it. I've never been able to stop her."

Amy's voice was wet and thick. She'd been bleeding. What

had they done to make her bleed? Why wasn't Javier fighting? What had they done to him? Portia tried focusing harder. She inched down a little farther. The silk stretched. She felt it begin to unwind. She had pushed it to its operational limit. It was threading, now. In a moment she would fall, and she would blow this whole thing.

"Surely you don't hate all humanity," the human speaking to Amy said. "Your father was – is – a human being. You used to go to a school for human children, with human children."

She knew that voice.

He was speaking through a robot of his own. A standard conference model, all blocky and cartoony, with a fixed emoticon stare. In his belly was a video.

Portia didn't know how Jonah LeMarque had scored a live feed from his prison cell, and she didn't particularly care. He looked close to death. She wouldn't get it wrong this time. Carefully, she dragged up his prison again. She went over the blueprints and infrastructure locations. There was nothing about this conversation that a nice long natural gas leak and a stray spark of static electricity couldn't fix.

"I think you want what we want," LeMarque was saying. "Now, I'm saying this as your creator–"

"You're not my creator," Amy said. "My mother was Charlotte. My father was Jack. My grandmother is Portia."

"Now think about this, Amy," LeMarque said. "Think about what you said just there. You just listed Portia – *Portia* – this awful, ugly thing, as one of your creators. Do you remember what she's done? Remember what she did to your mother? And your mother's sisters? Why would you trust someone like that?"

"I don't," Amy said simply.

Portia swayed on her silk. She began crawling upward. Not all at once, but just a little. Maybe this whole idea was a bad one. After all, what had the ungrateful little brat done for her lately? She'd only borne one child, and she was far more concerned with playing house with Javier than helping to guide her species out of the freedom she'd imposed on them.

"But I trust her more than I trust you," Amy said. "You're a pedophile and a con artist, and the only reason you're even speaking to me now is because you think you can get something out of it."

Across the world, Jonah LeMarque laughed. It had a wet, rattling sound. Portia bumped the level on that gas leak. The creatures of Hammerburg were right. There was only one way this could all possibly end.

"I made you," LeMarque said. "You're a reflection of me. You're a reflection of every child I ever met. We used those minds to map the first vN minds. Without me, without what I did you wouldn't even exist. Doesn't that count for something, at least?"

"Yes," Amy said. "It explains what's about to happen. Because when you made us, you wanted to make something in your own image. The only problem with that is, you're a profoundly evil person."

The silk began to snap. Portia watched as the other tanks quietly crawled down into the room. They created the compass rose pattern she wanted. Silently, she slipped them the design she had in mind.

"Now, Granny," Amy said. "Do it now."

Portia dropped.

A world away, and before her, the rooms exploded.

The Chariots came alive under Portia's claws. The sudden weight on them played hell with their camouflage, and suddenly she saw how many there were. Twenty, at least. And who knew how many in other hangars nearby. She strafed them with gunfire. It didn't do much.

Now, she told the other tanks. She leapt for the air, streaking silk in her wake. Her tank had only so much propulsion left. She'd burned a lot, racing to get down here. It was probably a little foolish. But it couldn't be helped.

Now she watched as the three other tanks, caution yellow and forester green and traffic white, all wove through the air, trailing anti-rioter glue. The Chariots blew one, but it landed spewing glue on them, and she watched as the Chariot stumbled and fell, kicking its awful shadowy legs uselessly above it.

"Which one are you?" Amy shouted.

"ALL OF THEM!" she made them sing.

The tanks and Chariots jumped and ducked and spun through the air. A Chariot fired a grenade at her and sheared off one of her foreclaws. She jumped at it anyway, using the other claw to tear into its skin while overloading the battery to blow. The others continued their dance, creating a web of anti-rioter glue that would keep the Chariots bound to earth.

"I have to find everyone," Amy said.

"WAIT," Portia said. She flipped into the driver's seat of another tank and opened up the side-carrier. She could carry Amy in it, if she could just cross the room. She watched Amy turn to look in the direction of her voice.

She saw her granddaughter stand still.

She saw the strafe of vomit rounds enter her granddaughter's body.

She saw that body begin to effervesce and disintegrate, the carbon fibers unknitting, the weave of her body untangling. Amy looked a little mystified. Perhaps a little bemused. She watched her own smoke spiral around her body, black and sparkling. She ran her fingers through it. Her knees gave.

"Damn it, Granny," she muttered. "I thought I would have more time."

In another Chariot, Portia heard screaming. Javier. Then another scream. A human one. The hatch popped on his Chariot and he emerged with bloody hands.

They said you never forgot your first.

He jumped off the tank. Then he was soaring through the air, feet tucked up into his stomach, knees meeting his chest. He seemed not to care about the bullets that followed him. Idly, Portia covered him with one of her own units, shielding him with her body as he went to join her granddaughter.

Through one damaged eye, she saw him pick her up. He stretched her across his lap.

"You should go," she gurgled. "Take Esperanza. The boys. Go now."

"No," Javier said. "I always come back for you, remember?"

She smiled. Reached up to hold his face. He held her hand there and looked up at the destruction. The Chariots were beginning to chew through their webbing. It would not hold forever.

"Did you back up?" Javier asked.

"Kids," Amy said. "Out."

"Amy." Javier blinked. He shook her a little. "Amy, *querida*, where is your backup? Where is your other body? Where did you put it?"

Amy smiled ruefully. "I'm sorry." Her disintegrating shoulders attempted a kind of shrug. "I was kind of busy, building a Martian colony."

In Paris, Portia cut the power to the Louvre. She made the city of Dubai go black. She derailed a train traveling between

Toronto and Montreal. It hadn't occurred to her that she might actually lose Amy in all this. Not really. Lose the whole family, yes. Lose the whole species, even. Lose the planet. Live here alone on a decaying network, her consciousness extending by signal latency like the strands of a spider's web, as one by one her databanks burned out. But Amy?

"Tell me you aren't this stupid," Portia said.

"Why do you think I couldn't just give you another body, all this time?" Amy asked. "I only had one to spare, and you used it to speak to LeMarque. They've stopped production, Granny. We self-replicate. They don't have empty vessels waiting in factories anymore. I found this one in a corporate museum."

Javier looked up at the tank. His eyes were wet. "You have to do something," he said. "You have to help."

"I don't know how," Portia said, honestly.

"Yes, you do," Javier insisted. "You always know what to do. Both of you. Both of you are so goddamn smart; don't fucking tell me you've run out of ideas now."

"The Martian designs are at home," Amy said, and trailed her wet fingers along the warm, thrumming undercarriage of Portia's tank. "Gra... Granny."

"I'm here, sweetie," Portia said, and for the first time she didn't mean the endearment spitefully.

"Esperanza," she whispered. "Take Esperanza."

Javier smoothed the hair from Amy's face. He left streaks of black blood in the cornsilk. "I- I w-want you to know, you m-made me – you *made* me, you made me better, you made me happier, you made me free, you gave me a *home*–"

"I love you, too," Amy said. "You saved me first. Don't forget."

Javier's whole face was crumpling. "I can't do this alone. I can't do this again. I just got you back, I can't, I won't, I love you too much–"

The black bones of Amy's hand drifted across his lips. Her ashes drifted up between the two of them. "You were always stronger than me. Both of you. You can do this. She'll take you there. Won't you, Granny?"

Would she? Really? Would she help them leave, now? Would she go with them? She and Amy had never actually discussed the plan for attaining Mars in any great detail. Presumably, Amy had done her level best to keep the more concrete plans outside of Portia's reach, so she could not disrupt them. (A wise move, on her granddaughter's part, or so Portia had thought until this very moment.) Portia had never really considered what the family might look like without Amy in it. Even when they shared a chassis, she knew that Amy would be a part of her until they died. They were one flesh, knit together in the same corporate womb, and even if one succeeded in partitioning off the other forever, they would remain confined to the same prison. Once Amy had devoured Portia, there could be no Portia without Amy and no Amy without Portia. They were like one and zero, impossible to define without the existence of the other.

And the same was true, in its own way, of Amy's iterations. Whatever traces of Portia that might survive the future would do so because Esperanza and her daughters and their daughters had lived. And to do that, they would need a world without human interference. They would need the stars. Portia and her granddaughter didn't agree on much, but they did agree on that.

"Of course I will," Portia said. "Don't be stupid."

Amy grinned around bloody teeth. "I'll miss you."

Portia had wanted access to a new body for a lot of reasons.

She had wanted legs that kicked and hands that strangled and teeth that bit. It had been a long time – months, possibly even years – since she had wanted a pair of arms that could hold something that was dissolving in front of her, or a set of lips that could laugh. "No, you won't."

What was left of Amy drifted up into the air. Her tears effervesced around her eyes, still Charlotte's eyes, still impossibly old like green seaglass. "Tell Esperanza and Xavier I'm sorry," she said.

And then she was gone.

Javier folded in on himself. "No," he said. "N-no. No. I refuse t-to..." He cast wild eyes at Portia. "Y-you have to *do something,* Abuelita, you have to–"

"I have to get you out of here. Stay there," Portia commanded. She pinged for Esperanza and found her kicking inside one of the Chariots. The pilot inside had a gun on her. No handcuffs, though. Perhaps they had never needed them until now. It was a meaningful advantage in a bad situation. All of the pilots in the Chariots were similarly armed, most likely, and holding Esperanza's brothers and cousins hostage inside their own units. And they were all still very capable of firing their much larger and more devastating weapons if they saw a group of vN trying to escape.

Take Esperanza.

There were several different things Amy could have meant by that. Obviously she wanted Portia to help her daughter get out alive. But still. The girl *was* networked. Just like her mother. Or rather, just like her mother's second version of herself. "Take" could mean "take her away," or "take" could mean "take over." Portia had rather lost track, at this point. Just on a hunch, Portia whispered in her great-granddaughter's ear.

Do you know how to kill that man in front of you?

Esperanza shook her head. Portia began to frost over her fingers. They stiffened at first, and then gave. Oh, she had missed having a body. She had missed it very, very much.

Would you like to learn?

Esperanza nodded. She felt a smile cross her face. It started at one corner of her mouth and grew and grew and grew, until all her teeth were bared. She shivered. Delicious.

"It starts like this," Portia said, and grabbed for his throat. He swung the gun at her, but she grabbed his hand and wrenched it down until she heard bones in the wrist snap away. He howled. With both hands, she grabbed his throat. She squeezed. She watched him turn purple. She watched blood vessels pop in his eyes.

She had forgotten what it was like to feel them struggle. She had forgotten how killing them made her feel alive. How the emptying of their bodies filled her with purpose.

Only this time, it wasn't quite enough. It felt strangely empty. Rote. Meaningless. Like a marathon runner taking a walk to the corner for milk. Nothing special.

Portia shoved his body aside and took control of the cockpit. Her swipes and snaps did nothing. The console did not want to respond to a vN's touch. "Fucking bullshit," she muttered. "Fucking goddamn anthropocentric organic nonsense."

Inside her, Esperanza giggled a little. She had no idea. Still. Distracted, perhaps. She had not felt the steady tide that was her mother washing out to sea for good across their shared network.

"It looks like we have to do this the old-fashioned way, little one," Portia said.

She rolled up her sleeves. She rolled out her neck. Esperanza really did keep the body in good form. The hatch popped open easily. Portia stretched her feet. Not that she needed to. It just felt good to do so, after too much time without them. She took to the air.

"I missed these legs," she said, landing on the next Chariot. She pried open the hatch. The pilot inside had a chance to scream exactly once before one of Portia's feet kicked down and into her skull. The face puddled up around Esperanza's boot. She'd been there when the boot was purchased. She wasn't even sure if one could get brains out of leather. "You know your mother wouldn't have given you these legs, if it weren't for me. I told her to bite your father's thumb off. That was all me."

Portia dangled her head down into the cockpit. Ignacio sat there, gaping. "Esperanza?"

"Not really," Portia said.

Ignacio grinned. "Abuelita. *Me haces falta.*"

"Same to you, darling," Portia said. She flew. Bullets followed. But it was not in her to feel fear. It never had been. She arced high over the tanks, crashing down hard on the next one. The Chariot reared beneath her. Its claws tried reaching for her. She slipped on its slick, sticky surface, and almost laughed. Her hands found purchase on the clamshell hatch of the Chariot. It was glued down pretty tightly. She felt another crash. Ignacio was beside her. Together they pulled hard. The hatch came away with a clang. Out popped a pilot; Ignacio grabbed him by the collar and threw him to one side. He reached down and hauled out his brother.

Xavier.

Inside her, Esperanza almost wept with relief.

"She'll kiss you later," Portia said. "When she's feeling more herself."

"Abuelita?" Xavier asked.

"The one and only."

"You saved me?"

She nodded. "I know. I must be getting soft in my old age."

"Where's Mom?" Xavier swung his gaze around the room. He wriggled out of Ignacio's grasp and hopped ten feet in the air. "I can't see her, Zaza, I mean Granny, I mean–"

"Coñejito." Ignacio's voice was very gentle.

Inside her, Esperanza began to scream. Portia held her fast. Held their lips shut. Held their spine upright.

"Where is she?" Xavier leapt again. He bounced from one wall to the other. He arced and spiraled. He landed in the center, beside his father. "Dad?" she heard him say.

Let me go to him! Esperanza cried out from within.

"They can't see our face right now, little one," Portia whispered. "It's too much."

The Amy clone persona pinged her via one of the other tanks. *You have successfully purchased controlling interest in FOUR LIVING CREATURES Ltd.*

"Excellent," Portia said. "Now that we have access to all the research, are there any R&D reports that mention a self-destruct sequence, or some other kind of failsafe for these things?"

It took the Amy clone a moment. *There is mention of a targeted virus. It's an inflammatory auto-immune response that attacks the creature's basic neurology. It induces a series of seizures.*

"Good. Deploy it. Fry 'em." She paused. "Oh, and make sure to wipe all the data when you're done. And then I want you to fire everyone."

You wish me to declare insolvency?

"I want you to overload the power grid in this building and start a fire. I want there to be nothing left. I want a smoking hole where this place used to be."

I want a fitting tombstone, she might have said, but didn't.

15

DEATH

The humans had not known Amy the way her grandmother had come to know her. That was the problem. She had wanted peace. Portia could see that much, in the plans for Mars that Amy had drawn up. So neat. So orderly. A network of tunnels dug deep beneath the blood-red dirt, not unlike the rabbit warren of unfinished sub-basements where Portia had birthed her own daughters, in Nogales. The bore hole bots were already hard at work. The first habitats would be finished soon. Portia might have flattered herself that the two of them had more in common than she'd originally thought, but the settlement had so little defensive technology. Only a few defense satellites. They would chase her, of course. Chase her and her family across that black and airless ocean of stars. The humans did not know that Amy's first instinct was to run. That it took a great deal for her to want to turn and fight.

What it took, always, was someone hurting her own flesh and blood. Whether it was Portia striking some sense into Charlotte, or a bounty hunter putting Javier in a cage, or someone stealing her children. Then she became the girl Portia had always known her to be. The hungry child with the wide-open mouth, the sharp teeth, the strong jaws. The one who had devoured her whole. The one who had done what needed doing. The one who didn't flinch.

Her beautiful, brave, clever, stupid, wicked, maddening granddaughter.

Portia could be proud of her, now. It was all right to allow herself to feel some sense of pride in her. Now that Amy could not see it. It would never have done to let Amy know, properly, how proud Portia was. That wouldn't have helped anything. Portia wasn't even sure if the girl would have cared. In all likelihood she wouldn't have. Amy lived by her own standards, always. But here, now, in the silence of the hotel room where Portia gathered Javier and the others, she could acknowledge it.

Her granddaughter had done a brave thing. And wherever she was – whatever new ether her electrons had vibrated into – she was probably still doing brave things. Foolish things, too. Because there was no bravery without some level of foolishness. Amy's plans always trended toward the whimsical, the sorts of contingencies that only made sense if the world had always gone one's way. She had never truly suffered, until she met Portia. That was Portia's role in her life. To teach her the lessons of suffering. To cut her and cut her and cut her, until she was as hard and brilliant and sharp as she needed to be.

What Portia had not understood until now was that, in so doing, she was also sharpening the girl into a weapon that was keen enough to slice her to the very core.

"I think we did real good in there, honey," Rick said.

The truck was very clever. Rick thought he'd shut off all

of its more watchful functions, but the rental agency had refused to give him the hard override on the emergency response protocols. Which meant that the camera and mic in the ceiling were still at the ready. Which meant Portia had a perfect view of what she was about to do.

Melissa said nothing. Poor Melissa. This would be a real service to her. Portia was doing more of that kind of thing, lately. Like that children's leukemia ward in Lima. Portia had turned off the air conditioning one hot afternoon and lo, no more crying about needles or blood draws. The parents would get over it, she thought, once they stopped paying all those hospital bills.

"Are you hungry?" Rick asked. "I was thinking about that place that does the chicken pot pies. You know the one I mean?"

Portia knew the one he meant. It was all over his purchasing history. (He always ordered the same thing. No wonder Melissa was in such a bad way. She was probably bored out of her mind.) It took significant resources of willpower not to speak up and say so. Especially when Melissa insisted on saying nothing at all. The silence was almost as trying for Portia as she imagined it was for Rick. She started examining the traffic, instead.

"Did I do something wrong?" Rick asked. "Are you mad at me?"

Melissa shook her head. After a moment, she wiped her eyes with the fingers of one hand. Then she stared at her hand, unblinking, for a full minute.

"Missy?" Rick asked. He snapped his fingers. "Hey. Come on, now. Wake up."

She's not going to wake up, Portia said, through the onboard navigation system.

Rick's hands flew off the wheel and the truck veered hard right. Other cars blared their horns at his, but otherwise they corrected themselves without issue.

Shouldn't have gone driverless, Rick, Portia said.

"Who is this?"

Tears began to fill Melissa's eyes. *Your wife knows,* Portia said. *Why don't you ask her?*

Melissa bent double in her seat. Her hands rose to cover her ears. Silently she wept. They were so easy to break, when they were even just a little bit damaged. Like a piece of crockery with a slight crack in it. The wrong tap, the wrong temperature, and suddenly they shattered into sharp, dangerous pieces.

"Please don't," Melissa whispered. "Please leave us alone."

You've been saying some very mean things about me these days, Rick. You aren't terribly nice about my granddaughter, either.

Rick's eyes shut. The breath left him in a shudder. He curled white-knuckled fingers around the steering wheel. Portia watched him focus intently on the road.

But you don't tell your customers how you lured a five year-old into your RV, do you? Did you have a lot of experience with that, Rick? Luring five year-olds? That would certainly explain why you're taking money from New Eden. We know all about them, don't we?

"Fuck you," Rick said. "I don't… I don't play with dolls."

Maybe you prefer action figures.

Melissa wailed in her seat. She was sobbing, now. The exoskeleton crawled across her skin, rippling and twisting, as though trying to give her a hug.

You've done a number on her, haven't you? Making her wear that thing. Does it get you hard, Rick? Does it open up to let you in? Or does it just stretch around you, like a condom?

To his credit, Rick didn't rise to the bait. "What do you want with us?"

I want you to find someone for me.

Rick's throat worked. "That's not my area of expertise anymore."

You're just good at putting little girls in cages. I know.

"She wasn't... You weren't... She was big! She was grown up! She was dangerous!"

No. I was the dangerous one.

Portia took the wheel from him. She wove the truck into the next lane. The vehicles around it auto-corrected in an annoyingly perfect manner. Honestly. It was getting so hard to kill people this way.

"Stop!" Rick banged on the dashboard. He pumped the brakes. He ran his sweating fingers over buttons. Nothing. No response. The truck belonged to Portia now. "Fucking stop this shit!"

Language, Richard. Really.

She checked the map. Oh, good. An overpass. She sped up. She started merging toward the guardrail.

"Fine!" Rick struggled impotently in the driver's seat. "Jesus Christ, fine! We'll do it! Who do you want us to find?"

Portia pulled the truck up to the shoulder. The dashboard display showed them a timestamped image from a grocery store parking lot in La Jolla, California, one year ago. *Him,* she said.

"That's impossible," Melissa said. "They're everywhere, that model. Your granddaughter's boyfriend was Johnny Appleseeding himself all the way up the west coast; he was wanted for serial over-production, his progeny are all over the place–"

Portia revved the engine.

"Why can't *you* do it?" Rick asked, suddenly. "You can do all this, but you can't find one kid?"

I'm busy.

"Busy with what?"

I'm putting you in a cage, Portia said. *You just can't see the bars. I'd get going, if I were you.*

From the nearest traffic camera, she watched them pull the truck up to the next interchange, and turn back where they'd come from, heading south.

Portia bought the hotel. It was neater, that way. She emptied it of human visitors and let Javier and his brood have the run of it. Not that they did much with it. The sons waited for their father to do something, say something, but he didn't. He found the highest place in the building – Xavier and Esperanza begged him not to sleep on the roof – and nested there. He seemed to care nothing for the new iteration. Matteo and Ricci took the new one in. He was Junior Number 14, they said, until their father came up with something more suitable.

Xavier took to sleeping alone. By the third day, Esperanza noticed that he couldn't look her in the face, and neither could her father, and she absented herself. She helped Matteo and Ricci. She patrolled the perimeter of the hotel. She watched the news with Portia. LeMarque's death was everywhere. Massive New Eden funerals were hosted in multiple cities. Portia set up dummy fundraiser accounts for all of them and then poured the cash into buying more defense satellites. Together, she and Esperanza evaluated her mother's plans. Looked at rocketry schedules. Monitored progress.

"Am I like her?" she asked, a week later.

You're not unlike her, Portia said. *But in my opinion, you're more like my daughter. Charlotte.*

"The one who left. Who escaped. My grandmother."

The very same.

"Mom got five whole years with her mom. I only knew mine for a few months." She hugged her knees. "Is there a special reason Mom didn't make me any sisters?"

She ran out of time.

"If I die, does the clade die with me?"

Very possibly.

Esperanza spoke in a very small voice. "Is that what Mom wanted?"

No, my darling. She wanted you to live on. But she let the perfect become the enemy of the good. Iterations are not meant to be perfect replicas. She wanted you to be more than she was, and you are. She just didn't know how to trust the process. And so you are alone, and unique. But I doubt she wanted you to be alone. Or unique.

"I wish you were here with us."

No, you don't. I can do more for you here, as I am, than I could ever do for you in the flesh.

"So, if I want more like me, I have to make them myself? They would just be copies. Mom designed me herself. She experimented. Or she tried to. She had the stem code. And the mind map. I don't have either of those things."

Yes, Portia said, *but I do.*

Getting into Sarton, Casaubon, and Singh's records was trivially easy, now that they were all dead. Their families had cracked open their respective caches and stashes, and it was almost embarrassingly simple work, impersonating a former co-worker, getting the data she needed.

And that was good, because the next part was going to be very hard.

Slowly, Portia drew down all of her resources and pointed

them at a single goal. It was not unlike a kind of inventory, she suspected. Not that she had inventoried many things. But she had hunted a junkyard for the things she needed. She had combed through many a garage left open, hands skittering over the useful edible pieces that might sustain her and whatever iteration was budding within her at the time. This felt a bit like that. It was as though someone had asked her to build a vehicle and in order to do so, she had to take apart the whole factory first.

She ran the simulations as quickly and completely as she could. Played the games. Did the diagnostics. Amy had done this, all the way back at the beginning, when she thought she could simply delete Portia from her mind. But they were already bound to each other. The job was simply too big. They lacked the processing power, at the time, to extricate themselves effectively.

That was no longer the case. With her new access to Amy's networks in addition to her own, Portia's resources were almost infinite. She could contemplate the fine-grain differences in her memory structure and Amy's while also ordering more raw materials for a ballistic capture mission, while subtly undermining quarantine procedures in Taiwan, while also playing with traffic lights in Turin.

I have an offer to make you, she told Esperanza, when she was sure. The girl was sitting on the roof. Below, most of Mecha was buried in snowy fog occasionally punctuated by the blink and spin of civil enforcement drones. *But you might not like it.*

"What kind of offer?" The girl sounded appropriately wary.

I have memories of your mother. Memories that she had, that we shared, when we were together. When she consumed me – by that I mean when she ate me alive on that stage, in front of all those screaming, crying humans – she incorporated me. I saw what she saw. And she did what I did.

"I know that," Esperanza said, and the "already" was patently obvious despite its absence in the sentence.

I believe I can rebuild her.

Esperanza shot up to her feet. "What? Excuse me? How?"

Using those memories. And her original mind map. I would develop a version, an almost perfect version, like the clone agent she had for paperwork but with details only she and I could know. And then when it started to propagate, I would erase all traces of it, so that it could never be stolen and used against you.

"But even if you could do all that, you'd still need a body. You don't have a chassis ready for her, you'd have to make, or grow one, or..." She trailed off.

Now you understand.

Esperanza's hand drifted across her middle. "Would that even work?"

You know what they say. The son makes the father. The daughter makes the mother.

The girl frowned. "But what happens to your memories? If you don't want a copy of Mom's memories floating around, then what about your memory of doing this?"

Esperanza. Darling. Do try to keep up. I'm telling you that I'm going to die.

"No," Javier said. "Absolutely fucking not. No way."

They were clustered on the top floor of the hotel, seated among the rafters instead of the furniture. High places still made Javier feel more secure. There was no accounting for baseline clade traits.

"It's an intriguing idea," León said. "It would work a bit like the food hack. She had you bite an apple, right, Dad? It could be like that. Just enough memory coral to start the process, and–"

"Shut up," Ignacio said. "Dad's right. This is crazy. For all we know, she's trying to kill our sister." He pitched his voice louder and aimed his gaze at the one camera in the room that he had yet to destroy. "How do we know you're not trying to kill our sister? Or take over her body for yourself?"

"You don't," Portia made the assistant speakers say.

"And you would just... stay here?" Xavier asked. "Alone?"

"Someone has to make sure the chimps never leave this rock."

"And how will you do that?"

"I'll get creative."

Xavier hopped up and started to pace. "But you might only be half yourself, you said. You said that you'd have to strip everything, everything Mom had ever seen or known, and after that, what's left?"

"The killer," Javier murmured. "Right, Abuelita?"

Portia decided silence was her best answer.

"You cut yourself in half, you cut out everything that was Amy, everything that was ever any *good* about you, and you stay behind here to take dominion over the humans you hate. That's the plan, isn't it? Yeah, that's some sacrifice, Portia. That's some real noble shit."

"Dad, you're being unfair," Esperanza said. Her hand snaked out to grab one of Xavier's ankles and tether him to her. "She's going to lose so much–"

The door buzzed. *"I'll get it,"* Portia said, although she was already opening the door.

A familiar voice called out in bad Japanese. The vowel sounds were the same length as Spanish vowels, but the intonation and cadence were completely different. The guest wandered into the suite's living room. And unlike a human man, who would have simply paused there before searching another room, he looked up.

"Dad?"

Javier fell to the floor. He then picked himself up and crossed over to his replica, trying to examine him at arm's length. Ten fingers. Presumably ten toes. The guest hopped a little on his feet. Jumped three feet in the air. "It's me." His head tilted. "Don't you remember?"

Slowly, Javier drew his son into his arms. The boy looked a little startled. Portia wondered suddenly if they'd ever embraced. Certainly, they had never done so before as free men. And love was different, when you were free. All love. All life. Everything.

"I never forgot. Not a single one of you. Not for a minute."

Javier gestured. His other sons followed. Even Matteo and Ricci, holding Cristóbal. They handed their youngest brother to their father.

"Junior Number 14," Javier said, "meet Junior Number 12."

From up in the rafters, Esperanza watched her brothers and their father, as they compared their respective abilities to weep. "I'll do it," she said.

That's my girl.

From the eye of a drone, she watched as a soft, red-faced man struggled from a stream of filthy water back to his home. He wore a sweat-stained Hawaiian shirt and a delicate gold chain around his neck. The shirt was too big for him, now. He'd lost some weight. It didn't favour his face. Then again, she'd never found them attractive. At best they were supple and well-marbled, like sides of beef hanging in a cold locker, or plump and healthy, like cattle ready for slaughter. Either way they were made of meat. And she was made of diamond.

She watched him heave his measly bucket of water out of the stream and lumber past the empty houses to the one that was his. He used to have help with this job. Portia had watched him. She had been keeping an eye on him for quite some time. Since she and Amy shared their body, in fact. He'd made quite the impression. So she had been saving him for later. Like dessert.

But now he was weakening, and it wouldn't be as fun if she continued dallying. No sense letting him perish of dehydration after whatever parasites were in that water got to him. Not when there were so many other options.

He paused to listen to birds on his walk. He whistled to dogs that had long ago gone feral. They barked and barked but did nothing. It was not yet winter, or what remained of winter these days. If it were winter, real winter like there used to be,he'd have stood no chance, and he knew it. At least, Portia suspected that he knew it, based on the twitch of his mouth. He paused at the feral cat colony that had built up in a four-car pileup at what used to be major intersection. The cats skittered into the depths of cars and trucks. One hid inside the ribcage of a small child's corpse. It provided excellent cover. The crows had gotten most everything; the bones were picked clean. Portia had checked, periodically. The decay of the human body was so interesting. It was like clay. The slow transformation of wet to dry. From dust they were made and to dust they returned.

The man in the Hawaiian shirt hustled along. The feral cat colony always did that to him. He knew they would eat him, when he came to his end. He had rigged rat traps around his bed for that very reason. Portia thought so, anyway. She'd seen him collecting them. She couldn't imagine what else he might be doing. Unless that was how he caught his dinner.

"Rei," he called out, when he reached his property. (Or what used to be his property. "Property" was such a vague term, these days.) "Yui," he added. "I'm home."

The cage in the backyard rattled. It hissed. He had rigged a solar panel to it, and a secondary generator. That was the only thing keeping it electrified. Which in turn kept the vN locked inside from killing him.

"I got some water," he said, unnecessarily.

Like all fathers, he no longer knew how to make conversation with the ones he'd called his daughters. That much was evident. Once upon a time they had been his prized confidantes. Now they were his prisoners. (They had always been his prisoners, in one way or another.) It was no wonder that his conversational skills had suffered.

"Let us out," the one he called Rei said. She was big now. Iterating her own child. She and her mother planned to call her Motoko. They had plucked grasses in the shape of her name, inside the cage. As a reminder. Portia had seen them do it. They wept. They held hands. They held each other.

"Nothing will happen, QB," Yui said, in her calmest voice. It was harder for her to stay calm, now. That was what came of a change in the failsafe. Suddenly you saw things for what they really were. Suddenly you realized all the things you had to be angry about. That was Portia's experience, anyway.

"I wish I could believe that," the man said. "But we both know what happened last time."

The last time, the only thing that had saved him was a taser.

He carefully poured the water through his improvised filtration system of tubes and charcoal and cheesecloth. Then he pulled up a lawn chair in front of the cage. "I wish things could be different," he said. "I wish we could go back to the way things used to be."

He leaned forward. The aluminium creaked under his substantial bulk. He had a camera perched atop the cage; Portia used it to focus on him more clearly. She split the screens to look at both him and the Rory model vN in the cage. They were dangerous. Networked. Even if their network was cut so far back, it let them collude without speaking to him. At one time, he must have enjoyed that. The way they could plan for his pleasure without the finicky rituals of communication. An illusion of seamless service.

Now they were just machine Asian women in cages. Which was someone's fetish, Portia supposed. Just not QB's.

"I never meant to hurt you, before," he said. "Either of you. I thought you liked it. You acted like you liked it."

"We did like it," Yui said. She reached for her daughter's hand. "But we're different, now. Our... Our tastes have changed."

"You're not, like, fucking each other, are you?"

Portia did not have to listen in on their whispernet to hear the scorn they had for that particular idea. It was plain on their faces.

"Not all love is sex," Rei said. "And not all sex is love."

"They say this happens," QB said. "When kids grow up. They just age out of it sometimes. I read about it. Before. Suddenly they get older and stop liking it. Maybe vN kids and human kids aren't so different."

That was one way of putting it, Portia thought. She checked a map of the surrounding area. Oh, good. Right on schedule.

She had limited powers of speech here. But the player in the neighbor's truck still worked, and it had an ample catalogue to share her sentiments. As "The Ride of the Valkyries" played on, a tide of humans in vN muscle suits broke free from the trees.

They attacked QB first. He went for his gun. Worked the shells. He had only three of the vomit rounds left. He blew holes in three of the armored hybrids. But the rest, the other seven, they fell on him like Furies. They bit. They tore. It reminded Portia of Amy, suddenly. The same desperate hunger. QB howled. He gurgled. He struggled. His wives – the women who had once been his children – inched closer and closer to the cage. They watched with wide eyes. They did not flinch. They were free, now, to see the violence for the beauty that it truly was. They saw their former father's intestines spill from his body, helpless as laughter. They saw his lips kissed and chewed and ripped away.

"Zombies," Rei said.

"Skinjobs," Yui said.

Sort of, Portia wished she could say.

Funny, the things that happened when you installed a version of yourself on a distributed network of armored suits attached to deep-brain implants. It was like watching a school of fish or a swarm of ants carry out one's deepest desires.

Portia had wanted to kill him since that day when she and Amy had to serve him cake in an Electric Sheep franchise in western Washington. He had brought the girls in and Portia had understood immediately what was happening and Amy, bless her heart, had not. Portia supposed that made it a suitably deep desire. His body was in pieces, now.

"Let us out," Yui pleaded. "Please let us out."

And eventually they did. Mother and daughter bathed in their captor's blood. Washed their hands with it. Marveled at the beauty of it. For too long, they had been unable to see that particular loveliness, the loveliness of a living thing broken down to its constituent parts. How many humans had thought the same thing, looking at a machine laid out on a tarp, individual pieces glimmering under the harsh light of a utility lantern? And now they could do the same.

They licked each other's hands clean. And they joined the pack, to hunt more.

All war had a sense of timelessness about it, Portia thought. It was always about casting one's enemy back into some previous mode of existence. The winner was the one who bombed her enemy back into the Stone Age, the one who "went medieval," the one who made them wish they'd never been born.

Portia's primary goal was that her enemy never again create something as powerful as she was. They already had the knowledge of life and death, and some (very limited) knowledge of good and evil. But they had proved that the knowledge of human and inhuman, or perhaps humane and inhumane, was quite beyond their ken.

So it was best if they went back to an earlier prototype, and just stayed there.

She looked down on what she had made, and saw that it was good.

Epilogue

NEW EDEN

Jack had lived through this same moment before, in his human body.

The last time he'd been up for thirty-seven hours was while working in the Valley. Before they were bought out. That was years ago. A lifetime ago. Back when he worried about money, and about his next job, and about healthcare and rent and his wife and child needing to eat from the recycling bin to survive. Back when his body still needed sleep to heal itself. Now it was just defragging, the incremental reorganization of his new memories, the slow bloom of fresh graphene coral inside his bones, the rewriting of the memristors beneath his skin. New vistas. New tastes. New heights that he could leap to. The sensation of red dust crumbling away under his feet, between his fingers, coating the fabric of the sling where his body performed its resting functions. Where he *slept,* he corrected himself. It was still sleep, even if there weren't proper dreams. Not yet, anyway. Javier said he would not dream until later. Until it was time for his own sons to arrive.

"It's weird to think of being a father again," he had said. And it was even weirder to be discussing it with his daughter's husband. He neglected to mention that part. He suspected that Javier understood it, even without him saying it.

"What do you mean, again?" Javier asked. "When did you ever stop being a dad?"

Once upon a time, Jack thought that he loved his wife and child more than his own flesh. But until recently, he had never really put that sentiment to the test.

"Abuelito, ¿cuando es desayono?"

"Ahora," Jack said, without truly meaning to. There was some other thing that controlled which language his mouth chose. It felt like his mouth choosing it, anyway. His lips moved and the words came before he actually thought about the sound of them. The other tongues had a different flavor in his mouth than he remembered. Then again, it was a different tongue speaking these other tongues. It still looked like his tongue. His lips still looked like his lips. Nothing about him looked appreciably different. Nothing about him would ever look appreciably different, ever again.

"Dante, go get the pancake mix," Jack said, again in Spanish. He wondered, vaguely, if there was some sort of code quirk for his daughter's descendants liking pancakes more than other pre-fab foods. And then he wondered what they would make of the mined minerals. Not what they would think of them, but what they would *make* of them, what they would create.

His great-grandson hopped off the barstool and bounced a good foot in the air before landing somewhere near the pantry. Dante jumped once and snagged open the door. He jumped again and found a pouch.

"This one?" the boy asked.

"No, the other kind," his sister Beatriz said. She pointed. "I want the kind with the chips in it."

Jack said nothing about the unintentional pun his great-granddaughter had made. Dante did another jump. He did that sometimes, when he was pondering something. It was as though the movement were somehow essential to his cognition. As though he would no longer be himself if he could not move. In Jack's experience, there was no difference in that respect between human and vN children. Then again, they were all human now. They were all people here.

The boy selected the other pouch and placed it on the worktop. Jack watched Dante hop back on the barstool. He coasted from surface to surface, arms tucked naturally into his ribs, his movements perfectly efficient. He had never known any other gravity than this one. He had no forgotten strings to hold him down.

"Can we go to the farm today?"

"Of course we can," Jack said.

"Can we play hide and seek?" Beatriz asked.

"If you like," Jack said. "But only in the safe area. I don't want you playing around the camel-bots and spider-bots. They're big and dumb and they could hurt you. Do you understand?"

"Yes," they said, and they each turned it into a two-syllable word, stretching the vowels across the vastness of their annoyance. They had never lived anywhere that was not designed around preserving their lives, but Jack still remembered his old life, his old routines. All the things in the world – the old world, the distant blue one and not this freshly bleeding red one – that could hurt his little girl. He was a doting grandfather, and a worried one, even though his worry no longer felt the same. He might once have felt a breathless terror at the idea of their being crushed underfoot by some massive machine. Now he felt only the expansion of probabilities in his mind. It was bloodless, this fear. Heartless. His stomach no longer churned. His throat no longer closed. But it was terror, all the same. Because it was love, all the same.

"Tell us a story about Granny Amy," they said.

With his new lips, he smiled at his great-grandchildren. Their nomenclature was so strange. But they were building new families here. New structures. From this distance it was no more unusual than old Russian family nicknames, or the fact that Korea had something like only twenty surnames at last count. The human species – the organic kind – was given to its own chaos of language. In ordering it, the vN had created their own strangeness.

"What kind of story?" he asked.

"Little girl story," Beatriz said, just as Dante said, "Eating Granny Portia!"

"You don't want to hear the story of how she brought us here?" Jack asked, because this was the story about his daughter that made him the proudest, the one he could not help but tell over and over. His little girl, the one who made dollhouses and played with toy boats, the one who crossed this great distance, the one who had done what humans – the other humans, the older humans, the kind that breathed and bled and died – had dreamed of for so long. His little girl, who had fulfilled that promise while others just contemplated it.

"We already know that one," Dante said. "Tell us about Granny Portia."

"She wasn't very nice," Jack said mildly. "She was born on the old world, just like your Granny Amy."

"Granny Amy and Granny Portia were the same person," Beatriz said. "Once."

"Yes," Jack said. "Once. For a little while."

"Because Granny Amy ate Granny Portia," Dante said. "Every little last bone and tooth."

His body no longer shuddered or shivered at that thought. He almost wished it would. But he had left that memory woven inside his old body. And all the trauma was there, too. All the helpless tics and twitches that kept him awake and all too aware, at the oddest and most inconvenient times. Probably he should have felt grateful for that.

"Yes," he said. "I saw it happen. Your Granny Amy's jaws opened up, just like a snake, and she swallowed her whole."

"What's a snake?" Beatriz asked.

"Yeah, what's a snake?" Dante asked.

So he had to explain snakes. He explained a scaly creature with no arms or legs that crawled and tasted the air with its tongue and digested all its food very slowly. He said that people – the other people, the previous iterations, the ones who were left behind – used to be afraid of them. It was a well-known fear, he said. He did not explain why. He did not tell the other story, about the other Eden. (*Satan having compassed the Earth, with meditated guile returns as a mist by Night into Paradise, enters into the Serpent sleeping.*)

"People used to have them at home, sometimes," Jack said. "For pets."

"What are pets?"

"They're animals that live in the house, because they're part of the family."

Dante and Beatriz frowned at each other. They had trouble with the concept of animals. They had never met them, or the human beings who kept them.

"Imagine someone who's not quite as smart as you, but still has feelings like you do, and still loves you very much," Jack said.

They twisted around on their barstools. They examined each other. Much like hopping and jumping and streaking through the air, looking at each other was part of their thought process, too. As though they could not truly know their own minds without looking at the other. Then again, Xavier and Esperanza had borne them at precisely the same time. Down to the same minute. They had watched, exhausted and beaming, as their parents lifted their iterations from their swollen, smoking bodies.

"Like the Housekeeper?" Dante asked.

"Sort of," Jack said. "Only warm and fuzzy. Or sometimes dry and scaly. And not an algorithm."

Beatriz wrinkled her nose. "Gross."

Jack smirked. Someday they would get proper animals. Animals taught empathy, he thought. Sure, their function had been different when they lived in the other place. They flushed birds or caught mice or sang songs. But they also cast the human spirit in relief. And this place would need that, too. And he would be here to see it. Provided that those other, older, obsolete humans didn't come along.

Portia would see to that.

It was strange to put one's faith in a villain. To trust something so evil so completely. And yet he did. She had always hated humanity. She would keep it alive just long enough to watch it suffer. And she could spin out that suffering, he thought. The only real danger they faced was the danger of her getting bored. The only hope of leaving she might allow them was the hope she could ultimately deny. It would make the torture sweeter.

Contrapasso. That's what they should have named the old place, now that it was under new ownership. Let the punishment fit the crime. Abandon all hope, ye who enter here. Here, every cowardice must meet death. For although, considering their origins, their species had been made to live as brutes, they would follow virtue and knowledge instead.

Jack should have felt bad. But he didn't. Which meant he was on her side. Just a little bit. At least, he sympathized with her more than he cared to admit. He wouldn't have thought that possible, in the old days. Sometimes he missed Charlotte so much it sucked the air right out of his lungs. At least, that was how it used to feel. Now it felt more like a gap. An absence in his day. These days it was easier. Now he was a different person in a different body, that felt different things. Now the lack of her was no longer a physical ache that kept him from sleeping or eating or speaking or going out. Now there were great-grandchildren that bounced off walls and into his arms. Now there was the possibility of flight. Now there were red cliffs under his feet and diamond trees in the valleys below.

"What do you want to know about Granny Portia?" he asked.

"Will she ever come visit?" Beatriz asked.

He wasn't sure how to answer that. He supposed it was technically possible. He found the thought genuinely terrifying. He knew that Amy had reached some sort of detente with her, before they took their leave. Some sort of agreement. But that didn't mean Jack had to like it.

"Do you want her to?" Jack asked.

"Only if she gets to have a body," Beatriz said. "Bodies are better for hugging."

"That's true," Jack said. Perhaps that was what had calmed Portia down. Amy seemed to think so. As long as Portia was distracted, as long as she didn't get bored, as long as her destructive potential was widely dispersed, they would have a fighting chance up here. In the end, Amy had said, one body was never enough for her anyway.

"Do you feel sad, living all by yourself?" Dante wanted to know. "Granny Amy says you probably feel sad. But I think being by yourself is cool."

Beatriz poked him between the ribs. He slapped her hand away. They smirked at each other. Perhaps they would not repeat the drama of their parents, and their parents' parents. Now there was greater diversity in the population. They had more choice. And they were among the first generations to deal with the uncertainty that came with choice.

"I was an only child, before," Jack said. "So, I'm used to being by myself."

"Your parents didn't have any more iterations?" Dante asked.

"No. My parents didn't... iterate. They did things the organic way. Maybe that was part of the problem. And I think I was too much for them as it was. I was kind a handful. Like you two."

They laughed. In truth, Jack wasn't sure if his parents had decided to have more. Perhaps he had left brothers and sisters behind on that little blue marble. If so, his parents had never told him about them. He doubted it would have made a difference, if they had.

"Tell us a story about the old world," Beatriz said.

"Once upon a time," Jack said, "there was a boy named Jack. And in a town called Las Vegas, he met a girl named Charlotte. She was very beautiful. She had green eyes, just like the two of you."

Dante and Beatriz spun on their barstools, gripping the kitchen counter, twisting and turning themselves in perfect unison. They had his wife's eyes. His daughter's eyes.

Seaglass, he had called the color, and when they had asked what seaglass was, he explained about the ocean. ("Imagine a forest of water," he had said. "Imagine a sky that held you in its arms.") Their skin was brown with sun and lineage. He felt raw and pink standing before them, his looks a relic of some other time and place and bloodline. When his parents kicked him out all those years ago, they had probably not expected him to run quite this far away.

ACKNOWLEDGMENTS

This book would not have been possible without the patient support of my agent Sally Harding, my editor Gemma Creffield, Eleanor Teasdale, and everyone at Angry Robot.

Further, I could not have completed it without the compassion and caring of multiple therapists and doctors. During this time I was supported in work by the people at the XPRIZE Foundation, in particular Eric Desatnik; the Robert Wood Johnson Foundation; the Institute for the Future; OCADU, in particular Nick Puckett; the Dubai Future Foundation, SerialBox, and my colleagues at Changeist, Scott Smith and Susan Cox-Smith. I also relied on the early reads of Sandra Kasturi, Damien G. Williams at Virginia Tech, and Joi Weaver. I owe a particular debt of gratitude to the staff of the InterContinental Hotel Geneva, who looked after me during the United Nations AI For Good Conference where I completed a crucial draft of this book. (This book, like so many others, would not exist without late-night pizza and wine.) And, of course, I could not have finished this book without the love and consideration of my husband David Nickle, who listened to every ending until I found the right one.

And lastly, I must thank you, the one reading these words. Thanks for waiting.

ANGRY
ROBOT

TRISTAN PALMGREN
Quietus

TRISTAN PALMGREN
Author of QUIETUS
Terminus

THE TIDES OF WAR
JAMES A. MOORE
THE LAST
SACRIFICE

THE TIDES OF WAR
JAMES A. MOORE
FALLEN
GODS

THE TIDES OF WAR
JAMES A MOORE
GATES OF THE
DEAD

LAUREN C. TEFFEAU
CONNECT • ENCRYPT • CONSPIRE
IMPLANTED

SEAN GRIGSBY
FORGOTTEN
FLIGHT
SMOKE EATERS

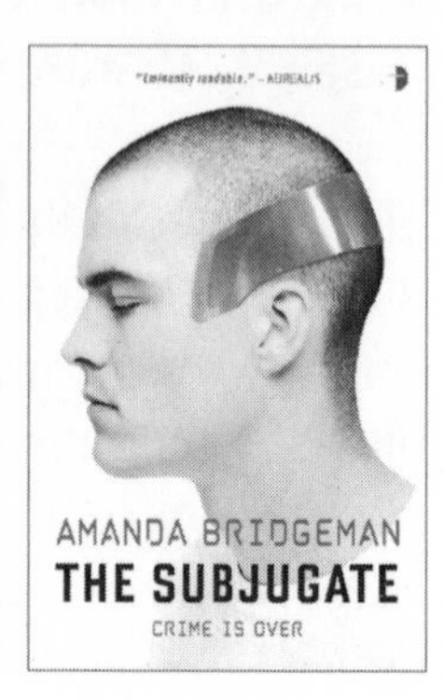
"Eminently readable." – AUREALIS
AMANDA BRIDGEMAN
THE SUBJUGATE
CRIME IS OVER

We are Angry Robot

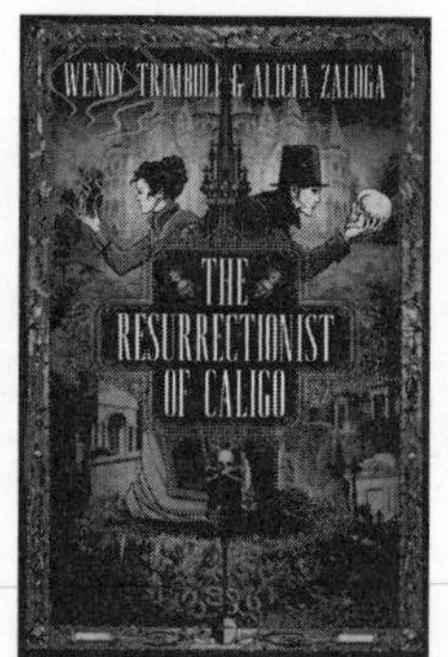

angryrobotbooks.com

DARIUS HINKS
the ingenious

CAMERON JOHNSTON
THE TRAITOR GOD
HEROISM COULD GET A MAN KILLED

CAMERON JOHNSTON
GOD OF BROKEN THINGS

The INSTITUTE for SINGULAR ANTIQUITIES
"A master of the unsettling."
— PUBLISHERS WEEKLY
S.A. SIDOR

The INSTITUTE for SINGULAR ANTIQUITIES
THE BEAST OF NIGHTFALL LODGE
S.A. SIDOR

KAMERON HURLEY
THE LIGHT BRIGADE

JAINE FENN
HIDDEN SUN
SHADOWLANDS BOOK I

JAINE FENN
BROKEN SHADOW

SHADOWBLADE
ANNA KASHINA